ALLAN BOROUGHS

Illustrated by Fred van Deelen

MACMILLAN CHILDREN'S BOOKS

First published 2014 by Macmillan Children's Books
a division of Macmillan Publishers Limited
20 New Wharf Road, London N1 9RR
Basingstoke and Oxford
Associated companies throughout the world
www.panmacmillan.com

ISBN 978-1-4472-3599-6

Text copyright © Allan Boroughs 2014
Illustrations copyright © Fred van Deelen 2014

The right of Allan Boroughs and Fred van Deelen to be identified as
the author and illustrator of this work has been asserted by them in
accordance with the Copyright, Designs and Patents Act 1988.

1 3 5 7 9 8 6 4 2

A CIP catalogue record for this book is available from
the British Library.

Typeset by Ellipses Digital Limited, Glasgow
Printed and bound by CPI Group (UK) Ltd, Croydon CR0 4YY

For Carol

CONTENTS

CHAPTER 1

THE WITCHES' TEETH

India Bentley stopped wading through the thick tidal mud and checked the horizon for any sign of southsiders. The first thing you learned when you lived on the North London shores was to keep your eyes peeled for southsiders. They'd come tearing across the water in skim boats and if they caught you unawares then you'd most likely get taken. Mehmet said it was the women they wanted mostly, them and the livestock. He said India shouldn't think she was safe just because she was only thirteen neither, 'cos a girl of thirteen was a woman as far as southsiders was concerned'.

But there was nothing much to see, just the vast swollen body of the Thames and the dead towers of the old city, sticking out of the water all hollow and bird-streaked, like witches' teeth in the distance. A lone scav-trawler sailed back and forth between the towers, dragging its iron grapple across the deep city beds in the hope of dredging up something useful.

She turned her attention to the small fishing net she'd staked out earlier. It was writhing and heavy to lift but she remembered to keep looking up while she worked. Only half-wits got taken by southsiders, she reckoned, mostly because they didn't check the horizon.

When she looked inside the net she sucked her teeth. Straight away she could see it was full of boneheads with yellow-dome skulls and blind eyes and needle-sharp teeth that snapped together like traps. Boneheads were no good to eat. They tasted rotten and sour on the day you caught them and they'd take a finger off if you weren't careful getting them out of the net.

Three summers ago, Tony Patel's dog had got caught in open water by a pack of boneheads. They dragged it under and stripped the flesh off it as it howled and thrashed in the water. Mehmet and his men were there but they just laughed and took bets on how long the dog would last until one of them finally put a bullet in its head. Then Mehmet said Tony should stop snivelling because it had always been a dumb excuse for a dog anyway.

She tipped the mutant fish back into the water, taking care not to get bitten. There were some sticklebacks at the bottom of the net that could go in the pot. They wouldn't make much of a meal, especially as Roshanne had a guest for dinner tonight, but Mr Clench never ate much and anyway, India couldn't care less if he choked on sticklebones. So she wrapped the little fishes in a damp piece of sacking, stuffed them in her satchel and then began to pick her way back across the tidal flats. She skirted the silted spoil heaps at the edge of the water where the trawlers dumped the unusable stuff: plastic bottles, twisted road signs and those mysterious orange cones they pulled from the water in their hundreds.

India wondered if she had time to fetch water from the well before the constable's men went on patrol. The sky was like a lead sheet but there was still some light left in it. She'd need to be quick though. Apart from a southsider, the last person you wanted to meet after dark was Mehmet, especially when he'd been at the wood alcohol and was waving a shotgun around.

She'd always liked going to the well. Her father had drilled it when he'd been home on leave. They'd sit together on the lid and he'd talk about a time before London was a lake, when it was a city with glass buildings and cars and everybody had enough food and fresh water. 'As much food as they wanted, India. Imagine that.' Then he'd sigh and look out over the water. 'The Great Rains washed it all away, though. All we've got left now is those dead towers.'

Then he told her stories about the cold country where he spent most of his time working, where a man could still have an adventure if he wanted it. It was a land filled with bears and wolves and ice people who hunted on reindeer sledges. A place where a hot cup of tea would freeze before it hit the ground. It was a place, he said, where ancient spirits lived beneath the mountains and living shadows stalked the forests.

When India arrived at the well she was not pleased to see someone was already there. An old woman was standing on the grassy slope, gazing upwards and holding out her arms.

'Chicken Licken!' she shouted to the sky as India drew near.

'Hello, Cromerty,' said India.

India's mother had never allowed her to call Cromerty a witch the way other children did. She said Cromerty was just an old person who needed someone to watch out for her. She had always tried to make sure the old woman had enough to eat in winter.

As India approached she saw Cromerty was wearing only a thin nightgown and a single slipper. Her hair stuck out like grey wire. The old woman fixed her with watery eyes and gave her a toothless smile.

'There's something wrong with the sky,' she said urgently. 'Can't yer see? It looks like iron.'

India glanced up at the uniform sheet of grey cloud. 'It's always that colour, Cromerty,' she said, 'it's just rain clouds.'

'Anyone can see the sky, deary,' replied the old woman. 'But do you really *see* it? There's iron in the sky if you knows how to look for it.'

'Well, I don't think I can see it, Cromerty. Look, if you don't mind, I need to get some water.'

The old woman was not to be put off, and shuffled along behind India. 'There's not many of us what's got the seein', deary. Maybe you got it, maybe not, but your mum definitely had it.'

4

India stopped and turned to look at the old woman. 'My mum?'

'Aye, she knowed the winds and the tides and she could tell if there were something wrong in the land just by listening to the earth spirits.' She brightened suddenly. 'Read your palm, deary? You never know – you might be going on a journey.'

India sighed. 'I don't think so, Cromerty. I really need to get on.'

'Well, let me know if you change your mind.'

'You should get inside the fence now, Cromerty. It's getting dark out here.'

The old woman ignored her and began to croon to herself. India guessed that Cromerty was having a bad day.

When India turned to the well, her heart sank. The lock on the lid was broken. Not just broken either: it looked as though it had been torn apart. 'Cromerty, did you see who did this?'

The old woman didn't reply. She was rocking back and forth, humming softly. *'First comes the iron and then comes the snow,'* she sang, *'and then comes the winter when nothing will grow.'*

India looked down the well. Mehmet often warned that southsiders might poison the water. She thumped the lid in frustration. The curfew was about to start and she ran the risk of being locked out. But the thought that someone might have poisoned *her* well made her burn inside.

'Cromerty,' she said to the old woman. 'Go back to the

village and tell Mehmet to keep the gates open until I get back. Tell him I'll only be a few minutes.'

'Watch out for the sky, deary,' called the old woman as she retreated down the hill. 'There's summat wrong with it, I tell ya.'

India shook her head impatiently. 'Definitely having a bad day,' she said to herself. She slipped the broken lock into her pocket and began to climb the grassy slope.

The other side of the hill was where the dead city started. It was running with wild dogs and full of houses that no one had lived in for a hundred years, rotting like the bones of dead animals. It made her shiver just to see them. Even Mehmet and his men avoided going there if they could help it.

Then she spotted them: two people about a quarter of a mile away picking their way across the rubble. There wasn't much light but she could tell that one of them was a man, tall and powerful-looking. She dived under a bush where she could watch them in safety.

Suddenly the big man looked up and stared right at the spot where she was hiding. She knew he couldn't possibly see her in the failing light but even so, he seemed to look *straight at her*. He turned to say something to the second figure – a woman, India could now see – and then pointed in India's direction.

She slithered down the hill on her backside. Southsiders, cack! They had to be southsiders, they couldn't be anything else. Her heart was going so fast that she had to stop at the bottom to catch her breath. The rules said she should run straight back to the village and report what she'd seen to the constable, but what if she was wrong? What if they were just a couple of mud grubbers from over Kilburn way or a pair of night fishermen? She could hear Mehmet now, laughing at her for having been so easily spooked. She paused.

The bank rose quite steeply where she was standing. She thought if she kept quiet and stayed near to the water, she might be able to get close enough to the strangers to get a good look at them. Then she could decide what to tell the constable's men.

She crept along the bank, staying low and trying not to make too much noise as she pulled her boots from the sucking mud. When she thought she was close enough she climbed the bank and peered over the top to take a look. The woman was less than a hundred yards away, looking at something in her hand. She had long hair, tied back into a ponytail, and she wore a leather flying jacket with a fur collar and heavy boots that came up to her knees. The tall man was nowhere to be seen. There was a motorcycle a short way off like the ones India had seen in pictures, a petrol burner, battered to hell and complete with sidecar. She shivered. No one in Highgate owned anything like that, which meant they *had* to be southsiders.

'You! Stay where you are!'

The voice made her jump and she slid down the bank into the wet mud. She glimpsed the man appearing from the gloom to her right and then she was off at a sprint. But the man was much faster than she had expected. Before she'd gone five paces a big hand came down on her back and sent her sprawling face down into the mud.

'I said stay where you are.'

She kicked her legs and spluttered muddy water but the hand kept her firmly pinned down. She was scared now too, scared and angry with herself. Because she'd done the one thing that only dumb people did: she'd got caught by southsiders.

CHAPTER 2

THE ONLY ONE OF HIS KIND

India struggled against the heavy grip to no effect. The more she kicked and thrashed, the more firmly she was held in place.

'Calculus, stop it, leave her alone!' The woman's voice sounded close by and India was immediately released. She wriggled away across the mud. But when she turned and caught sight of her attacker she cried out in alarm.

The creature was taller than anyone in her village, with a face that was hidden behind a long helmet. The body was slim and smooth, wrapped in a flexible metal skin that suggested a ripple of muscle and fibre beneath. The powerful legs were tensed and the midsection was pulled into a tight spring-steel abdomen. This was not a man at all but something else altogether, something she'd only read about in musty, waterlogged books, something she knew to be dangerous.

She scrabbled in her pocket for a small metal tube and

felt its familiar weight in her hand. When she flicked the button on the side it crackled to life and the tip glowed with a blue light. 'Get away from me,' she growled. 'This shock stick's got a full charge. It'll take your head right off.'

The creature looked at her curiously.

'Stand down, Calculus.' The woman scrambled down the bank towards them. She was lean and muscular, with a strong face and brown skin that suggested she had spent a lot of time out of doors. She frowned at India. 'Why were you spying on us?'

India could tell she was American because her dad had often imitated the voices of the Americans he worked with. He called them 'Yanks'. This was the first time India had ever heard one for real. 'Why did you steal my water?' she shot back, sounding braver than she felt. She threw the broken lock on the ground. The woman held up a small water bottle.

'We only took what we needed,' she said. 'You don't need to be afraid, we're not southsiders.'

'I'm not afraid,' said India. She noticed that the woman wore a pistol on her belt.

The woman fumbled in her satchel and then lit a small cigar. 'I have business with Mrs Roshanne Bentley,' she said, exhaling blue smoke. 'I was told she lives on the North Shores. Do you know where we can find her?'

'Who wants to know?'

'Verity Brown.' The woman held out a small card. 'I work

for the Trans-Siberian Mining Company. Perhaps you've heard of it?'

India had certainly heard of it. She darted forward and snatched the card from the woman's fingers. It was white, with the words 'Trans-Siberian' in blue, circling a map of the northern globe. The same picture she remembered seeing on the front of her father's overalls. Underneath, the card read: *Verity Brown (Mrs) – Salvage Agent*. The woman folded her arms and waited for an answer while the machine creature stood patiently at her side.

'That's a robot, isn't it?' said India.

'He's not a robot, he's an android, the only one of his kind left. He's my bodyguard.' A tiny smile appeared at the corner of Verity Brown's mouth. 'Doesn't hurt to have protection. You never know who's going to come after you with a deadly weapon, do you?'

India lowered the shock stick slowly and put it back in her pocket. She wasn't quite ready to trust these people yet but she was pretty sure they weren't southsiders. She stood up and wiped the worst of the mud off her canvas trousers, taking a closer look at the android as she did so. She could see he was old, really old, from a time before the Great Rains when they'd known how to make things like that. He had a large dent in his skull and the surface of his body was scored and pitted. There was a crack across his visor and a panel in his chest had been replaced by a piece of rusty sheet steel held in place with rivets. He was the most incredible creature she had ever seen.

11

'Can it talk?' she asked.

'Of course I can talk,' said the android. His voice sounded richly amplified from somewhere within his body.

India thought she might have insulted it. 'I'm sorry,' she said. 'I've never met anything, I mean anyone, like you before.' She wondered what was the proper way to address an android. 'He's pretty cool,' she said to Verity. 'Does he kill people for you?'

'Perhaps you could just tell us where to find Mrs Bentley's house,' said Verity, avoiding the question. 'I need to talk to her about her husband.'

'What d'you want to know about my dad?' said India, then she quickly bit her lip.

'Ah!' said Verity. 'So you must be one of the daughters.' She looked at the piece of paper in her hand. 'Bella, maybe or . . .'

'India.' She cursed for having given herself away. 'We live down there.'

Verity Brown looked along the shoreline where India pointed and stamped out her cigar. 'We need to visit your mother, India. I need her help with an important matter.'

'She's not my mother,' said India quickly. 'My dad remarried after Mum died.'

Verity nodded thoughtfully. 'OK, well we need to see your stepmother then, but we need to do it quietly. The village guards won't be happy if they see us.'

India looked from Verity to the android and back again.

'You'll never get as far as our house,' she said. 'The guards have got dogs and guns.'

'Don't worry, Calculus will get us past them.' She flashed a smile. 'But I need to know that I can trust you, India. It's important you don't give us away before we speak to Mrs Bentley. Can you do that?'

India looked at the strange couple again. 'Maybe.'

'I guess that'll have to do,' said Verity. 'Let's shake on it.' She extended a hand, which India shook awkwardly. 'We'll wait out here until it gets a bit darker. Tell your stepmother we'll be along to the house later. Will anyone else be there?'

India thought about Roshanne's perfectly arranged dinner party for Mr Clench and smiled. 'Oh, no!' she said. 'We've got nothing planned for this evening at all.'

She watched the two strangers disappear back into the surrounding gloom and then made her way back to the village, her head dancing after the strange encounter. Verity Brown was so completely different to anyone she had ever met and as for the android, well, if you had a bodyguard like that, she reckoned you could do just about anything you wanted. She smiled as she thought what she could do to Mehmet if she had her own android.

She was so busy with her thoughts that she didn't notice she had arrived at the village gates, a pair of heavy iron and oak doors, set into the fortified earthworks surrounding the village.

'Who goes there?' The voice snarled at her from behind the closed gates.

'It's me, India,' she said in a small voice.

The door groaned open a crack and three burning torches emerged, wielded by three burly men. Mehmet stood in the middle, holding a black dog that grunted and whimpered on the leash; the other two held shotguns.

'India! What're you doing out?' growled Mehmet, glaring at her. 'It's an hour past curfew. You'll get yourself shot and I won't be held responsible.'

'Didn't Cromerty tell you?' she said. 'I got held up. I had a bit of trouble at the well.'

'Trouble?' The word carried electricity. The men bristled and stroked their guns. 'What sort of trouble? Did you see anyone out there, India?'

She gulped. Looking at Mehmet's red eyes and the grim looks on the faces of his men, she felt suddenly afraid for Verity Brown. 'No, nothing like that. The lid got stuck, that was all. It just took me a while to get it free.'

But Mehmet wasn't listening. He pushed past her and peered into the gloom. 'Southsiders was up at Holloway yesterday,' he said. 'They took some goats and shot Gab Watling in the leg.' He stared into the distance and growled. 'They're out there again tonight, I can smell 'em.' He turned to his men. 'Go and get the rest of the dogs and fan out along the shoreline. We'll flush them troublemakers out and string them up in the trees.'

'No!' said India, too quickly. 'I mean there's no one there. I'd have seen them if there was, you can see all around here from the well.' She was further into the lie than she wanted

14

to be but she couldn't back out now.

Mehmet studied her for long seconds. 'All right,' he said, dismissing her with a jerk of his head. 'Get home then.'

Relieved, but still worried for Verity Brown, she pushed her way through the ugly group.

'I hear your mum's got Mr Clench coming over, *again*,' Mehmet shouted after her. The way he paused before he said 'again' said everything about what he was thinking. The other men sniggered.

'Roshanne's not my mum,' India shouted back over her shoulder.

She walked quickly down a rutted lane, past the tangled heaps of salvaged steel waiting to be fed into the flaming jaws of the village smelter. The stink of burning rubber made her hold her breath.

Their cottage was a damp, stone building that stood apart from the others near the edge of the water. Her heart sank as she walked up the path and saw her stepmother standing by the kitchen door, radiating impatience.

'What sort of time do you call this? I've been waiting all afternoon for those fish. This dinner won't cook itself, you know.' Roshanne Bentley's untidy smear of red lipstick was coming off on her cigarette. She wore a pair of satin slippers and her best lounging robe. Once richly embroidered, it was now threadbare and faded to a ghost of its former colour. The hem was damp and muddy from the house puddles.

India pushed past her stepmother and dropped the wet

sacking on to the kitchen table. 'That's all I could get. The rest were boneheads.'

Roshanne looked distastefully at the crushed and broken fish inside the damp parcel. 'Is that *it*? How am I supposed to feed our guest with that? Where the hell have you been all afternoon?'

'I just went to check on the well,' she said. 'That's all.'

'What, *again*? Sometimes I think that wretched well is just an excuse for you to sit around on the hillside while I slave away after you and your sister.'

India snorted at the thought that her stepmother might slave after anyone. Roshanne never emerged from her bedroom before midday and certainly never bothered with anything as mundane as housework.

'Why don't you just put chemicals in the water like everyone else?' said Roshanne. 'Then you might have time to give me a bit more help around here.'

'The chemicals kill off the fish,' said India wearily.

Roshanne picked a stray bonehead from the sacking and dropped it outside the back door with a shudder. 'A good thing too,' she said. 'Personally I couldn't give a stuff about the fish and I'm sure your hole in the ground would still be there if you left it alone for one night. I have to say I'm heartily sick to death of working my fingers to the bone in this ghost town of a village. It's no way to live for someone with my background.'

India sighed. Roshanne was not entirely wrong about the emptiness of the village. As the southsider attacks had got worse, so more and more of her friends' families had moved away. It didn't help that the few people who were left tended to avoid their house because of Roshanne's snobbery. India had got used to spending a lot of time on her own.

'It's tough for everyone,' she said in a weary voice.

'Not everyone, India.' Roshanne parked the cigarette in the corner of her mouth and began to sever the heads from the little fish and pull out their insides. 'Fortunately there are still some people who understand the importance of good breeding.' A clump of ash fell on the chopping board. 'At least Mr Clench knows how to live with style.'

The previous year, Thaddeus Clench had bought the largest house on the north shores and instantly became the subject of great discussion in the village. Some said he'd been a slave farmer in the West Country, while others said he'd made a fortune as a pirate rigger – or that he was a gold prospector who'd once killed a man in cold blood. He had first appeared in their house at her father's memorial service, when he'd stayed behind after the other guests had left, to 'comfort the grieving widow'. Then he had put his arm around India, urging her in a beery voice to 'call me Uncle Thaddeus'. After that he had started to come to dinner regularly in spite of Roshanne's truly disgusting cooking.

India dug her hands deep in her trouser pockets and curled her lip. 'I'm not that hungry tonight. I thought I might just stay in my room.'

'Oh no, young lady!' Roshanne wagged the knife at her. 'Mr Clench will arrive in one hour and I need you here.'

India's suspicions were aroused. 'Why do I have to be here?'

Roshanne rolled her eyes and let out one of her 'give-me-strength' sighs. 'You might not think it's important to have influential friends, India, but one day you'll learn the value of being well connected. When Mr Clench arrives I want you to be well presented so please make an effort. Why don't you wear a dress for a change?' Her voice took on an oily tone. 'You'd look nice in a dress.'

India wondered if now would be a good time to tell Roshanne about Verity Brown but decided it probably wasn't. She picked up one of the oil lamps and escaped upstairs. She found her sister Bella sitting on her bed, scribbling in a dog-eared sketchbook.

'What are you drawing?' asked India.

'Southsiders eating Tonya Solomon.'

'Southsiders don't eat people.'

'They do too! Levi Sloat said they ate his dad.'

'Levi Sloat's dad got drunk and fell down his own well.'

Bella thought this over for a moment and then shrugged. 'You're in my room,' she said.

India dutifully took a step backwards and watched her from the doorway. 'What do you think of Mr Clench?' she asked casually.

'He's OK, I guess,' said Bella, without looking up from

her scribbling. 'He talks to me sometimes, when I see him out. What's for dinner?'

'Sticklebacks,' said India. 'It's all I could get.'

'Stinky sticklebacks?' Bella wrinkled her nose. 'Are you sure about that? It smells like roast chicken to me.'

'With roast potatoes?' said India with a smile. They played this game whenever they were hungry. They played it a lot.

'Yeah, and parsnips and peas and onion gravy.'

'And apple pie and custard?'

'Ice cream!' said Bella blissfully. 'Let it be ice cream.'

They both fell quiet, lost in thoughts of food.

'So what does Mr Clench say to you?' said India after a while.

'Oh, I don't know,' said Bella, going back to her drawing. 'He just asks about Dad's job and stuff.' She suddenly brightened. 'He's got a cat and it's going to have kittens. Do you think Roshanne will let me have one when they're born?'

India shrugged. 'I shouldn't think so. What sort of questions does he ask?'

'I don't know! Just stuff, that's all. Mind your own business and get out of my room!'

India retreated to her own spartan-looking room and frowned at the floral dress Roshanne had laid out on the bed. She wiped her filthy hands on it and balled it up under the mattress. Then she swaggered in front of the mirror with a pencil stuck in the corner of her mouth like a cigar, squinting at her reflection through narrowed eyes. She wondered idly where she might be able to get hold of a pistol and a leather jacket.

She changed into a fresh work shirt and ran her hands through her thick black hair, pushing it into a set of wild peaks until she was satisfied with the effect. Not wanting to go downstairs, she picked up a picture from the mantelpiece and sat down on the bed. Tall and blue-eyed, John Bentley stood in the centre of a group of tough-looking men in overalls. He had the same half-smile he always wore when he sat in India's room at bedtime.

'Read me a story,' she'd say.

'Which one?' he'd say, teasing.

'You know which one.'

'What, *again*? OK. Which part would you like me to read?'

'The part when she meets her friends. You know, when they follow the yellow brick road.'

When he was finished she'd pull the sheets closer as he tucked her in.

'I'd like to have an adventure one day,' she said. 'But what would happen if I got trapped in the witch's castle, like Dorothy?'

'Then I'd come and rescue you,' he'd say, smoothing her forehead and kissing her goodnight.

'And if you got trapped in a witch's castle I'd come and rescue you too.'

India reached instinctively for the small metal pendant

inscribed with her name that hung on a leather cord at her throat. Bella seldom wore hers, but for India the little pendant was the last thread that linked her to a happier time.

A burst of adult laughter from downstairs startled her and she realized she had been daydreaming. She supposed she should put in an appearance and, as if on cue, there was a familiar shriek from the hallway.

'In-di-a! Are you up there? Please come down at once! Mr Clench has arrived.'

CHAPTER 3

UNWELCOME VISITORS

The kitchen was thick with cooking steam that smelled of fish. Mr Clench sat with his back to the door, telling a story while Roshanne and Bella sat in rapt attention. There was an open bottle of home-made wine and a bowl of apples on the table. India looked hungrily at the fruit but thought she would rather starve than eat something Clench had brought with him.

'So the Great Siberian Wastes are a land of opportunity if you've got the grit and the gumption for it. I mean, look at me. I was like all the other nobodies around here until I went east.'

'I'd love to see Siberia,' said Bella, wide-eyed. 'Will you take me there?'

Clench snorted with laughter. 'Good grief, it's no place for girls! It's full of wild beasts and primitive savages who'd chew on your bones if they got a chance. Did you know the ice people still believe in magic? They talk to the trees and the mountains, of all things!' He spotted India and jumped from his seat. 'India, wonderful to see you again.'

She ducked to avoid his embrace and moved to the opposite end of the table.

Clench wore explorer's clothes, heavy trousers tucked into long brown boots, and a multi-pocketed waistcoat over a checked shirt that failed to conceal his soft stomach. The clothes looked too clean and well pressed to have seen any serious action. He glanced down at India's shabby work clothes and muddy boots. 'You look as glamorous as ever, India. What have you been up to?'

'Checking up on that wretched well of hers *again*,' said Roshanne, giving him a lipsticky smile. She had applied a great deal more make-up, which now clung to her face in greasy clots.

'Still doing things the old-fashioned way, eh?' said Clench. 'I tell you what, I got hold of a cheap barrel of industrial disinfectant the other week from a guy who runs a dredger over in Wembley. He said it was the strongest stuff you can find. I'll dump it in the well for you tomorrow and you won't have to touch it again for a week.'

'Why, Thaddeus,' said Roshanne, 'that's very sweet of you.'

'Wait a minute,' said India, feeling her face flush. 'I work hard to keep chemicals out of our well. I don't want him touching it.'

'Enough now, India,' said Roshanne, tottering back from

the stove. 'Move out of the way so I can put this saucepan down.'

Clench grinned smugly while Roshanne slopped runny fish soup and gritty spinach into their bowls. India's stomach tightened into an angry knot.

'Well, isn't this lovely!' said Roshanne, sitting down. 'I always think there's nothing nicer than the company of friends and family.' She gave Clench another syrupy smile, which made India feel quite queasy. She wished Verity Brown and her android would arrive. 'And now that we're all here,' continued Roshanne, 'Thaddeus and I would like to make a little announcement.'

India put down her spoon. She had a bad feeling about any announcement that Roshanne and Clench might have to make together.

'As you know, Thaddeus and I have become very close over the last few months.' She smiled at him and dabbed her eyes with a small handkerchief. 'Thaddeus has been such a comfort to me in the last year that I have come to think of him almost as a member of our own family.' India thought she would definitely be sick. 'And for that reason, we have agreed that we would all benefit from an alliance.'

India's senses reached high alert. 'What sort of alliance?' she said.

There was an exchange of glances between the two adults.

'We felt that a joining of our families would be good for all of us. Thaddeus would gain a family and we would have the security and protection of a man – something that we've missed so badly during the last year.' Roshanne took a deep breath. 'Thaddeus has confided his feelings to me. He has made an offer of marriage and I have accepted.' She said it quickly, as if in a hurry to get it out.

Bella gasped. India groaned inwardly. The thought of Roshanne and Clench together was physically repulsive but the prospect of seeing him every morning at the breakfast table where her father used to sit was horrible beyond words.

'Well, what do you think, India?' said Roshanne.

None of what India was thinking was repeatable. She anticipated the cold poison she could expect from Roshanne if she objected.

'I think it's great,' she said in a flat voice. The lie made her eyes burn.

Her stepmother blinked at her, surprised. 'You approve?'

'Yeah, really,' said India. 'I hope you'll both be very happy together.'

Roshanne looked puzzled and shook her head. 'Oh no, India, you don't understand. The proposal of marriage was not for me. It was for you. Thaddeus wishes to marry *you* – isn't that exciting?'

The words felt like a rush of ice through her veins. When she spoke, her voice sounded very small. 'Me?'

'Yes dear,' said Roshanne. 'It'll be perfect for all of us.'

'But I'm not old enough!'

'Nonsense, you're only a bit younger than I was when

I married for the first time, and look what it did for me.'
She nudged Clench and made a horrible cackling noise. 'So
what do you think about that then, Bella? Your big sister's
going to get married!'

Bella was confused and looked to India for confirmation.
'When's the wedding?' she said in a whisper.

'How about two weeks from today?' said Clench, rising
from the table. 'I don't go in much for long engagements.'
He started to pursue India slowly around the room as India
tried to keep the table between them. 'Come on, India, try
to look a bit more cheerful about it. I'm still in my prime,
you know. Here, feel that.' He tensed a thin bicep and
invited India to squeeze it.

She stared at it as though it was a snake.

'Hey, Bella!' he said, turning to her sister. 'When you
come to live in my house, how would you like to have a
pony?'

Bella's eyes opened wide. 'Really? Could we? A real
pony?'

'Absolutely! We'll find you the best little pony in England,
a chestnut perhaps, with white socks. Provided your sister
agrees to marry me, that is.'

They all turned to look expectantly at India.

'Stop it, all of you!' cried India. 'It's disgusting. I'm not
going to marry him and you can't make me.' Her voice
cracked and she wiped her cheeks angrily with her sleeve.

'Well actually, India, I can,' said Roshanne, her voice
suddenly cold. 'Now that your father's dead, I'm your legal

guardian. Mr Clench and I have agreed on a contract and there's nothing you can do about it.'

'Missing!' said India through gritted teeth. 'He's missing, not dead.'

Bella looked from India to her stepmother as her bottom lip trembled. Roshanne rolled her eyes.

'Not this again! How many times, India? He disappeared over a year ago in the middle of Siberia. Face the facts, he's gone and he's never coming back. And now it's time I had some fun and laughter in my life, India! You're going to marry Mr Clench and we're going to live in his beautiful house and that's all there is to it.'

'Perhaps,' said Clench with a nasty grin, 'you'd prefer it if I did things the old-fashioned way, India?' With deliberate, comic clumsiness he sank to one knee and placed both hands over his heart. He cleared his throat, making his Adam's apple wobble in his skinny neck. 'India Bentley,' he began in a dramatic voice. 'My heart was like a desert until you came and watered it with your love.' Roshanne sniggered. 'Would you do me the honour of consenting to become Mrs India Clench?' Then he laughed, a long mocking laugh that filled the room, and Roshanne joined in, cackling at what a splendid joke it all was.

Unable to bear the horror a moment longer, India turned and fled from the kitchen. But she got no further than the kitchen door, where she ran straight into Verity Brown standing in the open doorway.

'Hello,' said Verity. 'I did knock but nobody heard me.'

The others gawped in shocked silence at the unexpected visitor. Just when Roshanne looked like she had recovered enough to speak, the towering figure of Calculus ducked through the doorframe and positioned himself next to his mistress.

'Good grief!' shrieked Roshanne. 'What *is* that? Who are you? What are you doing in my house?'

'Verity Brown,' said Verity, extending a hand that nobody took. 'I hope you don't mind us dropping in like this? India said it would be OK.' She smiled, displaying an even set of white teeth.

'I most certainly do mind,' said Roshanne. 'You're interrupting an important family occasion. And what do you mean, "India said it would be OK"?' All eyes turned to India.

'Mrs Brown works for the Company,' she explained. 'She needs our help.'

'Well, now is not a convenient time to ask for it,' said Roshanne. 'India, you've no business inviting this woman here with her . . . her —' she pointed to the android — '*contraption.*'

India smiled, enjoying Roshanne's discomfort.

'Don't mind him, Mrs Bentley,' said Verity, looking at Calculus. 'He's harmless, just a puppy really.'

'I think he looks kind,' said Bella, smiling at the android.

'It's a bloody robot, is what it is, and I don't want it leaking oil in my kitchen. Make it go out – go on, shoo, shoo, you ghastly thing.'

'Actually,' said Calculus, 'I am an android, not a robot. It's a very different thing altogether.'

Verity glanced at Calculus and jerked her head imperceptibly. The android stopped talking and made a curious gesture, placing his palms together and bowing slightly. 'Perhaps,' he said, 'it would be better if I waited outside. Please call me if you need anything, Mrs Brown.'

'That's some machine you have there, Mrs Brown,' said Clench when Calculus was safely outside. 'I expect not much could stop *him* in his tracks, eh?'

'Not much,' said Verity. 'Could we sit down? I won't intrude for long.'

Roshanne and Bella quickly cleared the remains of the meal while India poured Verity a cup of acorn coffee from the pot on the stove.

'Like India said, I represent the Trans-Siberian Mining Company,' said Verity when they were all seated. 'I'm here on business.'

'Ah! So you're from Angel Town,' said Clench.

'I'm from New York, Mr Clench, or what's left of it. But I go wherever I can find work. I see you know about Angel Town. Have you ever been there?'

'Well, er, maybe once.' Clench looked uncomfortable. 'A long time ago, I can't say I remember it very well, though.'

'It's a frontier town, the last big outpost before you reach the wilderness. Every rigger in Siberia brings their iron and oil to sell in Angel Town, and Trans-Siberian owns the whole damn place.'

'And what do *you* do in Angel Town, Mrs Brown?' said Clench.

'I make my living by finding things,' said Verity. 'Old things that used to be valuable, lost under the mud and the water.'

'You mean you're a *scavenger*?'

'I didn't say that, Mr Clench. Scavengers are only interested in *dead-tech* – junk that's good for nothing but scrap. But I'm a licensed salvage operator, a tech-hunter. It's a different thing altogether. My customers will only pay for stuff that's still in working order and that's very hard to find these days, unless you know where to look.'

Clench seemed impressed. 'A tech-hunter eh? That's a difficult job for a woman.'

'Only the difficult stuff is worth doing, Mr Clench,' she said. Her eyes held a glint of steel.

'Mrs Brown,' said Roshanne. 'My husband was a mining engineer and I know perfectly well what Angel Town is. Now why don't you tell us what you want so you can get back to bloody Siberia.'

India realized Roshanne was a little drunk.

'Trans-Siberian is owned by one man,' said Verity. 'Lucifer Stone. He built the company from nothing and now he's the richest man on the planet, the first person to become a millionaire after the Great Rains. He calls himself "The Director".' She took another sip of coffee. 'But what Mr Stone is really interested in is technology from before the rains. Let me show you what I mean.'

Verity opened her satchel and started rummaging around, heaping various items on the kitchen table. India watched as the pile grew to include a wrench, several pieces of wire, a pair of pliers, a screwdriver, a glass valve, a circuit board, a small box with tiny buttons on it and some plastic disks that reflected the colours of the rainbow.

Clench picked up the little box and tried the buttons. 'What does this do?'

'It's a speaking device,' said Verity. 'It's called a "fone". If you had one of these you could speak to anyone in the world, wherever they were.'

Clench looked at it with wonder. 'Can I try it?'

'You're welcome to give it a go,' she said with a small smile, 'but it's been under fifty feet of water for over a century, so my guess is you're not going to get through to anyone.'

Clench put the device down with a sniff.

'Here we go,' said Verity, finding what she was looking for. She unfolded a large map and spread it out on the table. It was heavily creased and worn through in places.

'That's Siberia!' said Bella proudly. 'My dad showed me a map like that once.' She prodded at the paper. 'That's the Ural Mountains and that's the Laptev Sea.'

'What are all those red dots?' said India.

'Tech mines,' said Verity. 'Concentrated pockets of old technology, lost under the water in cities, factories and hospitals. Most of it is low-grade stuff, waterlogged and useless. But occasionally one of these mines turns

31

up something that's worth good money. Computational engines, telegraphic devices, rocket propulsion systems—'

'A fully working android?' offered Clench.

'Precisely so, Mr Clench,' she said. 'I found Calculus buried in a factory in China and I rebuilt him with my own hands. I'm very good at what I do.'

'I don't understand what this has to do with my husband,' said Roshanne, pouring herself another glass of wine and spilling some of it on the map.

'I was coming to that,' said Verity. 'Mr Stone wants to acquire as much working technology as possible so his people can take it apart and find out how to replicate it. He pays top money for it too.' She lowered her voice. 'What I'm going to tell you next is a closely guarded secret.'

Instinctively they drew closer.

'There's a story that says when the old-world governments knew the Great Rains were coming they built an underground storehouse out in the wilderness. Somewhere that would be safe from the floods. Then they filled it with the most valuable things in the world. Everything they'd need to rebuild society when the waters went down.'

'You mean like the Ark in the Bible stories?' said Bella, her eyes shining. 'What sort of things did they put in there?'

'Well, what would you put in it?' said Verity. 'Books? Medicines? Great works of art? A way to feed the hungry? Nobody knows for sure. The project was codenamed "Ironheart" and only a very few people knew about it. But then after the rains, the Hunger Wars started. The Chaos Years followed and amidst all the panic, the records about Ironheart were lost. As far as we know it's still out there waiting to be found.'

Clench snorted. 'That's just an old rigger's dream, Mrs Brown. Every drunk in Angel Town has a story to tell about the legend of Ironheart, not to mention a map that they'll sell you, for a price.'

'And that's all it was, Mr Clench,' said Verity, 'just a legend. But that's where John Bentley came in. A few years ago he was surveying for oil out here.' She pointed to a desolate-looking spot on the map, surrounded by mountains. 'It's so remote it doesn't even have an official name. The ice people call it *Uliuiu Cherchekh*. Hardly anyone has been there since the Great Rains. While he was there, he met a tribe of nomads who told him about a secret location under the mountains they called *Aironhart*. He became convinced they were talking about the same place. He made several more trips to the area to look for it. Unfortunately we have no record of what he found because most of his files were destroyed in a fire just before he went missing.'

A silence fell on the room. India remembered the day the news had arrived. It had been a simple letter, just stating the facts: John Bentley had gone missing in the mountains and there was no hope left of finding him alive. The letter had said what a fine employee he'd been, and his final pay cheque had been enclosed. The Company had subtracted the cost of the uniform he'd been wearing when he disappeared.

'No one gave Ironheart any more thought,' said Verity. 'But then two weeks ago some of John Bentley's old papers turned up unexpectedly in a packing crate. It was mostly survey notes and rock samples but in among them we found this.'

She placed a flat piece of iron on the table. It was a nameplate, the sort you might put on a door or a gate post. It was black and pitted and inscribed with one word. *Aironhart.*

India ran a finger over the rough surface. 'What does it mean?'

'It may be nothing but it could mean your father found what he was looking for,' said Verity. 'If he did, then he decided to keep it a secret for some reason.'

'But why would he do that?' said India.

'Well, Angel Town is a dangerous place. Perhaps he had enemies there. But Mr Stone is very keen to learn what your father knew. That's why he's paying me to find out.'

'Paying you?' said Clench, suddenly alert.

'Why don't Trans-Siberian just go and look for Ironheart themselves?' said India.

'They've tried,' said Verity, 'but it's a vast and remote territory. In the summer it's a swampland filled with biting insects and in the winter the temperature is minus sixty and the ground is frozen solid. If Ironheart is there, it's probably buried deep underground. You could be standing on top of it and never know. Mrs Bentley,' she said, turning to Roshanne. 'If I can find out where your husband was looking, I can help the company to mount a proper expedition.'

Roshanne drained her glass. 'Well, good luck, Mrs Brown,' she slurred. 'But I really don't know what any of this has to do with me.'

'I was hoping he might have left you with some personal record of his work. Navigation charts, a diary perhaps? Something that could give us a clue as to where to start looking.'

'What about Dad's journals?' said India. 'Whenever he got home he'd always update his notebooks.'

Verity seized on her words. 'His journals? Yes, I think that might be the very thing – may I see them?'

'Let's not be too hasty.' Clench narrowed his eyes. 'Those journals are the property of this dear lady and her recently bereaved family.' He adopted a pained expression. 'There might be personal revelations in there.' He turned to Roshanne. 'I think, my dear, it would not be wise to share them with this woman.'

'Mrs Bentley,' said Verity firmly. 'When the Great Rains came, they stopped human civilization in its tracks. Since then we've gone back to the Dark Ages, scratching a living from melting down old junk and eating poisoned food.' She glanced at the cooking pot on the stove, which was still emitting vile smells. 'Ironheart just might hold secrets that could help us feed the world properly again. It could save thousands, if not millions, of lives.'

'Feed the world?' said India. 'Dad always said they knew how to do that before the Great Rains.'

'And we might learn how to do it again,' said Verity. 'So I'm asking you, Mrs Bentley, to please help me find this place. Do it for the memory of your husband.'

'The memory of my husband! Let me tell *you* about the memory of *my* husband, Mrs Brown. Five years I was married to that man. Five years of waiting for him to come home from yet another wretched expedition while I dragged up his brats in this mud hole.'

'Roshanne!' said India, shocked.

'I understand,' said Verity slowly, 'that it must have been very difficult for you.'

'You understand *nothing*.' Roshanne took another slug of wine and rubbed her eyes, smearing black grease across her face. 'After five years of being a loving and devoted wife I got nothing for my troubles, not a penny! That man was a complete waster, so don't give me any of this "Do it for the memory of your husband" rubbish. If you want something from me, Mrs Brown, you and your *Mr Stone* are going to have to pay for it!'

India looked at Bella. Her little sister's blue eyes had filled with tears as Roshanne ranted about their father.

'That's enough!' said India, jumping to her feet. 'I won't let you say those things about Dad. He looked after us and kept us safe – which is more than you've ever done!'

'What do you know about it?' slurred Roshanne. 'You're just a child!'

'I'm old enough for you to marry me off to that sleazebag, just so you can live in a nice house!'

'You poisonous brat!'

'You drunken old witch!'

Roshanne lunged unsteadily at India, lost her balance and collapsed to the floor with a squeal. 'You little minx!' she yelped as Clench helped her up. 'You're not too young for me to thrash your backside.' She attempted to chase India around the table, leaning on Clench for support.

The farce might have gone on for some time if Bella hadn't screamed. She was standing beside the window looking panicked. 'Stop it, all of you! There are people outside our house and they've got sticks and things.'

No sooner had Bella spoken than a windowpane shattered and a small rock rolled across the floor. Bella squealed again and ran to hide behind India. They peered through the broken window and saw an angry-looking group of people gathered a short distance from the house carrying sticks and burning torches. Mehmet was standing at the front of the group.

The sound of the kitchen door bursting open made them all jump again as Calculus ducked quickly inside. He slammed the door shut and pressed his weight against it.

'You had better come quickly, Mrs Brown,' he said. 'We've got big trouble outside.'

CHAPTER 4

HONEST FOLK

It looked like nearly all of the village had gathered at the end of their path and they did not look happy. The men swung sticks and farm tools restlessly while the women hung back, arms crossed tightly across their chests.

'What's happening?' whispered Verity as they stepped outside.

'A group of locals, Mrs Brown,' said Calculus. 'Apparently they have found our motorbike and assumed we are southsiders. They demand the release of our "hostages".'

'How many?'

'I count forty-seven people in all. They have various farm implements, six projectile weapons, mostly shotguns, and one machine gun. But I very much doubt that it's working.'

'Very reassuring,' said Verity. 'Well, so much for getting in and out without being seen. I'll go and talk to them.'

'Wait,' said India. 'They're shore dwellers and they're suspicious of strangers. Let me talk to them.'

She started down the path, with damp palms and a dry mouth. Most of the families in their village had lost people in the last year. If the crowd really thought they had the chance to take revenge on a pair of southsiders, it might be difficult to control them.

At the front of the group stood Mehmet, picking his nose. Cromerty was next to him, grinning toothlessly as though she was out for a pleasant stroll.

'Hello, deary, lovely evening, ain't it?'

'Where's your mum, India?' said Mehmet, ignoring the old woman.

'Roshanne's inside,' said India. 'She's OK. We're all OK. What are you all doing here?'

The constable wiped his fingers on the seat of his trousers and drew himself up to his full height.

'We've come for the southsiders. Two of the boys found their *machine*.' He pointed to the motorbike which lay overturned in the shallow waters at the bottom of the hill. 'Now we're going to teach them a lesson once and for all.' The crowd grumbled and pressed forward. From the corner of her eye India saw Calculus shift his position slightly.

'Wait, Mehmet, these people aren't southsiders. They're from Trans-Siberian Mining, where Dad used to work.'

'Then why did they sneak into our village at night unannounced?' He jabbed a finger towards Calculus. 'With a military droid?'

'It's true what India says,' said Verity, coming to her side.

39

'We're here on business. We just want some information, that's all.'

'We don't give information to strangers,' said a young man with a face full of ripe pimples. He yanked out an ancient pistol that was thick with rust. 'A raiding party took my sister last year,' he said, pointing the gun at Verity. 'So now I'm going to shoot me a southsider.'

India flinched. But before she could speak, a blur of motion rushed past her. Something impacted heavily with the boy, who went flying backwards. India blinked; a moment earlier, Calculus had been standing ten feet behind her, but now he was crouching over the boy, who was groaning and clutching his chest.

The crowd pushed forward aggressively and a man at the front swung an axe at Calculus. He side-stepped it with ease and swept the man off his feet. A rock sailed over the heads of the crowd and thumped on to the path beside India.

'Stop it, stop it!' she cried. But her voice was carried away on a tide of anger.

'Come on, India,' said Verity, pulling India away. 'Let's go – quickly, before someone gets badly hurt.'

'See, I told you you'd be going on a journey, India,' laughed Cromerty. She began waving a handkerchief in a gesture of farewell.

'Calculus!' Verity called out as they retreated. 'Hold them off – but no fatalities, please.' She dragged India back to the house and pulled her into the doorway, out of sight of the crowd.

'Will Calculus be all right?' said India. 'Shouldn't we help him?'

'Never mind about him,' said Verity. 'I've put you in danger by coming here. The sooner we leave, the better for all of you. Can you help me get to my bike?'

India's mind raced. 'What about Dad's journals? That's what you came for, isn't it?'

'You'd give them to me?' said Verity cautiously.

'I might, but you'd need to do something for me in return.' India took a deep breath. 'I want to come with you, I want to get away from here and go to Siberia to find my dad.'

Verity shook her head. 'Sorry, India, I don't take passengers. I can see what's going on here, but believe me, there's far worse things that could happen to you than marrying Mr Clench. At least here you'll be safe.'

'You don't understand,' said India. 'Nobody knows what happened to my dad and nobody seems to care except me.'

'Put it out of your head, India,' said Verity firmly. 'Siberia is the most hostile place on Earth and I'm afraid Mrs Bentley was right: your dad is probably dead.'

'Everybody says that! But you don't know my dad – he's smart and he knows how to survive. Besides, I made him a promise that if he was ever lost, I'd come and find him.' She stopped. For the second time that evening she had said more than she meant to. 'All right then,' she bargained. 'If you won't help me find my dad, how about you just take me as far as Angel Town? I'll give you the journals in return

41

for a cut of the money and then you'll never have to see me again. But if you don't take me, I'll make sure you never get the journals. I'll burn them myself if I have to.'

'Jeez,' said Verity, blowing out her cheeks. 'You do drive a hard bargain, don't you? All right then, get me the journals. I'll take you to Angel Town and give you ten per cent of my fee, but then you're on your own, understood?'

'Fifty per cent,' said India, giving her a hard look.

'Twenty, and that's my final offer. Otherwise you can stay here and become Mrs Clench, for all I care.'

India nodded and they shook hands solemnly.

Back inside the house, Roshanne and Clench stood behind the kitchen table looking like frightened animals. India looked into Bella's wide, unblinking eyes and tried to give her a reassuring smile.

'I'll get the journals,' said India. She moved towards the stairs but Clench grabbed her.

'Now, wait just a minute,' he said, looking at Verity. 'Mrs Bentley is the proper owner of those journals and they're staying here until I can negotiate a fair price for them on behalf of the family. As for my fiancée –' he took a tighter grip on India's arm – 'she will learn to do as she's told.'

India twisted frantically in Clench's grip. 'Get off me, you pig!' she shouted. 'I'm not staying here! You don't own me and I am NOT your fiancée!'

'Damn it, India,' he said. 'If I'm going to be your husband you need to understand what obedience means.'

He struck her hard across the face. The slap made a

noise like a pistol shot and everyone froze in shock. Bella turned deathly pale and even Clench seemed taken aback by his own action. India stared at Clench in disbelief and touched her red-hot cheek. Then a rage took hold of her. She flew at Clench and raked his face with her nails. He struggled to control the spitting, screaming girl and raised his hand to strike her again. But she was too quick for him. In an instant the shock stick was in her hand and she jabbed him with it hard between his eyes.

There was a sound like a piece of dry timber being snapped in half and the smell of electrical burning filled the room. Clench's body flew backwards with a violent spasm. He crashed across the table and lay spreadeagled on the floor, twitching and jerking, a string of snot running from his nose. There was silence, save for the crackling of the shock stick.

'Stay here,' said India to Verity. 'Don't you *dare* move.'

Upstairs, she collected her father's satchel and stuffed it with the things she thought she might need in Siberia. Clean clothes, bottled water, her father's hunting knife. Then she went to her father's bookcase, which held twenty identical black journals, one for each year he had worked in Siberia. She pulled out the last two and put them into the bag before dashing downstairs, pulling on her thick, waxy jacket as she went.

Clench was still on the floor, groaning. India stepped over him and went to Bella, who sat hugging her knees in an armchair.

'Are you leaving?' said Bella in a small, frightened voice.

India nodded. 'I'm sorry, Bella, but I have to.' She looked at Clench. 'You understand why, don't you?' Bella nodded dumbly. 'I'm going to find Dad, Bella. I'm going to find him and bring him back – then we'll be a family again. You'd like that, wouldn't you?'

'Can I come with you?' said Bella in a whisper.

'I'm sorry, it's too dangerous,' said India, trying desperately not to cry in front of her sister. A thought struck her and she pulled out her pendant from beneath her shirt. 'Here, do you have your pendant? The one Dad made you?'

'In my room,' said Bella.

'I want you to do something for me. Every night when you look at the stars, I want you to hold your pendant and think of me and I'll do the same. Every night until I get back with Dad – can you do that?'

Bella nodded miserably. India hugged her little sister and then turned away so that Bella wouldn't see her tears.

She ignored Roshanne, who scowled angrily but made no move to stop her as she went to the door. But as India stepped over Clench, he reached out and grasped the leg of her trousers.

'You won't get far . . .' he croaked. 'You'll come crying back to me before you've gone ten miles.' Then he flopped backwards on to the floor, gasping for breath.

India stopped and kneeled down beside him. 'You'd better not be here when I get back,' she hissed into his ear. 'Because I'm going to fetch my dad.'

She stared at him contemptuously for a moment, then stood and hefted the bag on to her shoulder. 'Come on,' she said to Verity. 'We're done here.'

She hitched up the window in the hallway and threw her leg over the sill in a practised move. After helping Verity, she led her swiftly through a thin line of trees down to the shoreline.

They waded as silently as they could towards the upturned bike and turned it over. It was caked with thick mud and the sidecar was partially filled with water. Verity cleared the mud from the exhaust pipe and swung her leg over the saddle as India kept an anxious eye on the crowd at the front of the house.

'Get in, quickly!' said Verity. 'They'll hear us as soon as I start her up.' India threw in her bag and clambered into the watery sidecar as Verity applied her weight to the kick-starter. The bike turned over noisily but didn't fire. She tried again without success. By now they had attracted the attention of the crowd and fresh shouting broke out. A group of men ran towards them, led by Mehmet. There was a loud pop and an angry insect snicked past India's ear.

'India, get your head down, they're shooting at us!' Verity kicked the starter again and this time the engine roared to life. She twisted the throttle and the bike accelerated through the shallow waters, scattering the villagers like a flock of birds. As they gunned up the hill, Calculus seized the opportunity to jump on the back of the bike and they swept past the mob and into the surrounding darkness.

'Nice to see you, Calc,' shouted Verity. 'Did you miss me?'

'I'm glad you could get here, Mrs Brown,' he said.

Verity leaned over the sidecar and shouted to India. 'You still in one piece, kid?'

India swallowed hard and nodded. 'I think so. Is everyone all right – back there, I mean?'

'Some broken bones and superficial injuries,' said Calculus. 'Nothing major, but I suspect your neighbours will not welcome us back any time soon.'

India sat back in the damp seat and waited for her heart to stop thumping as the bike slithered down the mud track, away from the village. That was true, she thought, that was very true.

CHAPTER 5

THE *AURORA QUEEN*

Verity drove like a woman possessed, and the motorcycle slithered and fishtailed along muddy tracks, barely slowing for bends. India got the impression that Verity had not been riding a motorcycle for very long and she had to throw her own weight around in the sidecar to stop them from overturning. Calculus had climbed off the bike and was running alongside them, easily keeping pace no matter how fast they went.

They drove for an hour through the broken streets of the dead city until the shattered buildings gradually gave way to open fields and muddy tracks. India longed to stretch her legs and she was glad when they finally pulled to a halt beside a broad estuary. They looked out over a sheet of oily, black water and stinking, tidal mud. Verity checked her watch.

'They're late,' she muttered. 'The *Aurora Queen* is supposed to be here by now.'

'The *Aurora Queen*?' said India. 'Is that a boat?'

'Better than that,' said Verity, scanning the skies. 'A plane, the fastest way to the cold country – and so it should be for what I pay the Smiley Brothers.'

Verity inspected the bike and kicked at the front wheel, which had gone flat.

'Damn! I'm going to have to repair it. The villagers took the spare.' She set about removing the wheel and dragging the punctured tyre down to the water's edge. 'Stay alert, Calc,' she called out. 'This is dangerous country.'

Calculus had taken the opportunity to build a fire. He opened a small tin and tipped some black leaves into boiling water. 'Would you like some tea?' he asked India.

India took the steaming mug gratefully. The tea was black and scalding and felt good as it slid down her throat. She watched the android carefully as he sat down. 'Are you all right?' she said. 'You were very brave taking on that lot on your own. Weren't you scared?'

'I am quite all right, thank you, India,' he said. 'And I am programmed to have no fear, otherwise I might hesitate in my duty.'

'Then it's true what Mehmet said?' she asked. 'You *are* a military droid?'

'I was once,' he corrected. 'But I no longer carry weapons and I have no wish to be remembered as a war machine.'

'What would happen if you were ordered to kill someone?' she said. 'Androids have to follow their programming, don't they?'

'That,' he said, stoking the fire thoughtfully, 'is a very interesting question.'

A long silence followed. India thought it might be polite to change the subject. 'Where did you meet Mrs Brown?' she said.

'She found me in a factory, where I had been buried in the mud for over a century. She reset my base codes and repaired my damaged parts.' He tapped the steel sheet in his chest, which rang hollow. 'She is really quite talented, you know.'

'Are there any others like you?' India thought again how cool it would be to have your own android.

Calculus made a noise that might have been a sigh and began to tidy away the tea things. 'No,' he said brusquely, 'there are no more like me.' He turned his back and began to pack the bags. India wondered again whether she had offended him in some way. Just then, Verity returned from the water's edge, cheerfully dragging the mended tyre.

'So what do you think of this baby?' she said, slapping the side of the bike. 'She's over a hundred years old. I borrowed her from a friend of mine and I think I'm getting used to her. When we get paid in Angel Town I might see if he wants to sell her to me, provided I can get the gas. God damn it!' She swore loudly as the spanner slipped, skinning her knuckles.

'Will Mr Stone pay you for the journals when we get there?' said India, wondering how much money was twenty per cent.

Verity laughed. 'I doubt it – I've never even met the

man. I just deliver the goods to his office and his minions give me the cash.'

'But aren't you interested in how he's going to feed the world and do all those other things you said?'

'My job is to find the stuff,' said Verity. 'I'm not paid to ask questions.' She stopped working and looked at India with a serious expression. 'When we get to Angel Town I need you to do exactly as I say. Tech-hunting attracts the worst lowlifes, murderers and cut-throats. I need to get the money and get out as quickly as possible without attracting attention. Do you understand?'

India nodded.

Verity went back to work on the wheel. 'Don't worry,' she said from under the bike, 'as soon as we get the cash, you'll get your share and then you can do as you please. Once you've got a bit of money to your name, creeps like Clench won't be able to touch you.'

'Perhaps, after I've found my dad, I could buy a scav-boat and go looking for salvage,' said India. 'Maybe I could even drill my own well.'

'Smart plan,' said Verity, giving the wheel one last tightening. 'OK, we're ready to go.' She wiped her hands on a greasy rag. 'Now where the hell is the *Aurora Queen*?'

They sat beside the water with chattering teeth and scanned the skies. After half an hour India jumped up and pointed excitedly to a silent, blue-white line scratching its way across the sky.

'That's just a shooting star,' said Verity. 'The ice people

believe every person in the world has their own star, and when you die, it falls to Earth.' India watched the fading streak and shivered.

'Twin engines,' said Calculus suddenly, 'approaching from the east.'

At first India could hear nothing, but then she caught the faintest hum of an engine carried towards them on the breeze.

Verity turned on the bike's headlamp. 'Get ready to move quickly,' she said. 'They won't want to stay down long in this neck of the woods.'

The noise was constant now, an unmistakable droning of aircraft engines. A bright light pierced the cloud and the dark shape of the plane appeared. Its broad body was shaped like the hull of a fishing smack with two big outriggers under the propellers.

'Flying boat,' said Verity with a grin. 'The only way to travel in a flooded country.'

The plane hit the water in a burst of spray and foam, and the smell of aircraft fuel wafted over the water. Verity lit another cigar while it taxied into the shallows, and India stared open-mouthed at the enormous machine.

Two men with oil-black hair and greasy overalls climbed from the cockpit and waded towards them. India guessed that they were the Smiley Brothers but they looked sullen and dangerous. They conversed with Verity in low voices, all the while casting suspicious looks at India. They were clearly unhappy at having to take another passenger but, after Verity passed them some money, it was agreed. With the help of Calculus, they started to manhandle the bike into the hold of the aircraft.

'Let's get a move on,' said Verity. 'The engine noise will have attracted every bandit within five miles of here.'

India gathered the bags and climbed the short ladder to the plane. She had never seen a plane up close before and she was utterly captivated by the *Aurora Queen*. The fuselage was painted a vibrant red and white and the cabin smelled of leather and polish. Verity led her to a functional canvas seat and showed her how to fasten her seatbelt.

The take-off was thrilling. The engines vibrated powerfully and the plane bounced across the water, breaching the waves like a porpoise, making greater and greater leaps until they were suddenly airborne. India's stomach dropped away as the plane climbed hard and banked into the night sky.

She was disappointed that there was little to see in the darkness apart from the fires of the tyre-burners strung out along the estuary shore. Verity was busy making notes and Calculus was sitting quietly with his hands folded in his lap. She reached into her bag and pulled out one of the journals. It was battered and dog-eared and filled with dense notes written in an engineer's copperplate script. She had often thumbed through the books, fascinated by the descriptions of remote landscapes and the diagrams showing cross-sections of the land and the inner workings of pump systems. But she had never seen anything in them that talked of a hidden ark, or nomads, or any of the other exciting things Verity had mentioned.

'You should let Calc take a look at those,' said Verity, reading her thoughts. 'If there's anything useful in there he'll find it.'

India shut the book with a snap and looked at Verity suspiciously. 'If I give them to you now, you'll have what you want and you won't need me any more.'

Verity sighed. 'And what do you think I'm going to do when I get my hands on your journals, India? Throw you out of the plane? Look, if you're going to be my business associate you're going to have to start trusting me because when we get to Angel Town, me and Calc are going to be the only friends you've got. Now, how about you let him have a look at those journals?'

India couldn't help grinning. 'Is that what I am then, your *business associate*?'

Verity laughed. 'Sure thing, kid. So how about it, can he have a look?'

'OK, but I want to look at them myself first,' said India. 'He can read them when we land.'

She returned to the book in her lap and tried to imagine a land filled with wild creatures, ice people and oil prospectors where the wind of adventure might blow across the ice at any moment and carry you away.

Then something caught her eye. Tucked away, at the bottom of a dull page describing rock strata, was a single sentence that her father had underlined. Her blood chilled when she read the words: '*There's something wrong with the sky.*'

CHAPTER 6

ANGEL TOWN

She struggled to pull her feet free of the thick mud as the southsiders chased her across the tidal flats. They leered and snarled through yellowed teeth and reached for her with bony, spidery fingers. But the more she looked back at their scowling, wicked faces the more they looked like Thaddeus Clench and Roshanne Bentley dressed in wedding clothes.

Just when it seemed certain they would catch her, the picture changed. Instead of the shoreline she now stood in a wide valley surrounded by tree-covered slopes. The mud was gone and the ground was covered in pure, unbroken snow.

She saw him then at the top of the hill. Too far away to see his face but something about the way he stood, hunched against the cold, felt so familiar. She heard her name carried softly on the wind and he beckoned her to follow him. But when she reached the top of the hill he wasn't there. She turned every way, desperate to catch a glimpse of him, but he was nowhere to be seen.

It was as though the very ground had opened up and pulled him in.

'Dad!' She sat up with a start.

'Sleep OK, kid?' Verity was awake, pulling a brush ferociously through her long hair.

India sat up and blinked. 'Uh, yeah. Just a dream, that's all.'

Verity leaned across her and looked out of the window. 'We'll be there in about an hour. We're going to land on the river, which means you'll get a great view of Angel Town.'

The early sun streamed through the plane windows and cast a fresh-washed brilliance across the sky. Far below, a scattering of icebergs sailed on foam-flecked waves and an iron-red cargo ship plunged through the swell, the seas washing her decks. India peered at the horizon as a dark coastline emerged from the morning mist and she had her first glimpse of Angel Town.

From the air, the town was an untidy collection of wooden buildings and pitched roofs covered in thick snow. The muddy streets converged on a busy harbour lined with bleached timber warehouses and skeletal cranes.

'That's where they bring in the raw materials from the rig yards to be processed,' said Verity, pointing to a row of blackened factory buildings sending pencil lines of smoke into the crisp air.

'Where are the rig yards?' said India. She was anxious for

a glimpse of one of the giant prospecting vehicles her father had told her so much about.

'On the other side of the mountains, in Salekhard,' said Verity, 'about a day's journey from here. It's cheaper to bring the stuff over the mountains by barge and rail.'

The *Aurora Queen* dipped her nose towards a strip of water and landed in another burst of spray before taxiing to the dockside. They spilled from the plane on to a busy harbour-front market where the air was thick with the smell of meat and wood smoke. Stout women argued over the price of plucked chickens and wet fish while gulls wheeled overhead like scraps of paper on the breeze. A group of men with brown faces and skin like creased leather stood apart at the end of the harbour. They wore thick jackets and boots and tended some shaggy-looking beasts. India stared at them, remembering her father's descriptions of the tribal people in Siberia.

'Are they ice people?' she said in hushed tones.

'Yes – although they call themselves reindeer people,' said Calculus. 'They live out in the eastern wilderness mostly and sometimes they bring their animals here to trade. I don't remember seeing so many of them in Angel Town before.'

'And who is he?' She pointed to an old man wearing a metal disc around his neck engraved with fierce creatures. Although poorly dressed, he looked proud and noble.

'He's a shaman,' said Calculus, 'a holy person. They say a powerful shaman can take the shape of a bird and fly across the land or even control a man's dreams.'

'Control dreams?' she said. 'That's just superstition, isn't it?'

'There are many things that cannot be explained,' said the android, 'but that does not mean they are not true. The shamans are greatly respected and feared in this country.'

India looked back at the old man and was disconcerted to find he was staring directly at her. She turned away quickly to follow Calculus.

They caught up with Verity outside a noisy bar. Even though it was early morning, the sounds of laughter and an out-of-tune piano spilled on to the street. A sign above the door read: 'Mrs Chang's Fine Dining Rooms and Guest House – Licensed to sell intoxicating liquors and explosives'. Underneath, another sign declared 'NO ROBOTS' in large red letters.

'Perfect!' said Verity. 'Why don't you guys go ahead and get checked in and I'll see about getting us an appointment at Trans-Siberian.'

'We're going to stay here?' said India. 'It sounds like they're actually fighting in there.'

'It's just high spirits,' said Verity. 'Half of them are getting drunk because they're about to leave town and the other half are getting drunk because they just got back.'

A gunshot inside the building made India jump but the music continued without stopping. 'Is it always like this?' she said.

'Hell, no!' shouted Verity over her shoulder as she disappeared down the street. 'You should see it on pay days. That's when it gets really wild!'

India looked up at the 'No Robots' sign. 'Maybe we should try somewhere else?' she said.

'There is nowhere else,' said Calculus. 'Unless you wish to sleep in the stables?'

She shook her head. 'No thanks, but maybe I should go in first?' She looked at the door nervously. 'I mean, what's the worst that could happen?'

'They might shoot you,' offered Calculus helpfully.

'They might shoot you too.'

'True, but of the two of us I am the only one who is bulletproof.'

'That's a very good point,' she said. 'OK, you talked me into it. I'll wait for you out here, but be careful.'

She stood in a side alley out of the way of the crowds, avoiding the man with the dancing bear, who kept leering at her as he rattled his collecting tin.

She was so preoccupied that she didn't notice the three men dressed in long black coats and wide hats who walked up the alley until they were right on top of her.

Two of the men reminded her of Mehmet's thugs. One had buck teeth and a lazy eye and he kept wiping his nose on the back of his sleeve. His companion had heavy eyebrows and stood with his mouth open, wearing an expression that suggested he had to concentrate hard to stay standing up. But the younger man who accompanied them was different – thin and wiry, with a pale face and a shock of black hair. He looked only a few years older than India but he carried a long-barrelled pistol in the belt of his overcoat. He was obviously in charge.

'So, who we got here?' said the youth. His voice was surprisingly soft, like a child's, thought India, but his eyes were hard. 'I've seen you before. You arrived with that Brown woman, didn't you?'

India wished she had stayed closer to the main street, and hoped Calculus would return soon.

'I asked you a question,' said the soft voice. 'What business have you got with the Brown woman?'

India grasped the shock stick in her pocket but all three men were carrying guns and she knew she could only use it as a last resort.

'She's a damned thief, that woman,' continued the youth. He leaned towards India. 'I wanted to go to London for them journals but she stole that job from me. Now she's back here and she's got you with her. Are you one of Bentley's daughters, is that who you are?'

'That's none of your business,' said India, sounding braver than she felt. 'I've got a military droid with me. He'll tear your arms off if you don't let me go.' The older men laughed oafishly and the youth gave her a nasty smile.

'Oh yeah, I've seen your big guy earlier but I don't see him now. Looks to me like you're on your own.' He looked at her bag. 'So what you got, girly? You got your daddy's

59

journals hid in there?' Before she could answer he grabbed hold of the bag and tore it open.

'You give that back,' she shouted. 'It doesn't belong to you!' She tried to snatch it from him but the heavy man grabbed her by the arms. Outraged, India stamped on his toe, causing him to yelp and hop around the alleyway until he crashed into his companion. Before she could run the youth pulled out his own pistol and pointed it at her.

'Silas, Cripps, quit dancing with each other and keep her covered.'

The two men let go of each other sheepishly and stood in front of India while the boy went through her bag. He pocketed her father's knife, then pulled out the two slim volumes and held them up. 'Are these your daddy's journals?' he said. 'I'm betting they are.' He flicked through the pages of one volume, scanning the words. India noticed he was holding the book upside down. 'Well, them's my journals now.' He snapped the book shut.

'They belong to me,' said India furiously. 'You're a lousy thief is what you are!'

The men laughed.

'Didn't your daddy teach you to be polite to strangers?' said the boy.

'Didn't your mother teach you not to steal!' she snapped back.

His smile vanished in an instant. 'W-what did you say about my m-ma?' His eye twitched. 'Don't you dare say nothing about her!'

The other two men exchanged terrified glances as a cold fury seemed to consume the boy. He advanced on India with a face full of hate. She felt her legs go weak but, before he could reach her, a deafening explosion reverberated up the alley. Everyone ducked. Standing in the kitchen doorway of the guest house was a middle-aged Chinese woman holding a smoking shotgun.

'Leave her alone or I let you have other barrel,' she said.

The boy glared at the woman and India was afraid he might fly at her. But the heavy man reached out and grasped the boy tentatively by the arm.

'Er, Mr Sid? I think now we got what you came for, we better get movin'.' The boy shook his arm away angrily but he allowed himself to be led away, still glaring at the woman as he went.

Seconds later Calculus came running up from the other end of the alley. 'India, are you all right?' he said.

She picked up her torn bag and groaned. 'Oh, Calc, they took my dad's journals.'

'But at least you are unhurt,' he said.

'No thanks to you,' she said, rubbing her arm. 'Some bodyguard you turned out to be.'

Calculus turned to the Chinese woman. 'Thank you for your help, madam. Might I know your name?'

She looked at him suspiciously. 'My name, Mrs Chang. But you can call me Mrs Chang.' She curled her lip.

'They told me inside I should speak to you about renting rooms,' said Calculus.

She put down the shotgun and folded her beefy forearms. 'Always rooms at Mrs Chang's,' she said.

'Oh, good,' said Calculus.

'But I not like robot,' she added grimly.

Calculus was taken aback. 'I am not a robot, madam,' he said, offended. 'Robots are mere machines. I am a sentient android. It is an entirely different thing altogether.'

'That just a fancy name for a robot,' said Mrs Chang with a scowl. Then she looked from Calculus to the miserable figure of India. 'You got money?' she said eventually. 'No good if you don't got money.' Calculus hastily held out a bundle of notes. She grunted. 'OK, this way.' She turned and walked back inside. 'Welcome to Mrs Chang's,' she added as an afterthought.

CHAPTER 7

THE PIRATE RIGGER

The inside of Mrs Chang's guest house combined a dining room, a bar and a general store. There were open sacks of flour and dry beans by the door and tinned foods stacked neatly on shelves. New steel buckets hung from the ceiling next to coils of heavy rope and the counter was packed with jars of jam, candles and, alarmingly, sticks of dynamite.

Large men were crammed around rough wooden tables, consuming jugs of beer and plates of meat and potatoes. The air was thick with cooking steam and alive with rowdy conversation. Hardly anyone looked up at the newcomers. Mrs Chang picked up plates from the kitchen counter and began slamming them down on the tables.

'Why you want room?' she shouted to Calculus over the din. 'Damned robot don't sleep, don't eat nothing, don't spend no money, just take up space, bad for business.'

Calculus assured her he would willingly pay for the food

he wasn't going to eat so that he could sit in her dining room.

'What about her?' said Mrs Chang, sizing up India with a critical eye. 'She gonna eat? She's as thin as a noodle, no good if she don't eat.'

India felt sick to her stomach about the loss of the journals but she nodded miserably and said she would try and eat something.

Despite her hard-faced exterior Mrs Chang turned out to be a kind soul. She took pity on India's miserable state and led her to a small guest room on the top floor where she drew her a hot bath. At any other time India would have been entranced with the novelty of getting hot water from a tap whenever you wanted it. But now she just sat unhappily in the bath and hugged her knees while Mrs Chang scrubbed her back.

'Who was that boy in the alleyway?' asked India.

Mrs Chang made a tutting sound as she pulled a brush from her apron and began to drag it through India's hair. 'That's Sid the Kid. He's a bad lot, just sixteen and already he kill five men. One of them right here in my dining room.'

India was shocked. 'But if he's murdered people why doesn't somebody do something about it? Don't you have a constable?'

Mrs Chang snorted. 'Not so easy, Sid is the Director's son. No one can touch him and he have plenty men in his gang who do whatever he say. They're all bad men but Sid, he's the worst of them all. You no want to tangle with Sid!'

'Well believe me, I wish I hadn't,' said India gloomily.

Mrs Chang found her some warm clothes and laid them on the bed. There was long underwear that India had to roll up at the bottom, a thick woollen shirt and a set of padded overalls. Mrs Chang explained they had belonged to her son whose rig had fallen through the lake ice two springs ago, drowning the whole crew. She said it in a matter-of-fact way as though death was always close at hand in Angel Town.

As India was getting dressed, the room gave a sudden lurch. She was wondering if she had imagined it when it happened again. The ground began to rumble and the glass in the windows rattled.

'What's happening?' she cried, holding on to the edge of the bed. The rumbling stopped as quickly as it had begun.

Mrs Chang looked out of the window. She muttered some indistinct words under her breath and made a curious sign in the air with her finger. 'Earth tremor,' she said, returning to the task of folding towels. 'Happen more and more these days. You ask me the Company take too much from under the ground. Not show enough respect to the mountain spirits.'

'Mountain spirits?' said India. 'Do you believe that's what causes earthquakes?'

Mrs Chang put down the towels. 'You soon find out this a damn strange country,' she said. 'There's gold and oil and iron under the mountains but that's not all. This an old country, really old, and there's things under the ground that best not be disturbed.'

'What sort of things?' said India.

'Living shadows – dark creatures that lived in this land before men,' said Mrs Chang. 'The ice people call them the Valleymen. Best you don't ask no more. Just hope you don't find out for yourself, that's all.'

Mrs Chang refused to be drawn further on the mysterious subject. She took India back down to the dining room and placed a steaming bowl of thick pea soup laced with salty cubes of ham in front of her.

The dining room had thinned out now. Calculus had been pacing the room awaiting India's return and announced that he was going to go in search of Verity to tell her what had happened. India had the impression he was feeling guilty about not having been there to protect her.

The hot food lifted her melancholy a little but she soon pushed the half-finished bowl of soup away and lay her head down on the table.

'Not eatin' that?'

She sat up suddenly. The man opposite was bristle-headed and powerfully built, with a thick neck and barrel-shaped body. He wore a maniacal grin as he pointed to India's bowl.

India shrugged and he pulled the food eagerly to his side of the table. She watched in fascination as he shovelled steaming spoonfuls of thick, green paste into his mouth as though he had been starved for a month. When the soup was finished he leaned back and let out an enormous belch.

'Much obliged to you, miss,' he said. 'I hate to see good

food go to waste. The name's Bulldog, Captain Aggrovius Bulldog.'

'Aggrovius?'

'Yes, well, my old mum thought it sounded exotic. Most people call me Aggro, though. They say it suits me.' He beamed and his eyes bulged like a wild man's.

Despite her worries, India laughed. 'I guess it does,' she said, holding out her hand. 'I'm India. I guess my mum thought it was exotic too.' His massive paw enveloped hers. 'What are you the captain *of*, exactly?'

'Ah, well, that depends on who's doing the asking.' He looked over both shoulders in an exaggerated display of caution. 'It wouldn't do if I found myself talking to someone from the Company, now would it?'

She assured him that she was not from the Trans-Siberian Company and he scrutinized her for a few moments before deciding to continue.

'All right then,' he said, pulling a pouch of tobacco from the folds of his jacket and rolling a thin cigarette. 'A freelance prospector, is what I am. Captain, chief executive and owner of *The Beautiful Game*, the finest rig in Siberia.'

Her eyes widened. 'You're a pirate rigger?'

'Well now, that's a word you don't use in polite company,' he said, looking shocked. 'Anyway, it depends on whose point of view you take.' He struck a match and sucked the cigarette to life, enveloping the table in a cloud of blue smoke. 'Now,' he said, settling back into his chair, 'them crooks that run Trans-Siberian is your real pirates. Call it an honest business to sell a man a prospecting licence and then take half of what he finds? No, I'm a free rigger. I run my own crew and we keep what we find. That's the way nature intended it.' He gave India another alarming grin. 'It's nice to hear a friendly accent. So what brings a fellow Londoner to Siberia?'

'I came with Mrs Brown and her bodyguard,' she said. 'I wanted to see Siberia but I guess that's not going to happen now.'

'Ah, so you're with the android,' he said. 'I've seen him about the place. He's a fine piece of hardware, he is. You must be the young lady what 'ad the run-in with Sidney this afternoon.'

'Good grief, does everyone in town know about that?'

'Most people around here make it their business to know what Sid the Kid gets up to,' he said, blowing a smoke ring. 'He gets away with murder, quite literally! I'd say you'd been pretty lucky.'

'Well I don't feel lucky. Thanks to him I'm probably going home. I thought I was going to like Siberia but I don't think much of it so far.'

'Well, that's 'cos you ain't seen the best of it,' he said. He reached into his pocket and spread a sheaf of grubby postcards on the table. They showed a variety of snow-covered scenes: mountains, trees heavy with white crystalline frost and icy lakes. '*This* is what Siberia's all about.'

She ran a finger lightly over a picture of a snow-capped

mountain. It seemed to gain a new intensity as she gazed at it – as though it was a living window through which she could climb. She imagined she could hear someone chanting, a hypnotic voice that seemed to pull her towards the picture. As soon as she lifted her finger the chanting stopped and the picture returned to being a faded and cracked photograph. She realized Bulldog had been talking.

'I'm sorry, what did you say?'

'I said Siberia's a beautiful place, but terrible too. It's minus sixty in the winter and as dark as a witch's armpit, with frozen lakes that can swallow a rig whole.' He exhaled another plume of smoke. 'But give me a clear day in the mountains with the smell of diesel in the air and any rigger'll tell you it's the best place on Earth.'

At that moment the door to the dining room swung open and Verity and Calculus walked in together. India could see right away that Verity knew all about her encounter with Sid. She looked as dark as thunder.

'India, are you all right?' she said. 'Calculus told me all about it. I could kick myself for leaving you alone. Sid could have killed you on the spot!' She turned her eyes skywards and groaned. 'And they're expecting us at Trans-Siberian to tell them what we know about Ironheart.'

'Ironheart, eh? said Bulldog. 'There's a fair few riggers have died chasing that dream.'

Verity turned sharply to glare at him.

'This is Captain Bulldog,' said India quickly. 'He's a free rigger!'

'Pleased to meetcha!' said Bulldog, extending a giant hand.

'Well it's not mutual, Captain,' she said, folding her arms, 'and this is a private discussion so, if you don't mind?' She raised an eyebrow and Calculus moved to stand at her shoulder.

Captain Bulldog pulled back his unshaken hand and grinned. 'Of course, of course, just on my way anyhow. I'll say this, though. If you go looking for Ironheart you'd best be careful on account of what's there.'

'Why?' said Verity suspiciously. 'What *is* there?'

'The thing you want most in the world,' he said. 'Whatever that is. Gold, diamonds, precious relics. They say it was the last resting place of the Siberian crown jewels. Others say it holds all the lost knowledge of the ancient world or technology a hundred years ahead of what we have now. Whatever you're looking for, Ironheart will promise it. But it's the song of the siren. It'll lure you in, but it always ends in death.'

Verity snorted. 'That's just rigger talk, Captain,' she said. 'I don't pay attention to superstition and rumour.'

'Izzat so?' he said. 'Well, here's some hard facts. There's something at Ironheart that Lucifer Stone wants badder 'n anything in the world, and him and his boy are as crazy as a pair of cornered snakes. If I were you, I'd watch my step! Good day, ladies.' He pulled on a fur hat that made him look like an overstuffed teddy bear and strode out of the dining room.

Calculus watched him go. 'It may have been unwise to engage that man in conversation,' he said. 'It is possible that he is not entirely trustworthy.'

Verity frowned. 'India, what the hell were you thinking? That man was a pirate!'

'Well you were the one who blurted out about Ironheart,' said India. 'In any case he was just being nice.'

'There is no such thing as "nice" in this town, India,' said Verity. 'Didn't your adventure this afternoon teach you that? You don't talk to anyone about our business, not unless you want to get robbed or cheated or murdered.' She took a deep breath and rubbed her palms over her face. 'Well, that's it then,' she said. 'By now Sid will have given his father the journals so we might as well pack up and go home.' She looked around the dining room. 'This place seems OK, we'll stay here tonight. Tomorrow I'll see if we can get you a cheap passage back to England on a freight ship.'

India felt sick with disappointment. She looked away out of the window so that Verity and Calculus wouldn't see the tears welling in her eyes and felt for the pendant at her neck. She wondered what Bella was doing at that moment.

'What is that, India?' said Calculus.

'It's nothing,' she said wiping her sleeve across her face. 'Just got something in my eye, that's all.'

'No,' said Calculus, 'I meant around your neck.' He pointed to her pendant. 'May I see it?'

'OK.'

He removed it carefully from her neck, without touching the metal. 'Where did you get this?'

'My dad made it,' she said. 'He gave it to me just before he came back here for the last time. He said it was my own piece of Siberia.'

Calculus passed the palm of his hand back and forth over the metal. 'Curious,' he said. 'Iron and nickel mostly, with traces of chondrites in the outer layers. This is meteorite iron.' He turned it over and held it up to peer along its edge. 'It's made of two pieces of metal pressed together,' he said. 'And there's something in between them.'

'Here, let me see.' Verity took the pendant from him and laid it carefully on the table. She pulled a small jeweller's eyeglass from her bag and began to examine it. 'There's a pair of jumper pins on the upper edge,' she said to Calculus, pointing to two tiny brass specks. 'And there's definitely something sandwiched in between the two metal pieces.'

'A micro-controller?' said Calculus.

'I'm betting it is,' said Verity with excitement. She took out a pair of tweezers and turned the pendant over. 'India, it looks like your dad went to a lot of trouble to hide something in here.'

'What sort of thing?' said India. She had worn the pendant for several months without noticing anything unusual about it.

'Possibly an integrated memory chip,' said Calculus, 'a

storage device used by old-fashioned computers. They were very common once.'

India watched closely as Verity rummaged in the bag and pulled out a battered-looking black box with a small meter on the front and a pair of brass terminals on the top. She took out several pieces of wire and some crocodile clips and proceeded to connect the brass terminals to the pendant. The needle on the meter didn't move.

'The chip must have deteriorated over time,' said Calculus. 'It will need something to kick-start it.'

Verity nodded. 'OK, give me a spark, Calc, but *gently*. No more than thirty milliamps.'

The android took the pendant carefully between his finger and thumb. There was a small *snap* as a spark jumped from his fingers to the surface of the metal. For a moment, nothing happened, then the needle on the meter flickered to life.

'I have an output,' said Calculus. 'It's a coherent data stream, there's information here.' The meter continued to flicker and Calculus was silent. At last he spoke again. 'It's another journal.'

Verity punched her fist into an open palm. 'Hot damn, this could be what we were looking for all along!' India, do you realize what this means? I'll bet those other journals were just a red herring and all the information about Ironheart is stored here.'

'What does it say?' said India.

'I'm not sure,' said Calculus. 'The message is encrypted.'

He held the pendant close to his visor. 'I will need some time to decipher it.'

'How long?' said Verity, checking her watch. 'Trans-Siberian are expecting us in half an hour.'

'That would be difficult even for me,' said Calculus. 'It is a complex cryptograph with over fourteen trillion possible combinations. Simply to count them would take a human being four hundred and forty-two thousand years, six months, twenty-eight days and—'

'All right!' said Verity. 'I get the point. Just get it done as quickly as possible. We'll need it soon if I'm going to strike a bargain with Lucifer Stone.'

India's heart began to beat faster as the prospect of a Siberian adventure opened up before her once more. 'Why would Dad have gone to all this trouble to hide this information?' she said.

'Perhaps because he knew he might not come back,' said Verity. 'And because he knew that what was at Ironheart was very valuable.'

'Or very dangerous,' offered Calculus. He disconnected the wires and handed the pendant back to India. 'Here,' he said, 'I have recorded the data from the microchip. Keep hold of it safely. If word gets out about this I think Sid might try to pay you another visit.'

CHAPTER 8

AN UNPLEASANT ENCOUNTER

The sun was low in the sky by the time they left Mrs Chang's and a bitter wind blew off the river. They marched through the streets to the eastern edge of town and the black, granite offices of the Trans-Siberian Mining Company. At the bottom of the front steps they stopped to look up at the two gas flames billowing like orange silk on either side of the oak doors.

'Stone keeps them burning because he can afford to,' said Verity. 'He likes people to remember who has all the wealth and power around here.'

India, who was used to never feeling warm in their dank London cottage, was shocked by the waste of fuel.

Inside, the building smelled of waxed wood and polished brass. Verity marched up to a fat guard, who was seated behind an ornate desk, cleaning his ears with a pencil. 'I need to see the Director immediately,' she said, flashing her business card at him and leaning across the desk menacingly.

'I have some important information that he's going to want to hear straight away.'

The guard inspected the end of the pencil and then peered suspiciously at Calculus. 'No weapons in the building,' he said flatly. 'That means the gun and the robot.'

'Actually,' said Calculus, 'I'm an android.'

'It's a very different thing altogether,' added India helpfully.

Verity tapped her foot impatiently. 'When can we see Mr Stone?'

The guard curled his lip. 'When the Director shares his diary with me I'll be sure to let you know. In the meantime, wait over there.'

They sat in the lobby on hard chairs and watched the guard scraping grease from under his fingernails with a paper clip. One entire wall of the entrance hall was taken up with a map of Siberia. It was studded with small flags bearing names that crackled with the promise of adventure: 'The Grace Under Pressure', 'The Lone Wolf', 'The Ice Queen'. The flags gradually thinned out towards the East until there were none left at all. India wondered where on the map Ironheart might be.

Finally, after a wait that felt like hours, they left Calculus in the lobby while another guard ushered them up the stairs and along a corridor, then up a spiral staircase to a flat rooftop. As they emerged into the icy brightness a gunshot scattered a flock of gulls into the air.

'Splendid shot, Mr Director, well done, sir.'

A group of well-dressed men and women at the far end of the roof applauded politely. They were drinking some kind of golden spirit from balloon-shaped glasses and some of them appeared to be quite drunk. In the centre of the group stood a short but enormously broad man, holding a smoking shotgun. He wore a floor-length fur coat, tied with a thick leather belt and had shaggy black hair with one furry eyebrow that ran right across his forehead. His beard was plaited into black ropes and there were pieces of bone tied into the ends. He looked like a story-book troll that had crept out from under a mountain.

'Not bad, if I say so myself.' His voice sounded as though he liked to gargle with gravel every morning. 'That's nine hits in a row. Who'll stake me a hundred gold Crowns I can't make it a straight ten?'

As they drew closer India's blood froze. Standing to one side, wearing the same furious look she had seen in the alleyway, was Sid the Kid. She felt his stare on her like a beam from a cold lighthouse.

The Director turned towards them. 'You'll be that Brown woman, I daresay.' He spat on his hand and held it out to Verity. 'Lucifer Stone.'

The hand was black and grimy but if Verity was dubious about taking it she never let it show.

'How was your trip to London?' he said with a smirk.

'It's an honour to meet you at last, Director,' she said, ignoring the sniggers from the group. 'I hear a lot of talk in the Northern territories about what you have achieved here.'

India noticed how all the men followed Verity with their eyes.

'I'm proud of this town, Mrs Brown,' he said. 'Twenty years ago there was nothing here but a few reindeer herders. Everything you see here has been forged from the mountains with my own hands.'

Verity looked impressed. 'Well, with all that going on, it's a wonder you can still find the time for target practice.'

Stone puffed out his chest. Something in the way he brandished his gun reminded India of Mehmet. 'This is still a frontier town, Mrs Brown, and I like to keep my skills sharp. Let me show you!'

At the far end of the roof stood a large contraption on wheels that looked like an old-fashioned catapult, designed for bashing down castle walls. Stone gave a signal and a man in overalls wound a handle which pulled back a flexible metal arm until it nearly reached the ground. He took a large green fruit from a pile and placed it into a basket at the end of the arm.

'Watermelons,' explained Stone. 'We have them specially imported. Nothing explodes like a watermelon when you shoot it.' He looked around. 'Except maybe a man's head, no?' The group laughed on cue. He hoisted the gun to his shoulder. 'Pull!'

The steel arm snapped to attention and the melon was flung in a high arc away from the roof. The gun blasted once and the melon burst into pink mist, casting a thousand fragments of red flesh into the street below. Everyone applauded again.

'Bravo, Mr Director,' said Verity.

India didn't clap. She didn't think there was anything special about being able to hit something the size of a watermelon.

'That's a bit of a waste, isn't it?' she said, earning a scowl from Sid. Verity flashed her a warning look, as Stone's eyebrow formed a thick V shape.

'Mr Director,' said Verity quickly, 'may I introduce my, er, business associate?'

Sid sneered and whispered something into his father's ear. Lucifer Stone examined India closely. 'Ah yes, the daughter of John Bentley if I am not mistaken. You seem to have inherited your daddy's unfortunate habit of speaking first and thinking later. I assure you our watermelons aren't wasted.' He walked to the edge of the roof. 'I combine my shooting practice with my welfare programme. Look!'

In the icy courtyard below was the most wretched group of men, women and children that India had ever seen. Despite the cold, they crawled on their hands and knees to pick up the shattered pieces of fruit from the filth and cram them into their mouths.

India's hand went to her mouth. She knew what it was like to go hungry and she understood how it could drive you to do just about anything. 'That's horrible,' she said. 'Why are you tormenting them? Why don't you just give them the fruit?'

Stone's eyebrow creased even further and silence descended on the group. He leaned towards India until she could see the dense crop of blackheads on his nose. From the corner of her eye India saw Verity reach for her gun before remembering it wasn't there.

'Because, Miss Bentley,' he growled, 'where would be the sport in that?' He turned and tossed his gun to an assistant. 'Don't feel too sorry for them, they are just primitives. They've been drifting into Angel Town for months now although heaven only knows why.' He went to the edge of the roof and glared down at the crowd who were now gazing up expectantly, waiting for the next melon. 'Vermin!' he roared. 'If I had my way I would exterminate the lot of you.' He turned away and pulled on his overcoat. 'Come, Mrs Brown, walk with me and we can talk business. Dr Cirenkov, please join us!'

A severe-looking woman in a black suit stepped forward. India noticed, uneasily, that Sid followed too, walking a few paces behind.

'Dr Cirenkov is my chief scientist here,' said Stone. 'It's her job to make sense of what you tech-hunters bring me. She has a genius for taking things apart to find out how they work.'

The doctor stretched her mouth into a thin-lipped smile that didn't reach her eyes and bowed low. Her sinuous movements and cold-blooded expression reminded India of a reptile. 'I saw your bodyguard in reception, Mrs Brown,' she said in a clipped accent. 'He is a very impressive machine, would you consider selling him to us? You could name your price.'

Verity raised her eyebrows. 'Really, Doctor? I'm surprised you'd be interested in such a relic. He's highly unreliable and well past his best. In any case, surely the great Lucifer Stone has no need of a bodyguard?'

'My need is not for a bodyguard, it is for an army,' said Stone. 'The doctor wants to take apart the metal man so we can learn to build others just like him. With an army like that, Trans-Siberian would be unstoppable.'

Verity looked perturbed. 'Take him apart? I don't think I could allow that, Director. I am sorry but Calculus is not for sale.'

Stone and the doctor exchanged glances.

Stone led them to the other side of the roof overlooking the harbour front and the railway sidings. 'When I came here twenty years ago I built my first factory with my own hands,' he said. 'Then came the roads, the refineries and the ports. Now my railways extend for five hundred miles into the wilderness and I have an Emperor-class engine, the *Tolstoy*, that can make the Obdoria run in ten hours straight!' He shook his head grimly. 'But it's not enough. At our present rate of progress it will take a hundred years or more to put the world back the way it was before the rains. If we find Ironheart we can do it in a fraction of that time.' He turned to Verity. 'So you understand, Mrs Brown, how disappointed I was to discover you had been so careless with John Bentley's journals.' He held up the two slim volumes.

'I think we all know perfectly well how they got here,' said Verity, glaring at Sid.

'And I think we all know perfectly well that they are worthless,' said Stone, tossing them back to Verity. 'So tell me why you're here. And don't give me any nonsense about expecting to get paid.'

'We know there's nothing in the journals,' said Verity. 'But we have something much better: a message from John Bentley that will take you straight to Ironheart.'

Stone's eye twitched. 'Really? So where are you keeping that information? Somewhere safe this time, I hope?' He shifted his glance to India and her heart beat faster. The metal pendant felt cool against her skin. 'No doubt you're about to tell me that this is worthy of an increase to your fee,' he continued. 'So what do you want?'

'A joint venture, Mr Director,' said Verity with a smile. 'First thing tomorrow I will give you the location of Ironheart in return for a small share of your profits. Shall we say thirty per cent?'

Stone made a hawking noise and spat on the ground.

'You would do well to remember that I control every inch of Siberia from here to Vladivostok. No one is going to find Ironheart unless it's in one of my rigs.'

Verity's smile stayed fixed. 'If you're not interested, Director, I could always find another buyer. The Chinese perhaps.'

'I'll pay you five per cent for your information,' he said, 'and that is more than fair.'

'How can you talk about what's fair?' said India suddenly. 'Is it fair that those people down there are starving and being used for sport?'

Stone growled at the back of his throat.

'Not now, India,' murmured Verity.

'My town is very well run, Miss Bentley,' said Stone, with simmering menace. 'Ask anyone here, they'll tell you they are all very grateful to me.'

'They'll say anything because they're all terrified of you,' said India.

Stone's knuckles tightened to bloodless knots. 'What did you say?' He advanced on India.

She tried to take a step backwards but found herself at the edge of the roof. 'I'm only saying those people deserve to be treated fairly,' she said, swallowing hard. 'They don't des—'

Her words were cut short as Stone grabbed the front of her shirt and hoisted her off her feet. She gasped as she found herself dangling over empty space and looked down to see the hard, icy cobbles, eighty feet below. 'Please . . .' was all she could manage to cry out.

'Mr Director, I'm sure we can do a deal,' said Verity rapidly.

'If you are so concerned for those people, Miss Bentley,' growled Stone, shaking her like a rag, 'why don't you go and join them?'

India's head swam.

'All right then,' said Verity quickly. 'I agree to your offer of five per cent, Mr Director. Do we have an agreement?'

Stone looked for a moment as though he had not heard Verity. He continued to stare angrily at India as she thrashed helplessly at the end of his arm. Then slowly, he pulled her back and deposited her on the roof once more. India's legs immediately buckled underneath her and she collapsed to her knees, panting for breath. Sid laughed openly at the terror on her face.

'Very good, Mrs Brown,' said Stone in a matter-of-fact way. 'We have a deal. And I'll not ask for proof of what you claim either. But if that information is not with me by the morning then I'll have both of your skulls for bookends.'

Verity helped India to her feet. India felt sick and her legs would not stop shaking.

'So!' said Stone brightly as he rubbed his palms together. 'How about we seal the deal with a glass of vodka in my office? Alone,' he added, with a final poisonous look at India.

'Of course, Mr Director,' said Verity, with a forced smile. 'I'll be right with you as soon as I have spoken to my business associate.'

Verity put her arm around India and led her quickly down a flight of iron stairs at the side of the building. When they got to the bottom she hugged the trembling girl. 'It's OK, India,' she said. 'It's over now. But what were you thinking? Stone is the most powerful man in Siberia. We were here to do a deal and you just picked a fight with him.'

India bit her lip. 'I'm sorry,' she said, wiping her nose on her sleeve. 'It's just the way he was treating those people made me so angry.' She took a deep breath. 'I'll go back and apologize. Perhaps if I talked to him again . . .'

'Oh no,' said Verity holding up her hands. 'You're not going anywhere tonight. Here, take my bag, Calculus will take you back to the hotel. I'll go and smooth things over with Stone. Let's hope Calc can crack the code and find the location of Ironheart by the morning or we're all in trouble. In the meantime you just concentrate on staying out of sight and looking after that pendant.'

Verity led India away to find Calculus before she joined the Director for a drink. As they left, India was surprised to see that Stone was still standing on the roof, deep in conversation with Sid and the doctor.

'Why d'you give 'em five per cent, Pa?' said Sid. 'They got nothing. Them journals were useless and now they've made up some story about a message but they got nothing.'

Stone lashed out suddenly. The blow from the back of his big hand sent Sid sprawling.

'You're a fool, boy! You got eyes and ears but you don't use 'em. Didn't you hear the way she threatened to go to the Chinese? You don't make that kind of threat unless you're holding good cards. And didn't you see the way she looked at the girl when she spoke? And how the girl kept touching her neck? If Bentley left a message then he most likely gave it to his daughter. Now get up!'

Sid picked himself up from the floor and dabbed his lip with a sullen expression.

'I'm not paying five per cent to anyone,' continued Stone, 'but it suits me to play along with Mrs Brown for now. If we don't find Ironheart in the next four weeks then the hard snows will set in and I can't afford to wait until next season.' He turned to Cirenkov. 'Doctor, I'll need your help to take care of Mrs Brown and her war droid tonight. That machine will be no pushover.'

Then he rested a hand on Sid's shoulder and spoke in a kinder tone. 'And I want you to do what you do best, son. As soon as it gets dark, round up your boys and get over to the China woman's place.'

A slow smile spread across Sid's face.

'Nothing fancy and no messing,' said Stone sharply. 'If anyone suspects what's under those mountains before we get there then we'll have a war on our hands. Just do it clean, find out what she's hiding and then drop the body in the vats. No one will ever question the disappearance of another runaway in Angel Town.'

Sid didn't need telling twice. He was away down the steps with his long coat flying behind him and the nastiest of smiles spreading across his face. Tonight, he thought to himself, he would teach that vicious little alley cat a lesson, and whatever his pa might say, it wasn't going to be quick or clean.

CHAPTER 9

ESCAPE ON THE *TOLSTOY*

She climbed to the top of the hill, cold air stinging her cheeks. A white reindeer stood at the edge of the trees, young and slender, unafraid. She stroked its neck and noticed it had one eye of ice blue and the other of the darkest brown.

'Do you know where my father is?' she whispered.

The reindeer spoke clearly. Its voice sounded inside her head.

'He rests among the heads of warriors, beyond the fast-flowing river. He is safe, for now, but he is not alone. Something waits with him and soon it will awaken.'

'How am I meant to find him?' she said.

'You must look for me first,' said the reindeer. 'Follow a red star to the East where it leads you over the mountains and I will protect you when you make the crossing. You must hurry, India Bentley. Find the heart of iron before the snows come or the winter will be ceaseless and without light. But now the wolves are coming and you must flee, quickly!'

'But how will I find you again?' she asked. There was no reply.

The reindeer was gone and only the endless, white silence of the snow remained.

She woke with a start in Mrs Chang's guest room. It was still dark outside, several hours before dawn, and the fire in the grate had faded to an ember. The half-remembered dream had left her feeling unsettled and anxious. She wondered if Verity and Calculus were back yet.

Calculus had said little on the journey back to the hotel and he seemed anxious to return to the Trans-Siberian Mining Company as soon as possible and check on his mistress. India's shakiness after her encounter with Lucifer Stone had given way to a headache and as soon as they arrived at Mrs Chang's she had gone straight to bed.

Unable to get back to sleep, she got up and pulled on some clothes before going to the window. The street was empty and shuttered and the boardwalks glittered with a coating of ice. She looked up and was startled to see a thin, white streak of light passing noiselessly across the sky to the East; a shooting star, like the one she had seen in London. A second streak followed and then a third. And then a whole swarm of fiery stars arced gracefully across the night sky towards the mountains. India realized she was holding her breath. Verity had said when someone died their star falls to Earth, so what did this mean? She clutched at her pendant and hoped that Bella was safe.

As the last shooting star faded away, a movement across the street caught her eye. She ducked behind the curtain as a lone figure moved briefly out of the deep shadow. She recognized the black hair and chalk-white face immediately. Sid! Downstairs the wood and glass front doors smashed inwards and the shards scattered across the hallway. She rushed from her room and peered over the banisters. Bearded men in long-johns were gathering on the landing below in confused groups and Mrs Chang could be heard shouting in the dining room.

'What do you want? I told you no come back after last time. Get out of my house!'

There was the sound of more breaking glass and then Sid's voice. 'Shut up, China woman. Tell us where the girl is and we might not burn this place to the ground.'

'What girl? There's no girl here. Are you crazy? You get out right now or I set Mr Chang on you.'

There was a sound of scuffling and then a heavy iron clang rang out, followed by a howl.

'Ow! Boss, she hid me. My node, id's bleeding.'

'Never mind your precious nose, Cripps. You and Silas, get upstairs and find the girl. Make sure you get all her stuff too.'

Heavy footsteps sounded on the stairs. India darted back to her room and slipped a chair under the door handle. She guessed she had a minute, maybe two at most, before they found her room.

The side window of her room looked down on to an alley, a bone-breaking thirty feet down and too far to jump. But when she leaned out, there was a narrow ledge running just under the sill, and a drainpipe that offered a possible route to the ground.

India pulled on her boots with shaky fingers, then picked up Verity's bag and stuffed her own things into it. Trying not to look down, she opened the window and lowered herself over the sill to the ledge, standing motionless on the icy beam. The sharp night air made her breath come in quick gasps. Out here, the ledge felt much narrower.

She began a slow, cautious shuffle along the beam, towards the iron drainpipe. The frozen metal of the pipe stuck painfully to her skin until she pulled the sleeves of her shirt over her hands like mittens. Then she started to climb down carefully.

Just when it seemed she might escape, her foot slipped on the icy metal and she pitched sideways into the alley. Her grip on the pipe was lost in a heartbeat and her arms and legs flailed wildly as the ground rushed up to meet her. The impact knocked the wind from her chest and something hit her hard in the mouth. She groaned and lay still until she felt strong enough to open her eyes.

A foul-smelling pile of rubbish had broken her fall, probably saving her life. She sat up slowly; all of her limbs seemed to be working normally. Her knee had been twisted in the fall and her lip was bloodied, but she was otherwise OK. She climbed shakily to her feet.

'You! Stop there!' Two more men turned into the alley and were running towards her. She took off in the other direction, hobbling on her injured knee.

The alleyways behind the guest house were dark and stinking and she soon became hopelessly lost in the twisting maze as she tried to shake off her pursuers. Her breath came in ragged gasps and tore at her throat. Just as she felt her legs were about to give way she rounded a corner and ran straight into a massive figure blocking her path. She jumped back in alarm and looked up at the shadowy outline.

'Calc!' she cried. She hugged his metal body, her arms not quite meeting around his middle. 'I'm so glad it's you. Where's Verity?'

'I was hoping she was with you,' he said. 'There was no sign of her back at Stone's place. What are you doing out here?'

She spilled out the story of her escape from the guest house while trying to keep her voice from shaking. 'Good grief!' she cried. 'You're shot!'

He put a hand to the three small holes in his shoulder armour. 'When I went back to find Verity, Stone's men were waiting for me. My self-healing mechanisms will take care of the wound but I was lucky to get away. Sid's thugs are all over the town and I fear for Mrs Brown's safety if she is still at Trans-Siberian.'

'Then we have to go and rescue her,' said India. 'What are we waiting for?'

'India, these people are not like the men in your village,' he said. 'They are trained killers and there are too many of them for us to deal with. If they have captured Mrs Brown there is nothing we can do right now.'

'But you're her bodyguard! Aren't you even going to try to rescue her?'

'There are times, India,' he said calmly, 'when a tactical retreat is the best strategy. If we went back to Trans-Siberian then we would almost certainly be captured or killed ourselves. Mrs Brown gave me orders to ensure your safety. When that is done I will consider how best to help her.' He looked up and down the alleyway and grasped her hand. 'Come on, we should head for the harbour. I'll try to find a cargo ship that will get you home.'

She allowed herself to be pulled along through the narrow alleys as they headed for the waterfront, reeling from the events of the last hour.

They emerged into a floodlit yard laced with rail tracks and India gave a small yelp of surprise before Calculus yanked her quickly back into the shadows. Their route across the tracks was blocked by a monstrous black train reeking of hot oil and wood smoke. It sat in the siding like a slumbering beast, exhaling great gasps of steam and splashing hot, hissing fluids on to the frozen ground. India was stunned by its immensity.

'It must be the engine Stone was bragging about,' she said. 'The *Tolstoy*.'

'We have to get past it,' said Calculus. 'It's the only way to the harbour.'

They picked their way along the dark tracks, stepping over railway sleepers and staying out of the yellow pools of light from the carriage windows as they made their way towards the engine. The *Tolstoy* was a beast. Each of its eight wheels stood taller than Calculus and the bearings and connector rods were as thick as a man. They passed a muscular, soot-covered man stoking the roaring firebox and walked carefully around the front of the train.

Calculus peered along the platform. 'Just a few passengers,' he said. 'I think there's an alleyway over there that leads down to the harbour.'

But India wasn't listening; she was looking at the front of the engine which was adorned with a large red star.

'Calc, I need to get on this train.'

'This train is going east, India, it won't help us.' He continued to scan the platform. 'Now, get ready to run as soon as the guard turns his back.'

'I know where it's going, Calc. It might sound weird, but I've dreamed about this. Actually, since my dad went missing I've had a lot of strange dreams. The one I had tonight told me to follow a red star over the mountains. It means I should get on this train, Calc, don't you see?'

He looked at the red star and then at India. 'No, I don't see. Why would you want to do something that will only take you further into danger?'

'You're not listening to me!' She took a deep breath. 'Look, you told me a shaman can control another person's dreams, so isn't it possible that's what is happening to me? I think someone is trying to send me a message. The dream told me my dad was still alive but there was something with him, something that shouldn't be woken. It said if I didn't get there soon something bad would happen. I have to go east, Calc, I just have to.'

Calculus gazed at her steadily. It was impossible to tell if he was buying into any of her story. 'It is possible,' he said eventually, 'that you are experiencing some sort of psychic phenomena. But have you ever considered that whoever is sending you these dreams may not be telling you the truth?'

This had not occurred to India, and it was a chilling thought. 'I'm sorry,' she said after a pause. 'But I'm still getting on this train, so you'd better leave me here.'

The android made a noise like a sigh. 'I can't do that,' he said.

'Well, why not? I'm fed up with being treated like a child. Give me one good reason why you can't let me go.'

'Because, after what happened this afternoon, Mrs Brown gave me orders to look after you. It was the last thing she told me to do before she disappeared. So now I have to make sure you're safe; it would go against my programming to do anything else.'

'Oh,' she said, taken aback. They were both silent for a moment.

'We'll find Verity again, I know we will,' she said. 'But I made a promise too. I promised my dad that if he ever got lost I would come and find him and I promised Bella I was going to bring him back so we could be a family again.' She went to the edge of the platform and paused. 'You coming?'

He shrugged his shoulders. 'If I get on the platform

with you I will be noticed immediately,' he said. 'I'll travel underneath the train.'

'Whatever works for you, Calc,' she said with a grin.

'Here,' he said. 'If we are going to be separated I want you to have this.' He touched a panel on his arm and a thin strip of metal peeled away from his wrist like a sliver of steel skin. 'It's a communication device. If you need me, just press the button on the side and as long I am functioning I'll be able to hear you.'

She placed the band over her wrist. It curled naturally around her arm and fastened itself with a small click. 'My very own bodyguard,' she said. 'I feel safer already.'

She hopped up from the tracks, wincing at the pain in her knee. On the platform, well-heeled passengers shared drinking flasks and breathed clouds of steam into the night air while busy porters ferried boxes. A station official checked his pocket watch and held a green flag in readiness.

Shouldering her bag, India started down the platform – then stopped in her tracks.

Silas and Cripps stood at the station entrance. The one with the lazy eye held a bloody handkerchief to his face. They were scanning the passengers as they arrived and no one dared to meet their gaze. India knew they were looking for her.

She turned away and focused on getting on the train. No sooner had she placed her foot on the bottom step when a hand fell on her shoulder and a red-faced ticket inspector barked something incomprehensible at her.

'He wants to see your ticket,' whispered Calculus from the dark space beneath the train. 'He said if you don't have one he'll have to take you to the office.'

The inspector called over the guard, who checked his pocket watch and frowned. 'Ticket,' he said.

India swallowed. 'Er, it's with my dad,' she said, her mind racing. 'He's already on board.' She gave them a broad smile.

'No ticket, no train,' said the guard. 'Give ticket or come with me.' Some of the passengers were looking and tutting at India and the exchange had attracted the attention of Silas, who was now peering gormlessly in their direction.

She looked around for an escape and was about to run when her eyes alighted on a familiar, barrel-shaped figure rolling up the platform. It was Captain Bulldog, deeply engrossed in a meat pie. She seized her chance.

'Dad!' she cried out. 'There you are, I've been looking all over for you.' Bulldog stopped in mid-chew, looking startled as India ran up to him and took his arm. 'This man wants to see my ticket, he really is being very tiresome.'

Bulldog's face remained locked in surprise and his eyes flicked between India and the ticket inspector. He quickly swallowed his mouthful of pie. 'Er, hello, dear,' he said tentatively. 'I was just getting something to eat.'

India laughed lightly. 'Thinking of your stomach again, Dad? I bet you forgot to buy my ticket as well, didn't you? You really are becoming very absent-minded.'

'Yeah,' he said, forcing a tight smile, 'I'll be forgetting I've got a daughter next.'

The ticket inspector looked unimpressed. 'No ticket, no train,' he repeated.

At the end of the platform, Silas and Cripps were now both peering in their direction. India hid her face and Bulldog seemed suddenly to grasp the gravity of the situation. He exchanged some words in Russian with the inspector and they laughed loudly together. 'Let me thank you for your trouble,' he said, taking out a roll of notes and peeling some off. The inspector and the guard grunted and touched their caps. As Bulldog returned the roll to his pocket, India noticed that, like Verity, he also wore a pistol in his belt.

Bulldog ushered India on to the train and waved cheerily to the porters as he closed the door. Silas and Cripps were both peering at them now. They attempted to push through the turnstile, only to be stopped by the red-faced inspector. 'No ticket, no train!' he barked, holding out an expectant hand.

While they fumbled for change, Bulldog quickly dragged India into the carriage. 'What the hell's going on, India?' he said. 'Sid's gang are all over town looking for a girl and a metal man. They must have stopped me six times on the way here.'

She blurted out her story in a disjointed, adrenalin-fuelled way, falling over herself and stammering, so that he made her take a deep breath and repeat it again more slowly.

When she had finished he asked her several questions, mostly about their meeting with Stone.

'Well?' said India after a pause. 'What do you think?'

'What do I think? This is a non-stop train to Salekhard. I think we need to get you off now before you get into any further trouble, that's what I think.' She started to protest but Bulldog was already leaning out of the window on the track side of the train. He was shocked to see Calculus's head appear beneath the wheels. 'Streuth!' he spluttered. 'What's he doing down there? I'm not supposed to be his dad too, am I?'

'I would advise against trying to leave the train on this side, Captain,' said Calculus. 'The alleyways are swarming with Sid's men and India would certainly be seen.'

India was becoming agitated. 'I'm not leaving the train on either side. I've told you both, I'm staying here, and nothing you say is going to stop me.'

'Is that so?' said Bulldog, folding his big arms. 'Well, believe it or not, young lady, yours is not the only opinion that matters around here. All I want to do is get back to *The Beautiful Game* and now I'm stuck with a runaway girl and an enormous android!' Any further conversation was silenced by a blast from the guard's whistle. 'Oh, that's just great,' said Bulldog, throwing up his arms in despair.

The engine snorted like an awakening horse and the train took up the slack along its length with a clanking jolt. Calculus ducked quickly beneath the carriage. The steam heart of the beast began to shunt them forward and thick coils of vapour enveloped the station.

But as the train picked up speed, the lumbering figure of Cripps appeared at the window, puffing to keep pace with the carriage and peering in through the glass. He caught sight of India and opened his mouth to shout out but failed to notice the signal post that stood at the end of the platform and ran headlong into it with a resounding smack.

Bulldog winced as he pulled down the blind and their carriage passed the end of the platform. He blew out a long breath and slumped heavily into one of the worn plush seats. 'Well,' he said with a sigh, 'we might as well get comfortable. We're here for the ride now.'

CHAPTER 10

A BOX OF FROGS

With her head pounding, Verity Brown awoke on a bed of fresh linen in a comfortable room furnished with antiques and expensive fixtures. She reached instinctively for her gun but her holster was empty. When she tried to sit up she found her other wrist was handcuffed to the bed.

The earlier part of the evening came back hazily. Stone had been on his best behaviour over drinks, but then what had happened? She remembered feeling dizzy and getting up to leave and then, blackness. Drugged, she guessed, but why?

She turned her attention to the handcuffs. They were slightly loose. She worked her wrist around in the steel bracelet, trying to twist it over the malleable bones of her hand. This would not be a painless escape, she thought. She was still twisting her hand when the door rattled and swung open. An armed guard loomed briefly in the doorway and then Stone rolled into the room like a great troll.

'I trust you're feeling refreshed after your sleep, Mrs Brown,' he said. He sat down on a delicate antique chair that looked like it would burst under his weight and leaned forward on his heavy walking stick.

'I feel like hell,' said Verity. 'What did you do to me?'

'I'm sorry about that. I know it's bad manners to drug a dinner guest but I was never much good at manners.' He paused to pick his nose. 'Besides,' he said, examining the end of his finger, 'I couldn't take the chance you would really go to the Chinese.'

Verity struggled to work her hand free behind her back.

'Are you all right, Mrs Brown? You look like you're in pain.'

'Just the company I have to keep,' she said sweetly.

Stone laughed. 'You remind me of my fourth wife, Mrs Brown. She never knew when to keep her mouth shut either!'

'So would that have been Sid's mother?'

He raised his eyebrow in surprise. 'Ah! Very good. She was my true love, Mrs Brown. It damn near broke my heart when I had to kill her. The least I could do under the circumstances was bring up the boy.' He gave her a nasty smile. 'You, however, I couldn't care less about, so you can only imagine what I will to do to you if you don't give me what I want.'

'I would have sold you the information about Ironheart. There was no need to kidnap me.'

'Unfortunately, Mrs Brown, I couldn't wait any longer

for this particular nugget of information. If my rigs don't leave for Ironheart immediately then the hard winter snows will block the eastern valleys and we will not reach it before next spring. My rigs are fully fuelled and ready to leave at first light. I need that information, Mrs Brown and I need it now!'

'What's at Ironheart that you want so desperately?' Her wrist was almost free now. 'It can't be the money; you already have more of that than you could ever spend.'

'Power, Mrs Brown,' he said. 'Enough power to make the Trans-Siberian Company the dominant force over half the globe! When I first heard the legend of Ironheart I dismissed it as a fairy tale. But then my spies discovered something that made me change my mind. The original government records of Ironheart from before the rains, documenting everything that had been stored there. It made *fascinating* reading.' His eyes glittered. 'Ironheart is everything you think it is, Mrs Brown. There is enough treasure to satisfy the greediest pirate, but there is much more. The men who built it chose it as the place to store their greatest achievements. I'm talking about weapons, Mrs Brown, old-world weapons of horrific purity. Missiles that can lay waste to entire cities, chemicals that will shroud the land in poison gas and diseases for which the cure would only be available to the highest bidder. All of these toys lie hidden at Ironheart – can you imagine what fun I will have with them?'

Verity swallowed. Looking into the crazed features of

Lucifer Stone, she could imagine it very well. 'I'd love to help, Mr Director, really I would,' she said as her hand slipped suddenly free of the cuff. 'But I make it a policy not to do business with anyone who is madder than a box of frogs.'

She lunged across the bed at Stone. Ordinarily she would have overpowered him in seconds but, weakened by the drugs, she stumbled. Stone swiftly recovered his wits and struck her hard on the temple with his stick. Pain and lights exploded behind her eyes as she crashed to the floor.

The guard was in the room in an instant, hauling her to her feet and applying a second pair of handcuffs tightly behind her back. Her injured hand screamed in protest.

'Now, tell me!' yelled Stone, his face only inches from hers. 'What was in John Bentley's message?'

'I don't know,' said Verity between gritted teeth.

Stone made a noise like a wild animal in pain. 'Clearly you don't appreciate how serious I am, Mrs Brown, so let me make you my final offer. Tell me the location of Ironheart and I promise not to feed you into my furnaces, feet first.'

'You can yell all you want,' said Verity defiantly, 'but that information is encrypted and I don't know what it says.'

Stone narrowed his eyes and stroked his beard thoughtfully. 'Well, if you don't have it then it must be with the girl and your metal man. Yes, that's it, isn't it? The girl has the message and now she and that metal man have gone to try and find Ironheart themselves.'

There was silence for a moment, then Verity began

to laugh. Stone looked appalled. 'What? Why are you laughing?'

'You mean they've escaped?' said Verity, still grinning. 'I'd say that was pretty careless of you. Calculus is a military droid with full stealth capabilities. Once they get out of the city you'll never track them down.'

Stone glowered at her. The veins stood out on his forehead and there were flecks of spittle on his lips. 'Don't underestimate me, Mrs Brown. I have spies everywhere. Miss Bentley and that rusty machine won't stop my plans. Things will just take a little longer, that's all.' He turned to the guard. 'Mrs Brown is unable to assist us further. Please take her up to the roof and use the catapult to fling her body into the city streets. If she survives the fall, then drag her back to the roof and keep doing it until the job is done!'

The guard yanked brutally on the cuffs, causing Verity to cry out.

'Wait!' she said as they reached the door. She took a deep breath. 'There may be something I can help you with after all.'

CHAPTER 11

THE FREE-RIGGER'S CONTRACT

The *Tolstoy* picked up a gallop and plunged into the night, leaving the lights of Angel Town behind. There was a small wood stove in the compartment that didn't quite take the dry chill from the air and Bulldog stoked it hopefully, sending sparks and resin smells into the carriage.

'Well,' he said when India had finished her story. 'Sid's friends are a dangerous bunch and now they're very interested in you. So what are you going to do now?'

India hesitated. Her plans had not extended much further than getting on the train, but now she thought about it, she was clear on the first priority. 'We have to find Ironheart,' she said. 'If we can get to it before Stone we can find my dad and maybe even use the treasure to bargain for Verity's life.'

'Whoa, whoa!' Bulldog raised his hands. 'What do you mean, "we"? Don't include me in your plans. *The Beautiful Game* leaves for the southern oil fields tomorrow. The water's lovely and warm down there and the crew are looking forward to it.' He caught India's pained expression. 'Look,' he said kindly, 'you have no idea where Ironheart is, so why don't you forget all about it and focus on how you're going to get back to London? Mrs Brown is a resourceful woman, she can take care of herself.'

'But I know the region where my dad was looking for Ironheart. Verity said it was called Uliu-something-or-other. And when Calculus deciphers the message on my pendant then I bet it'll tell us exactly where to find it. Most probably.'

Bulldog reached in his satchel and fished out two huge sandwiches, handing one to India. 'It's called Uliuiu Cherchekh,' he said. 'It means "The Valley of Death" and it's over fifteen hundred miles from here. How exactly do you think you're going to travel that distance, on your own, in winter?' He took a bite from his sandwich that would have choked a horse.

'You're a pirate rigger, aren't you?' she said matter-of-factly. 'You could take me.'

Bulldog spluttered breadcrumbs across the carriage. 'Take you? Fifteen hundred miles is the maximum range of my rig with a full fuel load. We'd get there all right, but then we'd be stuck on the ice until we froze to death or until Stone caught up with us. Forget it, India.'

She wasn't about to give up. 'But you *could* get us there and back. There are pirate oil refineries out on the tundra where you can buy fuel if you know where to find them. It's called "long rigging", Mrs Chang told me all about it.'

'Oh, did she now? And did Mrs Chang tell you what it's like to be down to your last hundred litres of diesel with a blizzard closing in? Or how to stay on the trail during a white-out or any one of a thousand other things that can go wrong when you take liberties with the Siberian winter?'

'No, she didn't,' said India. 'But you know how to do those things and I know how to find Ironheart. So I know you'll do it because that's what pirates do, isn't it? They look for treasure!' She took a bite of her sandwich.

Bulldog squinted at her, impressed by the raw passion that came spilling out of this girl. However crazy this journey might sound she certainly seemed to have enough steel in her backbone to survive it. He weighed the risks involved. If they ran into one of the heavily armed Company rigs in the ice forests, that would almost certainly be fatal. But Bulldog knew all about *risk* and how it often went arm in arm with its more attractive sister, *profit*. If Stone wanted something this badly then you could be sure there was money in it. Then, of course, there was the girl's pendant. That might just be the thing that tipped the balance in their favour.

His ears began to feel warm, as they always did when a money-making opportunity presented itself. Perhaps, he thought, a journey to the eastern mountains might be a worthwhile investment after all. 'Well now,' he said. 'If you're determined to ignore what I say, I reckon I may as well profit from the deal.' He stroked his bristly chin. 'I'll have me own expenses to think about, not to mention my crew, who'll want a cut of whatever we find. So here's what I'll do. Give me the pendant and I'll take you to find Ironheart. But once you've got what you need to bargain for Mrs Brown's life, I get to keep whatever else we find there.'

'We'll split what we find evenly,' said India, narrowing her eyes. 'The pendant stays with me and Calculus will give you directions as soon as he cracks the code.'

They stared at each other across the carriage.

'All right, missy, you got yourself a deal.' He spat noisily on to his palm and held out his hand. 'But you be mindful now! This is a free-rigger's contract you're shaking on and we takes it serious in these parts.'

She nodded solemnly and held out her own grubby hand. She couldn't help wondering what Roshanne and Thaddeus Clench would think of her making her own way across Siberia and doing deals with pirates. She grinned as they shook hands. 'It's a deal.'

Meanwhile, outside the relative warmth and comfort of the carriage, the big android clung grimly to the axles of the moving train. He ignored the fearsome shaking and rattling that threatened to throw him off like a piece of rotten fruit, and focused instead on the message he had finally finished deciphering.

John Bentley had wanted the location of Ironheart kept secret for a good reason. There was treasure hidden there all right, but there were other things too. Terrible things. The worst products of a paranoid age. These were things that Calculus had hoped were gone forever and that he would never have to see again. Part of him wished that he had never seen the message, or that he could destroy the pendant so that the location of Ironheart would be forgotten for eternity. But he knew that would never happen. Ironheart was like a genie that would not go back into its bottle, and Stone and his army wouldn't rest until they'd found it. There was only one option: he would have to go with India and hope they got there before Lucifer Stone. If they failed, it was entirely possible that what was hidden at Ironheart could destroy every living creature on the face of the Earth.

And if that happens, he thought, I might be the only one left alive.

CHAPTER 12

THE BEAUTIFUL GAME

The rig yards of Salekhard marked the point where the Ural Mountains met the frozen mouth of the Ob river. It was here that the mammoth prospecting rigs rolled in off the ice to disgorge their cargoes of tarry crude oil and red iron ore into waiting goods trains for transport to Angel Town. The yards themselves – an untidy scattering of cranes, oil tanks and heavy machinery – had been built by men with an eye for practicality over beauty.

It was late afternoon and already dark when the *Tolstoy* clanged and hissed to a halt. The passengers shielded their faces against the freezing sleet as they collected bags and packing crates. India and Bulldog climbed stiffly from the carriage on to the wooden platform.

India was desperate to look beneath the train and check on Calculus. She chewed her lip nervously while heavily clad riggers unloaded the trucks and the crowd thinned. Then she ducked down quickly while Bulldog kept watch. 'Calc, are you all right?' she called. 'Oh please be all right.'

The underside of the carriage was black with grease and soot and, for a desperate minute, she thought he had fallen from the train. But then, slowly, a grimy block of darkness detached itself and began to crawl towards her.

'Calc! Thank goodness you're OK!' She threw her arms around the big android and hugged him tightly, covering herself in grime in the process. 'I'm so sorry,' she said over and over. 'I thought there was nothing more important than getting on this train but I never meant to put you through such an awful journey.'

'I am fine, thank you, India,' he said getting to his feet. 'Although I would not recommend it as a way to travel.'

They followed Bulldog across the open sidings to a low, concrete building. He made them stand out of sight while he tried the door to an office and stepped inside. While he was gone, India quickly told Calculus about the deal she had struck with Bulldog.

'I need to tell you something, India,' he replied. 'I have deciphered most of your father's message. It provides a map reference for Ironheart and it describes what he found inside. It contains treasure all right, but there is something else there too, something that must never fall into Lucifer Stone's hands.'

'Well, what was it, what did he say?' said India, hungry for information.

'It contains weapons, India,' said Calculus. 'The sort of

old-world weapons that would give Lucifer Stone the power he craves more than anything else.'

'Are you saying we shouldn't go there?' India had never known Calc to sound this serious.

'On the contrary,' he said. 'I was a soldier, India. I have seen what those weapons can do. I think it is essential that we get to Ironheart before Stone does.' He dropped his voice as they spied Bulldog emerging from the offices. 'One more thing. I think it is best if we do not share this information with these pirate riggers just yet. If they know too much then they may refuse to take us.'

Bulldog returned carrying a large hooded coat which he held up against Calculus to check for size.

'It's amazing what people will leave lying around in an empty office,' he said. 'Here, son, wear this so you look a bit less conspicuous.'

Calculus put it on. Far from being less conspicuous, he looked like a giant android wearing a coat.

'Perfect!' declared Bulldog. 'No one will look twice at you in that. Now stick close to me.'

He led them past rusting oil tanks and overhead pipe gantries that leaked steam and hot liquids. They emerged on to a wide expanse of frozen ground, lit with harsh electric lamps. Despite the fierce wind blowing off the bay, the yard was swarming with men attending to more than a dozen rigs.

India stared open-mouthed at her first sight of the immense prospecting rigs. The nearest one towered above them like a huge mechanical insect, heavy and greasy and leaking sticky puddles from its belly on to the ground. It had a blunt head section, a thick central body and a vast abdomen at the rear which, Bulldog told her, was used to store the oil and minerals it extracted. The whole rig rested on steel tracks that compressed the frozen ground beneath them.

Maintenance crews clambered over the rig like industrious monkeys and a cutting torch sent showers of blue sparks into the night that hurt your eyes. The air was filled with diesel fumes, and burning rubber mingled with the cold smell of the mountains. India breathed it in deeply and it made her heart beat faster. It smelled of adventure!

On the far side of the yards India spied a group of rigs that looked sleeker and better maintained than the others. Their tracks gleamed with an oily sheen and they carried heavy guns on their roofs.

'Company rigs!' said Bulldog, spitting on the ground. 'The big one is Stone's personal rig, the *Prince of Darkness*. Officially they're supposed to protect the fleet from pirates but they're not above piracy themselves. If they come across a lone rig they don't recognize they'll steal the cargo and send the crew to the slave factories.'

India shivered at the thought of the *Prince of Darkness* bearing down on them in the wilderness.

Bulldog led them on to a remote corner of the yard where the rigs looked older and more dilapidated, each one a patchwork of spare parts bolted crudely into place. 'This is a less glamorous neighbourhood, where people don't ask too many questions. And this,' he said, spreading his arms wide in front of the last rig on the row, 'is my baby. Say hello to *The Beautiful Game*!'

India stared. *The Beautiful Game* was smaller than most of the other rigs. Long ago it had been painted red and white but now it was streaked with rust. The upper decks were a rat's nest of equipment and cables that spilled over the sides, and the entire hull looked as if it had been pounded with a giant hammer.

'Does that thing really move?' said India.

'Steady on, that's my pride and joy you're talking about.' Bulldog looked offended.

'It really is very impressive, Captain,' said Calculus.

'Well thank you, my mechanical friend. At least someone here appreciates true beauty.'

'In fact,' said Calculus, 'I believe parts of it may be even older than I am.'

India bit her lip to keep from laughing.

Bulldog led them up a set of steps and through a low hatch where they gathered in an uncomfortably small living area. There was a table with bench seats and the walls were lined with navigation charts, crew rosters and a poster for a bar in Shanghai. A photo on the wall showed Bulldog's face peering from the hood of a bright-red parka trimmed with white fur. It was simply labelled: 'North Pole, Christmas Day'.

'Ahoy there!' A young man with a friendly smile stuck

his head out of a doorway. 'Welcome aboard *The Beautiful Game*.' He started when he saw Calculus. 'My God!' he cried. 'A mechanical man. Well, aren't you a beauty!'

'Thank you,' said Calculus, 'although I think I may be a little past my best.'

The young man looked at him blankly for a moment and then roared with laughter. ' "Past his best," ' he says. 'A mechanical man with a sense of humour!' He wiped his eyes and shook hands with India. 'Assistant Engineer Pieter Von Braun, at your service.' He bowed low. 'Tashar went to the bar,' he said to Bulldog, rolling his eyes, 'and I've been preparing some goulash, my mother's recipe. Are you all hungry?'

Bulldog's sandwich was now a distant memory and India nodded enthusiastically. Pieter disappeared back into the galley.

'Where's Rat?' shouted Bulldog. 'I need him to run an errand.'

A hunched creature appeared at the doorway, wearing a flight suit that was too short for him. His eyes nearly popped out of his head when he saw Calculus. 'Matsushito 5000 combat droid,' he said quickly.

'That is absolutely correct,' said Calculus, 'you clearly know a great deal about—'

'Height, two metres, weight one hundred and ten kilos without armaments, four parallel-track neural processors, sealed power unit with—'

'Rat!' snapped Bulldog.

The boy silenced himself immediately. He looked like a small mammal that was afraid it would be eaten.

'You'll have to excuse Rat,' said Bulldog. 'He likes facts and figures but he's not so good with people. Rat, go and find Tashar and tell her to drink up – we're leaving.'

Rat backed out of the door, still staring at Calculus, then fled down the stairs.

Bulldog gave them a guided tour of the rig while they waited. Behind the living area was a small galley, now fully occupied by Pieter and his pan of goulash. Beyond that were the crew's sleeping quarters and the main engineering section where several pairs of Bulldog's baggy underpants had been hung out to dry on the hot pipes and a hammock had been strung between the pressure gauges. ('Rat's sleeping quarters,' explained Bulldog.)

At the very front of the rig was the cockpit, which Bulldog showed them with relish. It was a cramped space, crammed with brass dials, lights and heavy levers, and it smelled of hot oil and sweat. Bulldog explained that when the rig was under way, he and Tashar would sit up front and manage the throttles and levers that controlled the caterpillar tracks. The equipment in the cockpit had been salvaged from a dozen different vessels.

'That pressure gauge came from the *Giselle* after an on-board fire. The drilling controls came from a Chinese rig that went through the ice in Dudinka, and this,' he said, sitting in a tatty, leather captain's chair, 'came from the *Excellent* after she blew up in the Urals.'

India felt increasingly nervous as the tour continued. The parts list of *The Beautiful Game* read like a catalogue of death and disaster. Calculus, however, seemed quite taken with the rig and was ready to accept Bulldog's invitation for an extended tour outside when Pieter called them for dinner.

Pieter produced huge quantities of potatoes and goulash from the galley and he and Bulldog attacked the meal like ravenous wolves. While they were eating, Tashar returned from the bar carrying a half-empty bottle of vodka and looking rather the worse for wear. She was very beautiful with high, Slavic cheekbones and long blonde hair that fell forward over her face. She was clearly displeased to find strangers on board her rig.

'So what is this, Captain? Now we have become a passenger ship?' She lit a black cigarette and poured herself a measure of vodka. 'You expect me to be a kid minder now? This is not in my job description, I think. You want us to be kid minders then we should get a bigger share.'

Bulldog shrugged, and sucked his teeth. 'No bigger shares,' he said. 'These are just friends of mine who've had a little run in with the Company, that's all.'

India smiled pleasantly but Tashar had clearly put her into a category marked 'unwelcome guest'. 'I know who they are, Captain. It's all over the yards that the Company is out looking for them. They say they're spies working for the Chinese and that they stole Company information. The reward on the robot alone is five thousand.'

'That's a lie!' said India. 'The Company hired Mrs Brown to find my dad's journals but then they kidnapped her and tried to kill me.'

'Actually,' said Calc, 'I'm an android—'

'Who cares?' said Tashar. She threw her head back and blew a lazy smoke ring. 'Either way, you're valuable property if we decide to cash you in.'

'That's enough, Tashar!' said Bulldog, suddenly cold-eyed and dangerous.

'So why are they here, Captain?' said Pieter, 'and what about our trip to the Caspian Sea?'

Bulldog pushed his plate away. 'There's been a change of plan,' he said casually. 'I've got a hot lead on a tech-mine. Easiest money we'll ever make, guaranteed. We're headed east towards Uliuiu Cherchekh.'

Tashar spluttered a mouthful of vodka across the table. 'Have you gone stinking crazy-mad?' she coughed.

'Er, Captain,' ventured Pieter. 'That's further than our operating range and long rigging in winter is no joke.'

Bulldog waved the objections aside and spread a large chart on the table in front of him. 'No worries. I know a few station captains on the way who'll let us have diesel. We'll stick to the forest trails and the river valleys to save fuel.'

'This is about Ironheart, isn't it?' said Tashar. 'Everyone knows that Stone is looking for it but there's no proof that it even exists. We don't need this craziness, we should turn these two in for the reward and then head south like we planned. Let's put it to a vote!'

'Enough!' Bulldog's fist crashed on the table. 'Damn it, Tashar, you're forgetting who gave you a job as a rig jockey when your licence was revoked. And, Pieter, you'd still be in a Company jail if I hadn't sprung you out. You were both keen enough to follow me then, so listen to me now. There's something valuable under those mountains, something bigger than we've ever seen before, and we're going to find it before anyone else does because, like India says, that's what pirates do. They look for treasure!'

There was a loud clattering up the stairs and Rat burst through the door, but then stood paralysed in front of the strangers. His mouth opened and shut like a fish. Bulldog took him gently by the shoulders.

'Rat! Calm down, son, what is it? Ignore them and tell me what's going on.'

Rat managed to squeeze out a few words. 'Men coming!' he blurted. 'Black coats, with guns!'

'Black coats? You mean Sid's boys? How many?'

'T-twenty-six. W-with guns.'

'He's right, Captain,' said Calculus, looking out of the door. 'There are several heat signatures headed this way from the direction of the loading docks.'

Bulldog swung into action and started handing out orders. 'Tashar, for crying out loud, sober up and get on the main deck. Pieter, run the start-up sequence. Rat, go outside and secure all the maintenance panels. Anything that can't be tied down, just leave it behind. Go!'

They jumped to their duties in a surprisingly well-disciplined way. India and Calculus pressed themselves to the wall as Rat scooted down the steps and Pieter disappeared into Engineering while Tashar and Bulldog hauled themselves into their driving seats. When Tashar turned on the electrical systems the wallboards lit up and the tractor engines burst into life with a deep-throated roar. The deck-plates rattled and vibrated and the smell of diesel filled the cabin.

Tashar pushed forward on a long lever and one of the tracks started to move, turning the rig slowly towards a range of mountains in the East. India clutched the table for support as the great machine began to roll forwards slowly, tracks clanging against the hard ground.

'More speed!' shouted Bulldog. 'Let's get to the mountains before they can send a patrol after us.' A loud clang reverberated off the hull. 'They're shooting at us!' he said. 'Step on it, Tashar!'

'Wait!' said India, shouting over the din. 'What about Rat? He hasn't come back in yet.'

Bulldog jumped from his seat and hauled open the main door, leaning out into the cold air as the rig began to pick up speed. The tiny figure of Rat loped along behind with arms outstretched, falling behind with every step as the guards accelerated towards him in an open truck.

'Tashar!' yelled Bulldog. 'Turn us around now.' The rig swerved and clipped a small maintenance shed, which immediately disintegrated, scattering wood splinters and equipment in their wake.

'We can't turn back!' yelled Tashar over her shoulder. 'We'll be overrun in a second. We have to leave him behind!'

'Damn it, Tashar,' Bulldog roared, 'if you don't turn this rig around now . . .'

He got no further. There was a blur of motion and he was pushed aside as a tall figure leaped through the doorway into the night.

'Calc!' shouted India.

The android rolled on the hard ground and started running towards the flagging boy. In a single movement he scooped up Rat and turned back towards the rig, legs pounding the ground like pistons. He drew level with the rig and leaped for the door, catching the sill with one hand. Bulldog and India pulled Rat inside but as Calculus clung on, the rusted steel frame of the door began to split and buckle under his weight. India reached out into the void and grasped the android's wrist with both hands as he dangled above the thundering caterpillar tracks a few feet away.

'No, India,' he said, 'I am too heavy for you.'

Her answer was to plant her feet either side of the door frame and grip him tighter. She cried out, afraid she would be dragged out of the door by his immense weight. Then Bulldog was there too, pulling hard and, in the next moment, Calculus had gained a handhold and hauled himself back inside.

Bulldog barely had time to jam the door shut before they ploughed through the steel gates of the rig yard. There was a screeching of metal on metal and they were all hurled violently around the little mess room.

The rig picked up a burst of speed and accelerated down a wide forest track. Tashar turned on the forward beams and steered expertly into a tree-lined valley, where she throttled back. The noise of the engine dropped to a tolerable level.

Bulldog sat in the centre of the room in a puddle of red gravy and potatoes, clutching the trembling Rat. India nursed her arms, which felt as though they had been nearly torn from their sockets.

'That was really very foolish, India,' said Calculus, wiping goulash from his visor. 'If I had fallen you would have been dragged to your death.'

'Well, you're welcome,' she said huffily.

The android sighed. 'I know you meant well, India. But I am quite used to being regarded as expendable.'

'Not by me. You're the last of your kind, remember? That makes you special.'

He looked at her for several seconds. 'In that case, thank you for saving my life.'

'That's OK,' she said. 'I guess it makes us even now.'

Bulldog clapped the android on the back. 'Not bad, metal man,' he said, 'not bad at all.' Then he slipped back into the captain's chair. 'All right! If everyone is finally on board, let's put some serious distance between us and the Company before they realize what just happened!'

CHAPTER 13

THE TESLAGRAPH

Sid the Kid clenched and unclenched his fists as he considered the wide swathe of damage left by *The Beautiful Game*. Silas and Cripps stood behind him, pleased that, for once, they were not the object of Sid's anger.

'So are you saying, not one damn Company rig gave chase to these pirates, Commander? Ain't that what my pa pays you for?'

The Commander, a lean and hard man made tough from thirty years of working in the wilderness, was afraid of no one. Nevertheless, something in this boy's eyes reminded him of a starving wolf he had once encountered out on the tundra. 'With respect,' he said, 'all of our vessels are being overhauled in preparation for departure tomorrow. The specific orders of your father, *sir*.'

Sid bared his teeth. 'You *lie*!' He pulled the pistol from his belt and took a step forwards. The Commander stiffened slightly but stood his ground.

'Don't take my word for it. Why don't you ask him yourself?' He nodded to a neat-looking man who was carefully carrying a wooden box as though it was filled with fine china.

Sid frowned and his two sidekicks crowded closer to get a better look.

'Whad's daht?' said Cripps, staring at the box. He had two black eyes and a wad of cotton wool stuffed up each nostril. There was a thick white sticking plaster strapped across the bridge of his nose.

'It's a portable Teslagraph,' said the Commander. 'One of Dr Cirenkov's discoveries. The Director had the foresight to install them in all of the Company rigs so he can stay in touch with his fleet.'

The man opened the lid to reveal a delicate pair of headphones and an ivory dial with fine black markings. He made subtle movements of the dial, as though tuning a musical instrument. The box crackled and made a sound like the sea rushing over gravel.

Sid squinted suspiciously at it. 'What's this? My pa wouldn't waste his time on that dumb contraption.'

The Director's voice rang out from the hissing box. 'Damn your stupidity, boy! You wouldn't recognize a useful piece of technology if it bit you in the backside! Now, tell me how a band of half-witted pirates managed to escape from my own rig yard.'

Silas and Cripps clutched each other at the sound of Stone's voice, as if he might materialize from the box at any moment.

Sid flushed red with the shame of being chastised in front of his men. 'S'not my fault, Pa.' He stooped to speak into a metal grille on the front of the box. 'This dumb-wit Commander was too busy taking his rig to pieces to chase them. D'you want me to shoot him, Pa?'

'I know where the fault lies, boy!' came the voice. 'It was you that let 'em slip through your hands. There are times I think I should have drowned you at birth!'

'It weren't my f-fault, Pa. That's not f-fair!'

'Fair don't come into it, boy,' roared Stone. 'You're a waste of space and always will be. Fortunately I have other ways to find that pirate rig. Now you stay put until I get there. If you want to do something useful, see what you can find out about *The Beautiful Game*, who they spoke to, their regular stopovers, anything useful. D'you hear?'

'Yes, Pa.'

'Good, I'll be there as soon as I've finished my business in Angel Town. Please resist the urge to shoot anyone until I get there.'

The voice clicked off and the static hiss returned. Sid thought he caught a faint smile on the face of the Commander. 'What're you finding so funny? My pa said I can't shoot you tonight, but there's always tomorrow. Now why don't you go and put your rig back together so it's ready for my pa when he gets here?'

The Commander clicked his heels smartly, then walked off into the night air while Sid returned to staring at the broken fence and the darkness beyond. He clutched the butt of his gun until his knuckles whitened. A vein in his temple throbbed painfully. It was at times like this that he felt his anger was a wild animal that might consume him and that if he gave into it, the part of him that was Sid might disappear and never come back again. Fighting to control his breathing, he slowly relaxed his grip on the gun. Soon he became aware that Cripps was still hovering at his shoulder.

'What is it?'

'Ethcuse me, sir,' honked Cripps, 'bud dere's a man here do see you. Says he's god information, bud he only wants to gib id do you.'

'Get rid of him. I don't have time for this.' Then he paused. His pa had told him to see what he could find out about *The Beautiful Game*. If there was even a small chance this man knew something useful then he should probably check his story. 'All right. I'll give him five minutes.'

The man looked tired and unwashed and wore several days of beard growth. He had a strange moustache that appeared to be crooked. And despite his new-looking cold-weather gear, he shivered continuously and kept his hood up. Sid guessed he wasn't used to Arctic weather.

'Good of you to see me, young sir!' he said as Sid approached. 'I know that you are a busy man but you won't regret it.' He rubbed his forehead nervously. 'I'm sorry, but I'm suffering a little with the weather. I wonder, would you have a glass of something warming available?'

Sid nodded to Cripps, who produced a small flask.

The stranger drank thirstily. 'Splendid.' He offered the flask to Sid. 'The restorative effects of a small glass of spirit. That's what keeps us men of the Arctic going, eh?'

'I don't drink,' said Sid. 'It brings the blood to the skin and gives you hypothermia. Now, tell me what you want.'

'Ah, indeed. Well, quite simply, I wish to do you a favour, young man,' he said, rubbing his forehead again. 'I understand you are seeking the whereabouts of a particular tech-mine and that certain persons may have absconded with this information?'

'What did you say?' said Sid, staring blankly.

'You want to find Ironheart and those pirates who know where it is,' said the stranger. Sid's face didn't flicker. That much of the story was common knowledge in the rig yard. The man was starting to annoy him.

'Perhaps you may be interested to know,' he continued, 'that India Bentley has information about the location of Ironheart embedded in a small pendant made by her father.'

Sid snorted. 'So how does that help me? That little witch is halfway over the mountains by now.'

The stranger rubbed his forehead again. 'Because the pendant is one of a pair. And I have the other one.' He held up a small, grey lozenge of metal, hanging by a leather thong. It was inscribed on one side with the name 'Bella'. 'It took me a little while to realize its significance but, believe me, you're going to want this when you find out what it is.'

Sid put his hand out for the twirling piece of metal but the stranger pulled it back quickly. 'Not so fast, young sir,' he said with a chilling smile. 'The previous owner was not happy to give this up and it was not come by without some significant difficulty on my part.' He paused. 'I expect some recompense for my time and trouble.'

Sid scowled and resisted the urge to reach for his gun. The pendant would have been easy enough to make and he had no reason to trust this soft-bellied fool. On the other hand, if the story was true then it might be a way for him to get back into his Pa's good books. 'What d'you want for it?' he said.

The stranger touched his forehead again nervously. Sid could see now that he had a large red weal between his eyes. 'Oh, very little in the scheme of things, young sir,' he said smoothly. 'A mere trifle. Perhaps we could go somewhere a bit warmer to talk about it?'

Sid thought for a moment and then nodded. 'All right then, mister, we'll talk. But I better like what you got to say.'

The stranger nodded enthusiastically. 'Oh, but you will, you will,' he said. 'And please, do call me Thaddeus.'

CHAPTER 14

THE MISMATCHED STARE

Two days out of Salekhard, life aboard *The Beautiful Game* had fallen into a regular routine. The crew had stopped arguing among themselves and went about their jobs like they were part of the machinery. The rig itself was like nothing India had ever seen before. She spent much of her time in the engineering section, fascinated by the network of polished brass pipes, oil-slicked pistons and flickering gauges that lined the walls. Pieter tolerated her endless questions and he allowed her to use the big grease gun to lubricate the bearings, provided she didn't touch anything else, and especially not the large red valves that directed cold water around the engines. 'You shut off the coolant in a baby like this,' he told her, 'then the whole thing's gonna blow apart in ten minutes flat, for sure.' But what she liked best was the cockpit. Although she was not allowed through the door, she stood on the threshold and admired the way that Tashar commanded the machine, coaxing the controls and feeding power to the tracks with a delicate touch of the throttles. India thought that, next to being a tech-hunter, driving an ice rig was probably the coolest job going.

Since the rescue, Rat had taken to following Calculus around like a puppy, asking endless questions about his technical schematics that the android answered with unfailing patience. As they talked in low voices, India wiped condensation from the windows with her sleeve and watched as the rig rolled steadily eastwards along wide forest trails. The land in all directions was covered in unmarked, crystal-white powder that softened the hills and transformed the trees into strange white shapes.

As darkness fell on the third day they pulled into a sheltered location and Bulldog prepared to secure the rig for the night. When India discovered he was going outside she pestered him to let her go with him until he gave in. So, a short while later, swathed in thick woollen under-layers and a borrowed deerskin coat, she waited impatiently for Bulldog to crack the seal on the external door.

As the hatch swung open, the outside silence rushed in to fill the little room and India stepped over the threshold into a cold and alien world. She shivered as the frozen air found the tiniest chinks in her clothing with needle-sharp fingers and recalled a time when she and Bella had played in the snow in London. She marvelled at the ice formations and the delicate frost patterns growing on the steel handrails. But when she slipped off her mitten to touch them, Bulldog yelled at her.

'Don't touch the metal without your gloves on! Your skin will freeze to it in a second and then there's only one way to get you off.'

'Which is?'

'You get a friend to pee on you.' He chuckled. 'Of course it helps if it's a *good* friend.'

India looked at the handrail and then slipped her glove back on. She didn't think she wanted that sort of help from anyone on board *The Beautiful Game*.

It was nearly dark when Bulldog had finished lashing down the equipment. He turned on the flood lamps and they stood for a moment, staring at the flakes falling thickly in the lights of the rig. India was struck by the intensity of the silence that came from a thousand miles of nothingness shrouded in thick snow.

'We'd better go in,' he said. 'You need to be careful out here, hypothermia creeps up on you and you don't even notice. The first sign is when you stop feeling cold and the tiredness takes hold of you. I knew a guy, got too cold one night and lay down to sleep on the roof of his rig. By the time the crew found him they had to chip him off with a crowbar.'

Inside, Tashar was poring over the navigation charts on the mess-room table. 'Fuel is down to thirty per cent, Captain, and we'll need to refuel at Gorki Station. Don't you think it's about time you told us where we're going?'

Bulldog turned to India and Calculus. 'I reckon you've had plenty of time to work on that pendant by now. So let's hear that message.'

India handed the pendant to Calculus, who laid it carefully on the table. 'This is a solid-state storage device,' he began. 'A microchip. It holds John Bentley's secret journal relating to Ironheart. As we hoped, the first part of the journal describes how to find Ironheart. It contains a map reference and a single word, "Nentu".'

'I never heard of a place called Nentu,' said Tashar.

'Nentu was the name of the Great Shaman of the North,' said Pieter. 'A famous wise woman who lived in these parts two hundred years ago. Could this have something to do with her?'

'I don't see how,' said Bulldog. 'Where's the map reference?'

'It's a point about one hundred and fifty miles along the upper reaches of this river valley,' said Calculus, pointing to a spot on the chart. 'It's very remote.'

The crew exchanged nervous glances.

'We know that place,' said Tashar darkly. 'It's in the dead country.'

'Nobody ever goes there, Captain,' said Rat, wide-eyed. 'The nomads say it's a bad place.'

'Well what better place to hide something you don't want found?' said Bulldog. 'What's the second part of the message?'

'It's an inventory of what John Bentley found at Ironheart,' said Calculus.

He paused.

'Well don't keep us in suspense,' said Pieter. 'What's there?'

Calculus glanced at India. She nodded encouragingly. 'Treasure,' he said. 'Gold, jewels, old-tech. It's all there for the taking.'

The pirates' eyes gleamed. Pieter and Rat grinned and punched each other on the shoulder, and Bulldog smiled thoughtfully.

'So once we find this place,' said Bulldog, 'how do we get in?'

Calculus shook his head. 'I don't know,' he said. 'Mr Bentley left no instructions for getting in.'

Everyone looked crestfallen.

'So basically,' said Tashar, 'we have to drive to the middle of nowhere to find this place, and then hope they left the key under the mat?' She rolled her eyes. 'My God, I preferred it when we just went rigging. By the time we get back to the southern fields we'll have lost six weeks of drilling time. That's half the season gone and money out of our pockets on a wild moose chase.'

Bulldog folded the maps. 'This is no *goose* chase, Tashar,' he said. 'This is the best chance we'll ever have to make it rich. Trust me, my ears never lie and this lead on Ironheart is hot. We'll press on as planned and, when we find it, then we'll figure out how we're going to get in. Perhaps John Bentley left some other clues that we haven't found yet.'

The meeting ended and Bulldog and Tashar began to plot the following day's course. While Rat and Calculus disappeared into Engineering for another technical chat, India helped Pieter to prepare the evening meal.

'If you want to be indispensable on a rig,' he said, expertly dicing some onions, 'then learn how to cook. Every rigger I ever met eats like a starved bear, even the women.'

India laughed. The longer she spent on board *The Beautiful Game*, the more the crew seemed to be like a large and badly behaved family. 'Do you have any children of your own, Pieter?' she asked.

'Sure,' he said. 'Four boys and they all want to be riggers like their dad.' He smiled proudly. 'But my wife's not so keen, especially when I have to travel this far east. She believes too many of the old stories about this place.'

'What stories?'

So as they worked, he told her ghost stories about the haunted places where the forest shadows would suck the life from a man's body if you accidentally stepped into them. He told her about the crews who caught glimpses of something behind them in the mirror and were driven mad with the thought that they were not alone.

He scraped the vegetables into the sauce and turned down the heat. 'Once, when I was a junior crewman on the *Snow Maiden*, we came across another rig rolling across the ice. We signalled them to stop but they didn't even slow down.' He shivered. 'When we finally got on board, every man was still at his post, stone dead, but their eyes were wide and staring as though they had seen the gates of hell.'

'Where was that?' said India, fearing she already knew the answer.

'That rig had rolled straight out of the Valley of Death.'

He fell silent, but when he saw her worried expression he gave her a broad grin. 'Hey, don't mind me,' he said. 'Riggers are just like sailors. They drink too much vodka and they start to see mermaids.'

They both laughed, but India shivered, as though something cold had touched her heart.

That night, her dreams returned.

She was riding the back of a great eagle, rising into the air on winds as cold as a blade. She gasped at the colours of the land as she soared over blue-pink mountains with peaks that seemed to float on the air like ghost ships. Then the bird plunged into the shadow of icy ravines, skimming the surface of the lakes and twisting through steep-sided valleys lined with green-black spruce dressed in their winter snows. She clung to the eagle's back, exhilarated by the powerful pulse of its muscles and breathing in the smell of the high nesting places that lingered in its feathers.

'They will leave you alone here,' it said, 'but you must not give up. Already the bringer-of-death rises in the East. If you stop now then it will be forever winter in this land.'

'But what should I do?' she said.

'You must feel for the spirit in the earth and it will lead you to me,' said the eagle.

And as it spoke, her senses stretched out into the landscape and she could feel the frozen river running through her blood.

'How will I know you?'

'By the sign of the shaman you will know me,' said the eagle. It

turned to look at her and she saw that it had one eye of blue and one of brown.

She woke in a sweat and couldn't get back to sleep. There could be no doubt now, the further east she went, the stronger the dreams were becoming. She couldn't escape the feeling that they were not her dreams at all, but that they belonged to someone else entirely.

The next morning was crisp and sun-washed and all thoughts of ghosts and spirits were banished by the smell of frying meat and eggs coming from the galley. After a relatively good-humoured breakfast, Tashar started the main engines and they got under way. It would be less than a day's journey to Gorki Station.

They turned off the main trail and headed south along a winding river. In the summer the area would have been impassable marshland but now, at the start of winter, the ground was hard frozen and easy going. What caused Bulldog more concern were the lakes. They had not yet become what he called 'iron-hard': frozen to a depth of a foot or more and able to take the weight of *The Beautiful Game* when it made the crossing to Gorki Station. India realized that the prospect of crossing the ice was worrying him deeply.

After an hour they reached a wide lake bounded at both ends by deep and impassable ravines. They parked on the shore and Bulldog and Pieter inspected its icy surface while the rest of the crew unpacked emergency rations, signal flares and additional warm clothing, which they hauled to the far side of the lake.

'Perhaps it would be wise to let me drive *The Beautiful Game* across the ice,' said Calculus.

Bulldog shook his head. 'That's the captain's duty, my friend,' he said with a grim smile. 'If this baby is going through the ice, then I want to be the one driving her when she does.'

They stood in the sunlight and watched Bulldog climb back into the rig by himself and start to drive slowly forward. The ice groaned like old timbers under the weight of the great machine and India found herself making tight fists inside her mittens. At one point there was a loud crack as the surface of the ice fractured and one of the rear tracks crashed through into the black waters. Pieter shouted urgent orders to Bulldog and, to everyone's relief, the rig lurched forward again, pulling clear of the hole. *The Beautiful Game* hauled herself up the snowy bank on the far side to a burst of applause.

Then Bulldog was out of the cockpit in great humour, slapping backs and telling tasteless jokes. He fetched a cold slab of chocolate from one of the outside food lockers and shared it out. India had heard about chocolate from the older villagers at home. She cracked the brittle bar with her teeth and savoured the wonderful, rich, melting sensation as it dissolved slowly in her mouth. All the worries from the previous night seemed to have evaporated. Even Tashar was smiling. At that moment, India thought there was surely nothing better than the life of a rigger, free to roam the wilderness in search of adventure. But almost at once a small cloud passed across her sky and she sat down on a nearby rock with a heavy sigh.

'Cheer up, India, it might never 'appen,' said Bulldog, his face still beaming in triumph.

'Sorry,' she said. 'I was just thinking about Verity. It doesn't feel right to be celebrating when Stone's still holding her prisoner.'

Bulldog nodded thoughtfully and sat down beside her. 'I understand,' he said. 'I've seen the Company do bad things to good people too many times. But we already gave them a poke in the eye when we escaped from Salekhard and we'll do it again when we find Ironheart. After that, Lucifer Stone will give us whatever we want. We'll get Mrs Brown back, no problem.' He gave her a reassuring grin.

'Thanks, Bulldog,' she said with a small smile. 'How much longer until we get to Gorki Station?'

'Not far now,' he said, 'just over the next rise and . . .'

His voice tailed off and she followed his gaze to a gap in the mountains where a thick column of black smoke was rising into the crisp, blue sky.

CHAPTER 15

THE *LONE WOLF*

Gorki Station was little more than a dirt road with some rough shacks and a few corrugated sheds arranged around the shores of a frozen lake. A small herd of reindeer were held in pens beside the main street and a lazy bullock wandered listlessly in the road. The wooden buildings in the centre of town had been reduced to smoking shells and there was no sign of human activity anywhere.

'What happened here?' said India, dismayed.

'I believe I may have an explanation,' said Calculus. 'Do you see those bullet holes in the side of that building? That's a heavy-calibre weapon, the same sort of gun we saw on the rigs in Salekhard. I think the Company has been here before us.'

'Brilliant!' said Tashar. 'The only advantage we had was that we were one step ahead of the Company. How could they know we were coming here?'

'We don't know that they do,' said Bulldog.

'We know it well enough,' she said. 'You've put us all in danger, Bulldog, and for what? Some dream you have about finding treasure. I say we dump these damned tourists of yours and head south now.'

Bulldog turned on her. 'What's the matter with you, Tashar? Do you really want to spend your life running from the Company? We've got a shot at finding Ironheart – but not if we keep bleating about how dangerous it is every time the going gets tough! Now go and find an oil tank so we can refuel and get out of here.'

'I think we have a more immediate problem,' said Calculus. 'Listen!'

They fell quiet and strained their ears to listen over the breeze. India thought she heard something, but it was more of a vibration than a noise.

'It's a rig,' said Bulldog. 'A big one, and it's coming this way. Whoever did all this is still here. Pieter, Rat, go and start the engines. Tashar, I need you up front!'

He held Tashar's stare for a moment before she turned and clambered up the steps.

As the engines burst into life another large rig appeared over the brow of the hill. There was a man on the roof sitting behind a heavy machine gun. The sleek machine began to turn slowly in their direction, revving its engines.

'It's a Company rig, the *Lone Wolf*!' shouted Bulldog, heaving himself into the captain's chair. 'Get us into the trees, Tashar, or we're sitting ducks.'

The Beautiful Game lurched off at a wild pace and India

pressed her face anxiously to the mess-room window. She heard a distant rattling noise followed by a metallic spattering on the outside of the hull.

'They're aiming for the fuel tanks, Captain,' shouted Rat from the back of the rig.

The trees were still half a mile away up a steep slope.

'We'll never make it before they catch us,' said Bulldog. 'Tashar, take a sharp right, now!'

'Are you crazy?' she shouted. 'That will take us across the lake. We'll go straight to the bottom.'

Another volley of bullets clattered off the hull.

Bulldog stuck out his jaw. 'Sometimes crazy is the only smart thing to be,' he said. 'The trees on the other bank are nearer. Do it, Tashar!'

Shaking her head, Tashar yanked one of the tall levers and *The Beautiful Game* swerved and plunged down the steep bank. The ice groaned as the enormous weight of the machine slammed on to it. India thought of the great care they had taken crossing the lake earlier. The *Lone Wolf* followed them down the bank, slipping and sliding as it tried to get traction but gaining on them all the while.

The ice gave way with a noise that echoed across the lake. From the window, India watched the other rig break through the surface and the front half of the machine plunge into the water.

Bulldog pulled *The Beautiful Game* to a shuddering halt on the opposite bank and threw open the cabin doors. 'They're in the water! Pieter, get your gear on and follow me.'

'You're not going to help them?' said Tashar. 'They were trying to kill us!'

Bulldog was already hauling on his coat. 'I'm going to get some answers,' he said. 'I don't believe they turned up here by coincidence. They knew we were coming and I want to know how.'

Then he was out of the hatch and down the steps, closely followed by Pieter and Calculus. India was still wearing her own cold-weather gear and plunged out of the door after them.

On the lake it was bitter. The sun had disappeared behind a leaden cloud and a cutting wind blew across the ice. The front of the *Lone Wolf* was completely submerged by the time they reached it and the back rested precariously on the edge of the ice hole so that the rig was pitched forward at a steep angle. Deep cracks in the ice were visible in every direction.

Bulldog and Pieter climbed on to the roof and pulled at the hatch while Calculus hooked his arm around one of the rig's sturdy supports to prevent it from slipping forward completely into the black water. The hatch appeared to be jammed and, try as they might, the two men could not shift it. From the corner of her eye, India spotted a movement. In the belly of the rig was a second hatch, partially submerged, and a lone hand flapped weakly against the glass porthole.

'There's somebody trapped down here!' she shouted, but the others were too busy to help.

She sized up the situation and then hopped across the

fractured ice to the hatch. Grasping the locking wheel, she heaved at it with all of her weight. The broken ice threatened to pitch her into the freezing water and all the while the hand clawed more desperately at the glass. Then the door burst suddenly outwards in a rush of black water and India found herself grasping at a pair of arms. Gradually a spluttering, bulky figure inched its way from the narrow opening. It looked like some strange creature being born on to the ice.

'I can't hold on any longer,' called Calculus. 'Stand clear!'

Bulldog and Pieter leaped away and India gave a last desperate heave to pull the man free from the hatchway. The rig juddered and began to slide forward into the water. India grabbed the man by the scruff of his jacket and used all of her remaining strength to drag him along the ice to safety.

With a last uprushing of air, the rig plunged into the foaming waters, carrying the remainder of its crew into the black depths. The group from *The Beautiful Game* stood in silence, looking at each other from opposite sides of the giant hole. The man India had rescued lay face down on the ice, groaning.

'Are you all right?' she said, leaning over him.

He rolled over and his eyelids flickered. He had an odd moustache that seemed to be peeling away from his face. She peered at the pale face under the hood of the jacket and then she jumped backwards with a shriek.

Doubting what she had seen, she leaned forward again

143

to get a second look. He looked paler than she remembered and wore several days of beard growth, but looking at his weaselly features, there could be no doubt.

The man she had rescued was Thaddeus Clench.

CHAPTER 16

AKA ARCHIE FENTON

India stared at Clench from the corner of the mess room and chewed her lip. She had not yet had a chance to tell the others who he was. Now, as he sat wrapped in a blanket, shivering and drinking Bulldog's brandy, the need to know why he was here was gnawing at her. Bulldog too had questions.

'Who are you and why did you attack us?' he demanded.

'I wasn't with them,' stammered Clench. 'I tried to get them to stop, really I did. India will vouch for me, she knows who I am.'

The others turned to stare at India.

'Is that true?' said Bulldog. 'Do you know him?'

India folded her arms. 'His name's Thaddeus Clench but he's no friend of mine. I don't know why he's followed me here, but one thing's for sure: you can't trust him.'

'I can verify India's story,' said Calculus. 'And I agree that Mr Clench does not seem particularly trustworthy.'

A black look flashed briefly across Clench's face, then

he forced a tight smile. 'Captain, surely you're not going to take the word of a tin robot and a child against mine?' he said. 'The girl's a runaway, I tell you, a wild child, and she's caused her family no end of grief.'

'Actually, I'm a—' began Calculus, but Bulldog raised his hand for silence.

'Half the people I know are running away from something, Mr Clench,' he said, 'but I judge people by what I see.' He moved closer so they were eye to eye. 'And this "wild child" has just saved your life. Now tell me, why do you look so familiar to me? Have we met before?'

Clench shrank back. 'Er, no, I don't think that's possible.' He licked his lips. 'I've never set foot in Siberia before.'

Bulldog snapped his fingers. 'I've got it!' he said. 'Your name's not Clench, it's Fenton, Archie Fenton. You're wanted in over half of Siberia.'

'*He's* Archie Fenton?' said Tashar incredulously. 'Well, he doesn't look that much, does he?'

'I don't get it,' said India. 'Who's Archie Fenton?'

'They used to call him Archie Cheap-as-Chips,' said Bulldog. 'He supplied mining equipment to the Company at rock-bottom prices. Then some of his drilling equipment caused a big accident that killed over a hundred people. It turned out that Archie was using faulty parts and selling them as new. They tried to arrest him but he skipped the country about a year ago.'

'That was when he came to London,' said India. 'He told us he was an explorer.'

Bulldog chuckled. 'Explorer, eh? I wouldn't say that. They tried him in his absence and sentenced him to hang. I'd say he's got a nasty surprise waiting for him when he gets back to Angel Town.'

Fear was written large across Clench's face. 'Please,' he said, clutching at Bulldog's jacket, 'don't send me back there.'

Bulldog scowled. 'A lot of us lost friends in that accident,' he said. 'The first inhabited place we get to, I'm turning you in.'

'Wait, wait,' begged Clench. 'If you take me with you, I can be useful. I can tell you how the *Lone Wolf* found you.'

Bulldog looked at Clench with renewed interest and India could see what was on his mind.

'Captain, you can't take him with us,' she said. 'He's a liar! He'd say anything to save his own neck.'

'Really now, India,' said Clench. 'You told these people you weren't a runaway but you left home in the middle of the night and your robot friend injured more than a dozen of your neighbours before you went. So you tell me which one of us is a liar?'

India's face burned.

'All right,' said Bulldog, 'enough of that. Clench, Fenton, whatever your name is, tell me what you know and I'll let you off somewhere you can hitch a ride on another rig. After that you'll be someone else's problem.'

Clench adopted the smug look of a man who knew the balance of power had just shifted in his favour. 'You've got a spy on board, Captain,' he said. 'An agent working for the Company. Someone on your crew is not what they seem.'

A shockwave ran round the little room.

'India was right,' said Pieter. 'He *will* say anything to save his skin. Let's throw him out now before he poisons the air with his lies!'

Bulldog raised his hand for silence. 'Who's the spy?' he said.

Everybody went quiet as Clench reached for the brandy bottle and poured himself another drink. 'I heard things,' he said eventually, 'while I was on the other rig. They said someone on *The Beautiful Game* had been sending them messages but they didn't say who. Apparently the Company has spies on lots of rigs and they've got some sort of dead-tech machine that lets them speak to each other over long distances.'

'How convenient,' said Pieter. 'A story you can't prove that gets you a safe passage out of here. Let's not waste any more time on him, Captain, let's just shoot him now.'

'You seem very keen to get rid of him all of a sudden, Pieter,' said Tashar, raising an eyebrow.

'What are you saying?'

'I'm just saying that if we have a spy on board then I'm looking at the man who was the last one to join the crew.'

'Only eight weeks after you did,' he snapped back. 'And haven't you been very keen to undermine the Captain lately?'

'Stop it, both of you!' cried India. 'Can't you see he's making you turn on each other?'

Clench sat quietly in the corner wearing a half-smile.

'India's right,' said Bulldog. 'He's probably just lying to save his skin. Lock him in the spare cabin and let's keep a close eye on him. If he's spent a week on a Company rig there may be other things he can tell us.'

After Gorki Station, *The Beautiful Game* turned off the forest trails and through the high mountain passes where, Bulldog figured, the rig would be harder to follow. On the Captain's orders, and much to Pieter's consternation, the rig drove day and night with Bulldog and Tashar taking turns to man the cockpit.

Outside, the scenery changed to an unending cruel landscape of rock, ice and flint-edged mountains that towered above them. The wind blasted the rig continuously and the sky was layered with dark grey clouds that matched India's mood. She watched nervously from the mess windows as the rig navigated impossibly narrow tracks through the high passes, dislodging giant rocks that went plunging into the ravines below.

At the daily crew meeting tensions were still running high.

'Everybody's tired,' said Tashar, 'and if we make a single mistake we'll end up at the bottom of a ravine. What's more, we're burning too much fuel in these damned mountains.'

'It's the quickest route,' said Bulldog. 'It'll take three

days off the journey and no Company rig will ever dare follow us up here.'

'For good reason,' said Tashar. 'No one's ever attempted to cross this mountain range in a rig before.'

'Ah! That's where you're wrong,' said Bulldog triumphantly. 'The last time I was here was fifteen years ago when I was part of Mad Don McNulty's crew. He swore blind there was a safe route over these mountains.'

'Didn't Mad Don McNulty take shelter in a cave and get eaten by bears?' said Rat.

'Well, yes,' Bulldog conceded. 'He was trying to prove that mountain bears are less ferocious than forest bears but it didn't quite work out. The crew lost interest after that and we all went back to Angel Town. But my point is, Mad Don's theory was sound, this is the best route across the mountains, you mark my words.'

'Well, I'm not liking this place one bit, Bulldog,' said Tashar. 'There had better be a lot of money at the end of this joyride or you will be needing a new pilot.'

Later that evening India went in search of Calculus. She found him alone in Engineering reading a heavy, leather-bound book and making neat pencil notes in the margins.

'What are you reading?' she said.

'Just a book I found in Captain Bulldog's library,' he said without looking up.

'Is it exciting?'

'It is very . . . absorbing.'

150

She leaned in closer and squinted at the dense text.

'My dad always used to read to me and Bella before we went to bed,' she said, giving Calc a meaningful look, 'even after we were both old enough to read for ourselves.'

Calculus put the book down with a sigh. 'I suppose I could read to you if you like,' he said.

She grinned. 'Would you, Calc? That would be great.'

He looked down at the page again. 'Where would you like me to start?'

'Well, most stories begin with "*Once upon a time*",' she said.

'Very well.' He straightened in his seat and held out the book in front of him. '*Once upon a time*,' he began grandly, '*laminar flows could be adequately defined through the application of the Navier-Stokes equations which allowed for the simulation of turbulent flows at moderate Reynolds numbers.*'

'Whoa, wait a minute! What on earth are you reading?'

He looked at the cover and then at India.

'*Basic Fluid Dynamics for Sub-Arctic Operations*,' he said. 'Captain Bulldog has quite an extensive collection of engineering manuals. If you prefer I could try a different one?'

'No thanks,' she said laughing. 'Perhaps we'd better skip the story tonight.'

He closed the book with a snap. 'You're up very late,' he said.

'I couldn't get to sleep,' she lied. 'Knee's playing up.'

'Let me bandage it for you,' he said. 'I have full training in field hospital techniques.'

She sat patiently while he fetched the bandages and then began to strap her knee with expert hands.

'I wish Verity was here,' she said as he worked. 'She wouldn't be afraid of Sid or Tashar or of ghosts in the forest. Do you ever think about her?'

He didn't look up from what he was doing. 'While I am capable of fully independent function,' he said, 'my anticipatory sub-routines do register Mrs Brown's absence from my immediate environment.'

India smiled. 'Yeah, I miss her too,' she said.

They were both silent for a moment while he carefully unrolled another bandage.

'What is your father like?' he said.

The suddenness of his question threw her off guard. 'Dad? He's brave and clever and he's always looking for ways to make life better for people. One year he built an irrigation system for our whole village. But then me and Bella tried to help and it went wrong and it flooded the house and all of Roshanne's shoes got ruined.' She smiled at the memory.

'You must miss him a lot,' said Calculus.

'Yes. But not the way everyone thinks. They keep telling me he can't still be alive and that I should just "let him go". But when I look up at the stars, Calc, it's like I just know he's looking up at the same sky somewhere. It's like we're connected somehow. Nobody ever seems to believe me though.'

'I believe you.'

India looked at the android in surprise.

'You once asked me if there were any others like me,' he said. 'And there were. Once I was part of a great army. There were many hundreds of us, we were strong and we fought many battles. Our minds were connected and we could hear each other's thoughts; I always knew I was not alone.'

India blinked at him. 'That's how it is for me,' she said breathlessly. 'Even though Dad's not here, I can always feel him. That's how I know he's still alive. So what happened to your friends?'

Calculus snipped the end of her bandage and tied it off. 'We were together for a long time,' he said. 'If we were damaged or destroyed our minds could be downloaded into a new body and we would go on living.' He fell silent.

India was entranced. 'So you can live forever?'

He snapped out of his daydream and began to put away the bandages. 'No,' he said quickly. 'After the Great Rains, the knowledge to transfer our minds was lost. One by one, over the years, the others all became damaged or they malfunctioned and fell silent. Now the only thoughts I hear are my own.' He turned and placed the medical kit on a shelf behind him. 'I was immortal once,' he said, 'but not any more.'

India felt a huge sadness for the android. She wanted to say something further but, at that moment, *The Beautiful Game* shuddered to an abrupt halt. The sudden silence from the engines filled the whole rig.

They found the others in the cockpit, looking out of the forward windows. *The Beautiful Game* had pulled to a stop on a steep slope at the head of a desolate, tree-lined valley. It was blanketed with a thick layer of unbroken snow and it looked as though no human had ever set foot in it.

'This is the start of the Uliuiu Cherchekh,' said Bulldog solemnly. 'It runs east for over a hundred miles. More than a dozen rigs have gone missing here so let's keep our eyes open, people!'

A full moon came out from behind a cloud, sending deep blue shadows across the valley floor.

'Is it me or did it just get colder in here?' said Tashar, pulling her jacket tighter.

'We need to conserve fuel,' said Bulldog. 'If we want to keep warm we'll rely on the wood stove. In the meantime, I'm going to check the tracks and the driveshafts. We took a pounding in the mountains and I want to make sure everything's in working order before we go any further.'

India stayed looking out of the window, feeling all of her courage drain away. Back in Angel Town it had been easy to talk about following the trail eastwards across the mountains. But now that she looked out on the Valley of Death she was reminded of Pieter's ghost stories. The valley looked like something from a bad fairy tale and the words from her dream came back to haunt her.

'*Already the bringer-of-death rises in the East. If you stop now then it will be forever winter in this land.*'

CHAPTER 17

THE ANDROID'S SCREAM

India sat in the mess room and waited impatiently while the crew checked the rig's systems. Bulldog and Tashar meticulously ran through every circuit in the cockpit, testing for any signs of damage.

'As soon as we've finished checking the main drive we'll get under way,' said Bulldog. 'Where's Pieter?'

'He went outside to fetch wood,' said Rat.

Bulldog's forehead creased into a frown. 'That was ages ago. I need him back here.'

'I could go and get him,' said India quickly, 'and Calculus could come with me.'

She was anxious to escape from the rig, if only for a short while. Bulldog looked dubious.

'Come on,' she said, 'I'm the only one with nothing to do. Besides, nothing bad's going to happen while Calc's with me, is it?'

'All right,' said Bulldog. 'Take one of the sledges with you and collect some firewood on the way. And take Mr Clench too,' he added. 'Make him do a bit of work around here for a change.'

Her heart sank. 'I don't want to go anywhere with him. He's a murderer, you said so yourself!'

'Well, like you say, nothing bad's going to happen while you're with Calculus, is it? Besides, I'm sick to death of hearing him whine about being cooped up. Perhaps a taste of the cold will shut him up.' He glanced out of the window. 'Just make sure you stay out of the forest, OK?'

'Why? What's in the forest?'

'Don't ask too many questions,' he said darkly. 'Now go, before I change my mind.'

Bulldog would listen to no further arguments, and twenty minutes later she stepped grumpily from the hatch into the fresh night air, followed by Calculus and Thaddeus Clench.

The sky was clear and the wind carried smells of fresh pine. The moon cast a light so silvery sharp that it almost tingled on the skin. They followed Pieter's footprints up a low hill covered with birch and pine while India collected dead branches and stacked them in a wicker basket on the sledge. Clench did little to help and walked behind, hugging himself against the cold and complaining bitterly.

'Outrageous,' he said over and over. 'Forcing a prisoner to risk his life like this in the middle of the night.'

India stomped up to the top of the nearest hill to get away from him. She paused to catch her breath and took in the view. Something on the far side of the valley caught her eye. A solitary light blinked once, like a flash from a rotating beacon, and when the moon came out from behind a cloud she made out an unmistakable black shape nestling in the treeline. She dropped quickly to her knees and waved to Calculus and Clench.

'It's another rig!' she breathed as they arrived beside her. She heard the faint whirring of sensors and magnifiers clicking into place behind the android's visor.

'The *Prince of Darkness*,' he said. 'Stone's personal rig.'

'How did they find us in this wilderness?' said India.

'That's how,' said Clench, pointing down the hill.

A short way down the slope a man lay in a hollow with his back to them. He was fiddling with a small wooden box.

'It's Pieter,' said India. 'But what is he doing?'

They watched him twist the dial on the front of the box and direct a thin metal rod towards the other rig.

'He's using a Teslagraph,' said Calculus.

'What did I tell you!' said Clench. 'He's your spy!'

India's hand went to her mouth. 'We have to stop him!'

She broke into a run down the slope towards Pieter with Calculus close behind while Clench hovered indecisively at the top of the hill. Pieter turned in surprise as they approached. He made a grab for the Teslagraph but Calculus knocked it from his hand and it smashed against a rock.

'Pieter, what are you doing?' panted India. 'Those are our enemies.'

Pieter scrambled backwards to get away from Calculus.

157

'They might be your enemies but they're not mine,' he said. 'You didn't seriously think I would choose a pirate's life, did you?' There was a hardness in his eyes that had not been there before.

India's face flushed. 'But how could you? The Company is run by thugs and murderers and if they catch us, they'll kill us all.'

'That's Bulldog's problem. I have four children and a wife to feed back in Omsk and the Company pays good money for information on pirates.'

A shout from Clench at the top of the hill made them turn. He was jumping up and down and waving his arms.

'What's he doing?' said India. 'He's going to get us seen.'

'Too late,' said Calculus. 'Look!'

On the far side of the valley, a swarm of two-seater ski vehicles had left the rig and started out across the valley floor, skimming across the snow like angry hornets. Each vehicle carried a driver and passenger dressed in broad hats and long flowing coats.

They were so distracted that neither of them noticed Pieter reach into his jacket pocket to pull out a pistol.

'Stay still and you won't get hurt,' warned Pieter, training the gun on them. 'I'll get an extra bonus for bringing in the girl and her pet robot.'

India and Calculus stood rooted to the spot as the noise drew nearer. Pieter glanced briefly in the direction of the ski machines – it took him no more than a second – but it was enough for Calculus, who lunged towards him. Pieter's gun fired once and the bullet glanced off the android's visor. But Calculus recovered his balance quickly and India watched with an absolute knowledge of what was about to happen but with no ability to prevent it.

'Calc, don't!' was all she had time to say.

The android's hand struck Pieter's neck with a dull crunch and his body went sprawling in the snow, where it lay motionless. The shock hit India like a bucket of cold water.

'You've *killed* him!'

Calculus grasped her by the arm. 'He was armed, India,' he said calmly, 'and he might have killed you.'

She backed away angrily. 'You didn't have to kill him. You could have just taken his gun away. He had a family – what's wrong with you?'

'I am trained to protect and I was protecting you.' The ski vehicles were advancing up the hill now. 'We don't have time for this, we need to go!'

India was not about to stop. 'You said you wanted to change, but you can't, can you? You're just a machine. A vicious, cold-blooded killing machine!'

The sound of approaching engines increased and the first ski machine burst over a snow bank. The man on the back levelled his rifle at Calculus. With blinding speed the android darted forward and seized hold of the machine, sending the riders tumbling into the snow. 'India, get away now!' he shouted to her. 'I'll hold them off as long as I can. Get back to the rig!'

India turned and ran back up the hill. It was heavy going and she sank up to her knees in the snow with every step. At the top of the hill Clench was hopping up and down.

'Let's go back while we can,' pleaded Clench, 'they've got guns.'

'I don't care,' she panted. 'I'm not going anywhere until I'm sure Calc's OK.'

They watched the battle unfold from the top of the hill. The ski machines began to circle Calculus. The android darted forward and overturned a second machine, hurling it on to the rocks, where it burst into flames. The air filled with the smell of burning spirit.

'Come *on*, Calc,' she cried. 'Let's get out of here while we have the chance.'

Calculus turned to look up the hill and motioned at her to start running. That was when the terrible thing happened.

One of the riders picked up a long metal lance and jabbed Calculus in the back. It made a sound like India's shock stick but a thousand times louder, a dry crackling noise that ripped the air. Calculus reared backwards as the charge coursed through his metal sinews. India started towards him but Clench held her back. 'Come on, for pity's sake, India or you'll get us both killed.'

A second man picked up his lance and jabbed Calculus in the chest, forcing him on to his back. His body spasmed violently in the snow. They pulled out a steel net and threw it over him, spearing him with the lances again and again until he thrashed around, losing all control of his limbs.

'Leave him alone!' sobbed India. 'Please just leave him alone!'

Just when she thought it could get no worse, came the terrible sound of the android's scream.

It started faintly over the noise of the wind, a high keening that sounded mechanical and human at the same time and grew louder and louder until the terrible screeching echoed around the valley.

She pressed her hands to her ears to drown out the horror. 'Stop it, stop it, you're killing him!'

Calculus finally stopped screaming and went limp. The riders stepped back and watched him twitching weakly on the ground. Clench tugged gently on India's arm. Even he looked shocked by what he had seen.

'Come on, India,' he said quietly. 'We have to get back to *The Beautiful Game* before they come after us.'

CHAPTER 18

THE REINDEER PEOPLE

For a moment, the scene was eerily still. The riders stood around the helpless android, admiring their handiwork. Up on the hilltop, India looked away from the terrible scene, half blinded with tears.

'The rig,' said Clench quietly, tugging on her arm again. 'We have to get back to the rig.'

She allowed herself to be led away. But when they had gone a few paces one of the riders looked up and noticed them. He turned his ski machine and started lazily towards them.

'Forget the rig,' said Clench, with panic rising in his voice. 'Head for the trees. They can't follow us in there on those machines.' He dragged her the short distance to the treeline and she followed, only dimly remembering Bulldog's warning to avoid the forest.

They pushed their way through the dense branches, searching for deep cover before the man on the ski vehicle arrived. As the forest closed in around them, they hid behind a thick bush and held their breath. A light dusting of snow fell from the branches above them, making India glance up nervously. When she looked back, the rider had pulled up and dismounted from his machine. He began to fight his way noisily through the whippy branches with his gun at the ready.

The leaves rustled overhead again. This time India caught a glimpse of something moving swiftly through the branches. Her eyes flicked nervously from the man with the gun to the overhead canopy. Now that she looked more closely, she could see several shadows converging overhead. They were bird-black with no discernible shape. Streams of smoky darkness trailed behind them like ragged silk.

'What *are* they?' whispered India, her insides turning to ice. But there was no reply.

She whirled around in a panic. Clench had gone.

'Thaddeus, where are you? Don't play games with me now!'

All at once the shadows rushed silently and fluidly from the treetops. The man from the rig looked up and realized his fate a split second before the creatures fell on him. His screams were cut short amidst a hideous chorus of hissing and rustling that filled the forest.

Her throat tight with fear, India watched as the writhing shadows swarmed over the man, completely blocking him from view. Her legs felt as though they were stuck in thick mud and she was unable to move. She had always thought her father's tales about living shadows were just made up to scare her but these creatures were real, horribly real. Part of her wanted to curl up into a ball and pretend this wasn't happening but she instinctively knew that would mean death. 'Come on, India,' she said under her breath, 'get a grip on yourself.' She reached for her pendant and thought of Bella and her dad, forcing the panic to subside in her chest. Moving slowly, she stepped backwards as quietly as she could on shaky legs. The creatures ignored her and continued their attack on the hapless man. She took another step.

She didn't see the figure standing behind her until a pair of powerful arms wrapped around her and a hand clamped tightly around her mouth. She tried to scream and all she could think was that she was about to die alone in this forest and no one would ever know what had happened to her.

But she did not die. Someone moved close and '*Shh'd*' in her ear. She stopped wriggling and the hand relaxed slightly. It smelled of earth and woodsmoke. She turned to look at her attacker. He was tall and weathered-looking, with supple, leathery skin creased into hard lines. She was reminded of the men she had seen in Angel Town.

The shadow creatures finished with their victim and his lifeless corpse fell to the forest floor. They moved away, making a noise like snakes sliding over one another. The tall man pressed a blackened finger to his lips and led her quietly in the other direction. But the path was dark and covered in forest litter, and when India stepped on a dry branch the shadows were immediately alert. They turned as one and began to weave back through the trees towards them.

The man broke into a run, pulling India behind him. When she stumbled, he scooped her up and threw her over his shoulder. The shadows poured through the trees after them like malevolent smoke. And, as if this horror was not enough, they began calling her name.

'In-di-aaaaa.'

The sound of a dozen hellish whispers chased her through the trees, clutching at her heart with fingers of ice. How did these foul creatures know her name and what did they want with her?

They burst into a moonlit clearing where a young boy stood holding on to the reins of two teams of reindeer harnessed to sledges. The terrified, sobbing figure of Clench sat on one of the sledges with a fur blanket pulled up to his chin. The man dropped India on to the second sledge and snatched up the reins. He flicked the hindquarters of the reindeer and they jerked forward through the snow at a rapid trot. The shadows did not follow them but gathered at the edge of the trees so that India could still hear their ghastly voices.

'They knew my name,' whispered Clench. 'How did they know my name?'

India took a deep breath. If Clench was going to be a trembling wreck then she would have to make a show of being calm and in control. 'I don't know,' she said. 'But they knew mine too.' She turned to the driver standing on the back of the sledge. 'Excuse me,' she said, 'but who are you and what were those creatures?' His attention stayed focused on the path ahead and he gave no indication that he had even heard her.

'It's the ice people,' wailed Clench. 'They're going to tear us apart for fresh meat, I know they are.'

'They're not cannibals,' snapped India, 'and they just saved our lives, so keep your voice down.' She tried the driver again. 'Thank you for saving us from those *things*. But we need to get back to *The Beautiful Game*. Our friend Calculus is in terrible danger.'

The two drivers said nothing and just stared straight ahead, sticking out the occasional foot to fend off a rock or a tree root that might break one of the sledge runners. India studied them closely in the moonlight. They appeared calm and focused. Both of them carried rifles, but they were ancient flintlocks that looked like they were only used for hunting. She gave up attempts at conversation and started to think about escaping. Even though these men didn't look like they meant her harm, she didn't want to find out the hard way.

The sledge was light and delicate, lashed together from sapling wood and bone. It moved at a fair pace but she could probably jump off into the soft snow quite easily. But then what? She had no notion of where they were or how to get back to *The Beautiful Game*. Even if she did escape, there was every chance that she would run into those *creatures* again. As the bitter night took hold, she realized that all she could do was curl up under the furs and wait.

A movement under the blanket surprised her and she realized that there was a sleeping dog in there, warm and thick-coated. She stroked it idly as her mind raced with the events of the last few hours. She was desperate to know if Calculus was still alive or whether her harsh words would be the last she would ever say to him. She buried her face in the dog's soft coat and wept.

After many hours the dawn broke: a pale, lavender line sending slanted rays through the trees. The dog yawned and jumped off the sledge and began bounding through the snow. Now that she saw it in the daylight she recognized it as a Siberian breed she had seen in Angel Town, a Samoyed. She noticed it had different-coloured eyes, one blue and one brown.

When they crested a low hill she saw a collection of conical tents, spread out by the edge of a frozen lake. Thin lines of peaty brown smoke rose from two of the tents but the rest appeared to be empty. There were no people to be seen.

The sledges pulled off the main path and stopped at a tent that stood on its own among the trees. It was painted with elaborate reindeer designs and hung with bunches of sage and brushwood. The dog barked and ran inside while the drivers moved away to a respectful distance and began to talk in low voices.

'Great. What are we meant to do now?' griped Clench.

India stretched her stiff muscles, seeking some small warmth from the dawn sun. The older driver pointed to her and motioned her towards the tent.

'You want me to go in?' she said uncertainly. She looked at the tent apprehensively and took a deep breath. It couldn't hurt, she decided, and maybe she would finally get some answers.

As she laid her hand on the tent flap, a tremor ran through the ground, dislodging small rocks and shaking the snow loose from the trees.

'Another earthquake,' said Clench, clinging to the sledge.

Every dog in the village below began to bark and howl at once and the reindeer had to be calmed by the drivers. Then came the wind, a wild breeze rushing through the trees and flapping the walls of the tent. India had to shield her face against a blizzard of snow and pine needles. As quickly as it had started, the ground stopped shaking, the wind died down and it was quiet again, except for the dogs, who continued to whimper softly.

'Dear God,' said Clench, 'what was that?'

'I don't know,' said India. 'I don't understand any of what has gone on tonight, or why we've been brought here but there's only one way to find out.' And with that she pushed her way in through the tent flap.

CHAPTER 19

THE SOUL VOYAGER

Inside, the tent was dark, save for the flicker of a smoky fire that smelled of burning dung. In the furthest, darkest corner, India could just make out a pale shape that rose almost to the roof and then descended to the floor in two graceful, pointed curves. She realized it was a giant skull, broad across the forehead with vacant eye sockets and huge tusks. It belonged to a creature that had not walked on the Earth for a long time.

A loud shriek behind her made her jump. Clench had stuck his head in the tent and caught sight of the skull.

'Put a sock in it,' she said. 'It's not going to hurt you. It's a mammoth skull – it must be ten thousand years old at least.'

There was a rustling at the base of the skull and a stick-thin creature stirred within a bundle of furs. India saw it was a woman, impossibly old and tiny, like a bird stripped of its feathers. She wore heavy amulets on her arms and a large metal disc on her chest engraved with a fearsome face. Thin strips of reindeer hide hung from a beaded headband, covering her eyes.

Ignoring Clench's nervous whimpers, India stepped forward. The old woman cocked her head and sniffed the air. Then she began to chant.

The words came in a thick, hypnotic stream, rising and falling like the smoke in the tent. It sounded like no language India had ever heard and yet it was familiar, as if the memory of it lived somewhere in her blood. When the old woman stopped chanting India took her chance.

'Hello,' she said. 'My name is India Bentley and this is Mr Clench.' The ancient creature unfolded herself slowly and shambled over to India. She carefully pulled back her beaded fringe, making India gasp. The old woman's eyes were clouded with cataracts and yet India could see quite clearly that they were different colours; one was blue and the other was brown, the same as the dog's. The dog itself was nowhere to be seen.

'Ask her who she is,' whispered Clench.

'I am Nentu,' said the old woman in a voice like dry leaves.

'So you-speaka-da-English then?' said Clench loudly.

India jabbed him with her elbow.

'I heard,' said India, 'that there was once a Great Shaman of that name.'

'I am the same,' said the woman.

India was puzzled. 'But that was over two hundred years ago, before the Great Rains.'

'And it was many years before that,' said the woman, 'when I first walked here.'

'She's off her head,' said Clench. Now that he had decided there was nothing to be afraid of, he pushed in front of India and puffed himself up for a speech. 'Look here, my good woman,' he said, 'my name is—'

She silenced him with a claw-like finger. 'You have many names,' she said, 'and they all hide who you really are.'

'What I mean to say, madam, is that I demand to know why we have been brought here.'

'Nothing has brought you here,' she said, 'except the choices you have made for yourself.'

'I'm looking for my father,' said India, pushing Clench aside impatiently. 'He went missing near here.'

The old woman shuffled back to the mammoth throne and retrieved a pipe from the furs. 'This I already know,' she said.

'Then can you help me find him?'

There was a long silence while Nentu drew on her pipe and blew out a plume of foul-smelling smoke that made their eyes water. 'He passed through Uliuiu Cherchekh three seasons ago, on his way to the caverns of Aironhart. I have not seen him since.'

India started eagerly at this news. 'Can you show us how to get there?'

Nentu wafted steam under her nose from a black pot

bubbling on the fire and then added some bits of dried bark and leaves from her pocket. 'I could show you and you might find him,' she said, 'but the Elder Spirit that lives beneath the mountains would not be pleased to see you. It does not welcome strangers.'

India felt she was not making much progress. 'I'm not afraid of spirits,' she said.

'Then you are a fool!' said Nentu sharply. 'From where do you think the Valleymen have come?'

India recalled a distant conversation with Mrs Chang about Valleymen. 'Are they the shadow creatures we saw in the forest?'

Nentu nodded. 'The Elder Spirit could destroy you in the beat of a bird's wing if it wished. For a hundred generations, soul voyagers like myself have kept peace with it.' She frowned. 'But we soul voyagers are not as many as we once were and it has not been an easy peace to keep.' Nentu drew in another lungful of greasy brown smoke. 'But now we have need of the Elder's help again. A bringer-of-death named Nibiru rises in the East and a man of blood comes from the West. Together they will clash in the Valley of Death.'

India was struggling to keep up. 'A man of blood? Do you mean Lucifer Stone?'

Nentu watched the smoke rising in the tent but did not answer. 'Very soon, the end of days will be upon us,' she said. 'Already the wild creatures in the forest are fleeing and iron has begun to cross the sky.'

'Iron in the sky?' said India, remembering something.

'Now we must ask the Elder for help again. But it has never cared much for short-lives like us and much depends on the way of asking.'

'Sorry,' said Clench, 'what exactly is supposed to happen if this *Elder* doesn't help us?'

'Have you not been listening?' said Nentu, curling her lip. 'Then Nibiru will come and she will bring a winter that never leaves.'

India's head was reeling. 'I'd like to help, but I still don't understand. What do you want from us?'

'Do you think it is easy to be over two hundred years old?' snapped Nentu. 'It is not! I have waited here for many years. I have extended my life with spells and magic and stretched out my life force to reach this moment. But now my magic is fading and it hurts my bones to be here.' There was a bitter note in her voice. 'A younger, stronger shaman must speak to the Elder in my place. Someone with the gift of a soul voyager.' The cataract-clouded eyes passed over India as though they were seeing another world. 'What of your mother?' she said suddenly.

'My mother?'

'The gift of seeing comes from the female. Did your mother have the gift of knowing the earth? A way with creatures, a knowing of the seasons or a telling of the weather?'

Something stirred a memory in India. 'The weather and the tides,' she said. 'My mother could predict them by listening to the earth spirits. At least, that's what Cromerty said.'

The old woman smiled and opened her mouth in a silent 'Ah!'. 'Then you have the blood,' she said. 'And have you not been heeding my messages?'

'Messages? You mean the dreams I had on the way here?'

Nentu nodded again. She seemed to have made up her mind about something. 'You have something of an untrained soul voyager. *You* will speak to the Elder in my place and, in return, I will tell you where to find your father.' The sightless eyes gazed right through her. 'You *must* promise it.'

India looked blankly at Nentu. No matter how strange this sounded, she told herself, if Nentu knew where her father was then she would have to play along. 'OK, if you show me where to find my dad then I'll do whatever you want. I'll speak to the Elder for you.'

As she spoke there was another trembling of the earth beneath their feet. The old woman seemed unconcerned. 'It is decided,' she said. 'Now you are expected. We must move quickly.'

She went to the back of the tent and pulled on a piece of rope. There was a rustling of straw, and a baby reindeer, with fur as white and soft as new snow, clambered to its feet on long, wobbly legs.

'It's beautiful,' said India as Nentu led the animal to the centre of the tent.

'A white reindeer is very rare,' she said. 'It carries strong magic. She will be your protector on the journey.'

Before India could ask how that was meant to work, Nentu's hand shot out and grasped her by the wrist. The old woman's grip was strong. With startling swiftness, Nentu pulled a long pin from her hair and jabbed it into the end of India's finger. India cried out and tried to pull away but the old woman held her firm and jabbed the same pin into the neck of the reindeer. She pressed India's fingers against the animal so that their blood mingled in its fur.

'What are you doing?' stammered India. Clench had backed into a corner, his eyes round and unblinking.

'This creature has now become your *kujaii*,' said Nentu, releasing India's hand at last. 'It will stay here with me while you travel onward. When you are threatened by bad spirits, the *kujaii* will attract the danger on your behalf. If necessary, it will die for you.'

India took a step back from the old shaman, holding her injured finger tightly to stop the blood. The reindeer moved closer and nuzzled up to her hand.

'Is that it?' said India in a shaky voice. 'Will you tell us what we want to know now?'

Nentu picked up her pipe again and blew a plume of smoke towards the roof, carefully examining the way it curled. 'You —' she turned to Clench — 'desire wealth.' Clench shrugged evasively. 'If you travel to Ironheart, you will become wealthy beyond your wildest dreams for the rest of your life.'

A slow smile spread across Clench's face. 'Are you sure

about that?' he said. 'I'm quite rich in my wildest dreams you know!'

'And you,' she said to India, 'will find your father but at a price you may not want to pay.'

India felt frightened but also a little angry that she was still not getting any clear answers. 'We've promised to help you, now tell me where my dad is,' she said.

Nentu pulled something from the embers that looked like a flat piece of bone from the shoulder blade of an animal. It was cracked and blackened from the heat of the fire. She laid it carefully on the floor and felt the cracks on its scorched surface with her fingertips. 'The bone map will show you the way,' she said. 'This line here is the valley between the peaks of the Bird's Foot Mountain. The track runs to the place of the fast-flowing river, here!' She pointed to a blackened smudge. 'There is Ironheart, where you will find your father.'

'But is he alive?' said India. 'I have to know if he's alive.'

'Use your gift,' said Nentu. 'What does it tell you?'

India took a deep breath. 'I don't know,' she said eventually. 'I've always believed he was alive somewhere but . . .' She tailed off.

'Wait. We're going to follow the lines on a *bone*?' said Clench. 'You have *got* to be kidding me.'

'Follow the bone map and you will find him,' said Nentu, 'but heed my warning: the man of blood also brings a son, a dark soul, filled with hatred.'

'That must be Sid,' said India. 'Well, don't worry about him, I'll give him a wide berth.'

'No!' said Nentu sharply. 'You cannot avoid him. Both of you go to Ironheart in search of a father's love and your destinies are entangled. Know that you will depend on him for your life before this journey is finished.'

India stared at Nentu. 'Depend on him how? Sid hates me, he wants to kill me.'

Nentu shook her head. 'You cannot avoid what is written in dreams,' she said, 'and you will not find success without him.'

India felt disturbed. She wanted to ask Nentu more but the old woman had turned away and was rummaging under the furs again. She produced a small bag and emptied it on the floor. It contained the vertebrae of a small mammal, a bird's feather and several small pebbles bearing painted runes.

'These have travelled with me,' she said. 'They carry a magic the Elder will recognize.'

Clench rolled his eyes.

'What should I do when I meet this Elder?' said India. 'Is there anything in particular I'm meant to say?'

The shaman jabbed at India's breastbone with her bony fingers. 'Say only what is in here! And *nothing* else. Do not try to fool the Elder with lies or you will bring ruin on all of us!'

India swallowed hard.

'Now go!' said the old woman, dismissing them with a wave.

'Is that it?' said Clench.

'You have two days in which to persuade the Elder to help us,' said Nentu. 'After that Nibiru will come and the winter of forever will begin.' She tapped out her pipe and returned to the mammoth throne. 'Go now. There is no more to say.'

Nentu closed her eyes as Clench scuttled outside and India gathered up the bone map and the pieces from the floor. But before she left, she had one more question to ask. 'Excuse me,' she said.

The blue-brown eyes opened again.

'But . . . I was wondering if you could tell me about my friend, Calculus. Will he be all right?'

Nentu breathed deeply and shut her eyes again. For a moment India thought she had drifted off to sleep. 'His soul is new and not yet complete,' she said eventually. 'He has a lesson to learn before he can continue on his journey.'

'What lesson?' said India.

'He has to die.'

'What?' gasped India. 'Why would you say such a thing?'

But the old woman did not answer. She had gone back to her meditation and begun chanting to herself. Their audience was clearly over.

India left the tent deep in thought and feeling troubled. Outside, Clench sat on a log, taking off his boot.

'Did you ever hear such a load of old tripe? Spirits and soul voyagers, pah! And did you see the way she lived? Disgusting!'

India watched him pull off his socks and pick at his yellow toenails. 'I really don't know if its true or not,' she said, 'but she knew about my dreams . . . and if there's a chance of finding my dad then I'm going to take it.'

'One good thing, though,' he said brightly. 'I'm going to be rich for the rest of my life. It couldn't happen to a nicer guy.'

India tried not to look at his feet. 'What do you think she meant when she said my destiny was entangled with Sid's?' Now she thought about it, this worried her more than anything else.

'Who cares,' he said waving a sock at her, 'but I'll tell you one thing. Your destiny had better stay entangled with mine because I've got something you're going to need.' He reached inside his shirt and pulled out a small pendant.

It looked just like hers. As soon as she saw it, India's hand flew to her mouth. 'It's Bella's!' she cried. She felt a stab of terror at the thought of how Clench might have come by it. 'What have you done to my sister, you monster?' She took a step towards him but he snatched the pendant away and sneered.

'Don't worry, the brat's all right. But after you left I realized the importance of this little trinket.'

'What do you mean?' said India. 'It's no different from mine.'

'That's where you're wrong, missy. See, after you'd gone, I discovered the microchip your dad hid in here. It's the sort of trick I should've expected from an engineer. It's the missing half of the message, isn't it, the one I heard the crew talking about?'

India bit her lip. She could have kicked herself for not realizing that her father might have hidden something in Bella's pendant too.

'So what?' she said, trying to sound like she didn't care. 'You don't know what's in it.'

'It makes no difference,' said Clench. 'All I know is that you need it to get into Ironheart. And that means you need *me*.' He grinned again. 'He was a clever man, your dad, I think that was the thing I hated most about him.'

She wasn't sure she had heard him right. 'What? You knew my dad?'

'Oh yes, didn't I mention it? We both worked for Trans-Siberian at the same time. When I found out he was looking for Ironheart I pleaded with him to share the secret with me. He could have let me in on it easily enough but he was obsessed with using it for the good of humanity. Humanity, pah! Then, when he went missing, I realized I had a chance to take what was rightfully mine.'

India's jaw dropped open as realization started to crowd in on her. 'That was why you came to London, wasn't it? To get close to our family and see what you could find out?'

'You have no idea how hard it was,' he said in a weary voice, 'sucking up to that sour old mare for a year. I took you under my wing, I offered you all a home. I bided my time so I could find out where John Bentley hid that information, only to watch you go waltzing off with that Verity Brown creature.'

She felt her flesh creep. 'You deliberately preyed on all of us. You're disgusting – a reptile!'

He pocketed the pendant and sat back with a satisfied smile. 'Call me all the names you want,' he said. 'But I'll tell you how it's going to be. I don't care what deals you've done with Verity Brown or that Bulldog animal, if you want to find your dad then you'd better play along and treat me with a bit more respect, otherwise you won't be going anywhere. D'you get it?'

India glared at him, her face burning. It seemed that there would never be a way to rid herself of Clench. She turned abruptly and marched back down the hill. Clench jumped up and tried to hobble after her.

''Ere! Hold on, let me get me boot back on, don't leave me here! India!'

CHAPTER 20

ON BIRD'S FOOT MOUNTAIN

At the bottom of the hill, the two reindeer drivers had built a fire and were boiling something in a large black pot. The man motioned India and Clench to sit down and the boy ladled them each a helping of grey meat that looked like boiled intestines. Clench pushed his around with a fork but, by now, India had learned not to be fussy and devoured the food, savouring its rich saltiness. She watched as the drivers examined Nentu's bone map and hoped that they would be coming with them to Bird's Foot Mountain. She felt comforted by their silent, down-to-earth presence.

When the reindeer had been readied, India and Clench climbed on board the sledges again and they started off, passing first through the almost deserted tent village. India wondered if the villagers had left because of the creatures that Nentu had called *the Valleymen*. When she cast a look back towards the old woman's tent she was surprised to see that the dog had returned and was sitting on a high rock watching them with the same mismatched stare.

Beyond the village she was struck at once by how little wildlife there seemed to be in the valley. In three hours of travelling she didn't see a single creature or hear any birdsong. The air felt dead, as though every living thing had fled from some impending disaster.

They followed the trail along the edge of the forest, occasionally switching to the bed of a frozen stream where the going was easier. As the sun reached the highest part of the sky, the driver pointed to a mountain with three distinct ridges that ran down to the valley floor. He made a claw-like sign with his hand which India took to mean that this was Bird's Foot Mountain.

Now that she looked at the bone map again, India could see there was a clear path up the central ridge to the top, where, she supposed, they would find Ironheart. It felt like the most remote place on Earth. She wondered what was happening on board *The Beautiful Game* and whether they would ever catch up with her or whether Tashar had finally persuaded Bulldog to give up and return to Angel Town.

Her limbs protested as she unfolded herself and descended from the sledge. To her dismay, the drivers began to make immediate preparations to leave. Despite her pleas for them to stay, she was forced to wave goodbye as their sledges pulled away and disappeared from view, leaving her alone in the wilderness again, with only Thaddeus Clench for company. She looked again at the bone map and hoped that she hadn't made a terrible mistake by coming here. 'Come on,' she said, trying to ignore the sinking feeling in her stomach. 'I want to be well away from these forests before nightfall.'

The valley was laid with fresh, virgin snow that came up to India's knees and she had to lift her feet high to take each step. After an hour her legs burned with the effort and by the time they reached the top of the ridge, they were both exhausted. The trail ended abruptly in a wall of sheer rock, too high to climb and with no apparent way forward.

'Now what?' said Clench.

India looked anxiously at the sun dipping towards the mountains and then examined the bone map, running her fingers along its roughened surface. 'There's a mark on here,' she muttered, looking up at the cliff face.

A little way along the wall was an isolated slab of rock that seemed to have fallen from the cliffs above. When she looked behind it she saw it was hiding a gap in the cliff face, a narrow canyon wide enough for two people to pass through.

She led the way through the gap with Clench hobbling along behind her.

'Slow down, why don't you? My feet are frozen through, I could get frostbite, you know. I might even lose all me toes.'

'A good thing too, from what I've seen of them,' muttered India under her breath.

But what they saw when they reached the other side

made them stop and gasp. The mountain ridge was actually part of a complete chain that formed the rim of a gigantic bowl. In the centre of the great circle, a frozen lake reflected the gold of the late afternoon sun.

'It's a hidden valley!' said India. 'You could walk all the way up here and never find it unless you had the bone map.'

'Look,' said Clench. 'It's another one of them shooting stars.'

They both watched the flaming streak cross the sky and disappear behind the far ridge of mountains. India was sure she felt a vibration in the earth as it struck the ground. '*First comes the iron*,' she murmured under her breath, wishing she could remember the rest of Cromerty's rhyme. She was still looking at the point where the meteorite had disappeared when she noticed something that had previously escaped her eye. 'There!' she said, pointing to a flash of colour in the barren landscape.

About a quarter of a mile away down the slope stood a green watchtower. 'That must be it!' she said. 'Come on.' She began to run down the slope, sliding in the loose scree as Clench puffed along behind.

They arrived at a small compound that comprised a dozen concrete buildings surrounded by a rusted chain-link fence. The watchtower stood in one corner, empty and paint blistered.

'Doesn't look like much,' grumbled Clench, rattling the gate. 'This is just a bunch of old sheds.'

'This must be it,' said India. 'There's nothing else for five hundred miles in any direction.'

They trampled down a section of the rotten fence and wandered in among the derelict buildings. They searched the compound for nearly an hour, opening sheds and storehouses, overturning empty barrels and peering into crates. But nothing looked like it might reveal an entrance to a secret underground complex of tunnels.

'There's nothing here,' griped Clench. 'This whole damned thing has been a wild goose chase from the beginning. It wouldn't surprise me if John Bentley just made the whole thing up.'

At any other time India might have argued, but now the exhaustion took hold and hot tears threatened to trickle down her face. She sat down heavily on a rock and looked at the bone map in the fading light. 'Following lines on a bone,' she muttered to herself. 'What an idiot.'

Abruptly she stood up and hurled the bone map as far as she could manage. She watched it clatter across the rocks below and then topple from sight. Curious as to where it had gone, she picked her way across the icy surface.

The map had fallen over a small ledge on to a pile of rocks heaped in front of a narrow cave. She peered into the dark space and her heart jumped when she spied something gleaming blackly in its recesses.

'Thaddeus, there's something here,' she called. 'Help me move these rocks out of the way.'

When the last stone was finally rolled away they found

themselves looking at a fissure in the rock about the height of a man. India scrabbled for the torch in Verity's bag and shone it down the hole. A few feet inside the cave was a tall, featureless rectangle of iron set into the stone.

'It's a door,' she breathed.

'Stand aside,' said Clench. 'This is a man's job, I think.'

He stepped up to the door and began tapping it and feeling for cracks in the ironwork with his fingers while India watched impatiently from the cave entrance.

'What are you doing, exactly?' she asked. 'It's getting dark out here.'

'It ain't my fault,' he grumbled. 'I don't know how this damned door's supposed to open. There's no handles on it. Perhaps this pendant can get us in.'

As Clench fumbled she glanced around anxiously at the deep shadows that had encroached up the mountainside. But when she shone the torch out into the darkness her blood chilled. Just outside the circle of light, a dozen wispy shapes floated like scraps of cobweb, gathering ominously around the cave entrance.

Clench turned to see what she was doing and caught sight of the creatures. 'Oh my life!' he wailed. 'It's them! It's the *Valleymen*.'

India's heart began to beat like a rig piston. While Clench whined and trembled, she tried to keep the creatures at bay with the torch. The image of the white reindeer flashed momentarily before her eyes, terrified and bleating. The Valleymen's soft, hissing breath was only feet away now.

But then a different sound cut through the night air. A bright light bounced up the icy slope and the shadows scattered like paper as a ski machine burst through their ranks, pulling up sharply in front of the cave. The rider pointed the machine's powerful beams at the creatures and drove them back into the shadows. Then he turned to India and pulled the scarf from his face.

'Bulldog!' she cried. She had never been so relieved to see anyone in her life. 'How did you find us?'

'No time for explanations now,' he barked. 'Whatever you were going to do, do it now. Those things are pouring out of the forest in their hundreds!'

CHAPTER 21

REUNION

Calculus lay still while his damage assessment programs reviewed the state of his body. Some of his critical circuits had been badly burned and would take several hours to repair. Other, less vital systems had been destroyed completely and he would have to make do without them. Only when he had completed his checks did he activate his motor functions and turn on his vision.

A bright light was shining in his eyes, blotting out the rest of the room. He switched to infra-red vision but that too was drowned out by the light. He was lying on his back on a steel table, arms and legs secured by heavy shackles that, to his surprise, resisted any attempt to break them.

'I'm sorry, my friend. This little set-up was designed specifically to neutralize your capabilities. Here, let me help you.' The bright light moved to one side and the face of Dr Cirenkov came into view above him. 'Welcome on board the *Prince of Darkness*,' she said, looking him up and down greedily. 'It's a real pleasure to meet such a fine example of old-tech. I'm looking forward to learning everything I can from you.'

'I am sure there is nothing much you can learn from an old robot like me,' said Calculus. His voice sounded distant and strangled.

'Oh, but you're so much more than that,' breathed the doctor as she slid closer. 'You are the last of the androids, Calculus. It's a very different thing altogether.' Dr Cirenkov's lips stretched into a thin smile as she snapped on a pair of rubber gloves.

'One moment, Doctor.' Lucifer Stone appeared in Calculus's line of vision. He sized up the android and nodded approvingly. 'Good, almost completely undamaged. Your electrical weapons worked well, Doctor. Now sit him up so we can talk.'

The doctor cranked a handle to raise Calculus to a seated position. He caught sight of two men standing by the door holding electric lances, and Sid, lounging in a corner, radiating menace.

'Let's make this easy on everyone, shall we?' said Stone. 'Tell me, tin man. I want to know where your friends on *The Beautiful Game* are heading. Where do they expect to find Ironheart?'

'Let me persuade him, Pa!' said Sid, moving away from the wall. He pulled the pistol from his belt and pointed it at the android's chest. 'I reckon a bullet through that old metal plate will kill him stone dead if he don't cooperate.'

Stone placed a restraining hand on Sid's shoulder. 'You know, boy,' he said affectionately, 'you are my only son and I love you dearly but you are without doubt the biggest moron in Angel Town, I swear it!' He struck Sid with the back of his hand, sending the boy reeling. 'Why do you think we went to all this trouble to capture him alive?' he shouted. 'A job like this requires more finesse than you can provide, boy.' He turned back to Calculus and pulled up a stool. 'Now then, tin man,' he said. 'The eastern valleys will become impassable within days and I have no time to waste on asking you politely. Tell me what I need to know or I will allow Dr Cirenkov to carry out some . . . *experiments*.'

Calculus noticed that the doctor was connecting some electric wires to a heavy steel probe. 'I would have thought that your spy would have already told you everything you wanted to know,' he said.

Stone chuckled. 'Ah yes, poor Pieter, one of my best operatives. May he rest in peace. It's good to see you can still be a creature of violence when you want to be, tin man. That will serve us very well.'

'I will not serve you at all,' said Calculus. 'I am a military droid and I am programmed to resist enemy questioning. My systems are secured with a quantum cryptograph and you will never be able to change them.'

Dr Cirenkov smiled and puffed out her chest. 'Ordinarily that would be true. If we tried to crack your programs we would still be at it a hundred years from now.' She gave a nasty chuckle. 'But not if we had access to your base codes.'

191

'My base codes?' he said, trying to keep his voice neutral.

Dr Cirenkov sounded very pleased with herself. 'The key to your root programs,' she said. 'The ones that govern your concepts of right and wrong. If we had access to them, anything would be possible.'

'But how could you get access to my base codes?' he said, fearing he already knew the answer.

Stone leaned in close to the android's visor and spoke in a low growl. 'You might think nothing can touch you, tin man. But I can take it away, I can take it all away.' He nodded to one of the men at the door who slipped out and returned with a dishevelled and dirt-caked figure.

Calculus felt a small surge of what he supposed was joy in his circuits when he saw her, but it was immediately tinged with regret. 'Hello, Mrs Brown,' he said, 'it's very good to see you again.'

'Hello, soldier,' said Verity, managing to raise a smile. 'I'm sorry about this, I really am.'

CHAPTER 22

IRONHEART

India ran her fingers lightly over the surface of the iron door. It was almost completely featureless save for two brass pins in the centre that stood proud of the surface. 'Jumper pins,' she murmured to herself. 'That's what Verity called them. Quick, Thaddeus, let me see that pendant.'

She snatched up the pendant from Clench's trembling fingers and located two identical brass points on its upper edge. Then she placed Verity's bag on the ground and fumbled around inside, pulling out the little black meter and several lengths of wire. Struggling to remember how Verity had done it in Mrs Chang's dining room, she used the wires to connect the pendant to the meter and then to the pins on the door.

Nothing happened.

'We're nearly out of time here,' called Bulldog from the mouth of the cave, where he was keeping the torch trained on the advancing Valleymen.

India stared down at the pendant in her hands. She could feel the panic beginning to rise in her chest. 'A spark,' she said suddenly. 'That's what it needs, a spark!' She fumbled through her pockets and pulled out the shock stick. Clench winced visibly when he saw it. Trying not to touch the exposed metal, she pressed the end of the stick lightly against the pendant. There was a brief *snap* and a curl of blue smoke rose from the metal. For a moment there was nothing, then came a clattering of relays inside the door as the ancient locking mechanism kicked into life. There was a hiss like escaping steam and a series of hidden bolts released their hold.

India whooped with delight and she and Clench heaved on the door, pulling it just wide enough to allow a person in.

'Both of you get in there, now!' shouted Bulldog.

India squeezed through the gap, with Clench following gingerly behind. Then Bulldog abandoned the entrance of the cave and charged after them, shoving Clench roughly out of the way and hauling the door firmly shut behind him.

There was much cursing and fumbling around in the pitch darkness of the tunnel. Bulldog struck a match and then inspected the door in its flickering light to make sure it was properly closed. A faint scratching could be heard on the other side of the metal. 'Well, we can't go back that way in a hurry,' he said.

'What are you doing here?' said Clench, jabbing him with a finger. 'Me and India have got a deal. See? Anything valuable in here is mine, you understand?'

'Steady on, Archie,' said Bulldog, lighting up another match. 'You may not have noticed but I just saved your miserable pelt!'

'Shut up, both of you!' shouted India, snapping on the torch. 'You're like a pair of kids.' She took a deep breath and turned to Bulldog. 'Captain, thank you for saving our lives.' He nodded graciously. 'But what *are* you doing here? And how did you find us?'

He leaned back against the wall. 'After you disappeared I took the snow bike and followed your tracks. I lost the trail and was about to give up when I met the hunters that had brought you here, high-tailing it in the opposite direction. My Yakut is a bit rusty but I could understand a few words and they told me how to get here.'

'Well hurrah for your rusty Yakut,' muttered Clench.

'I left markers for *The Beautiful Game* so they could follow on. I'm hopeful that they will get here by tomorrow.'

'Tashar agreed to come and rescue us?' said India incredulously.

'Well, not *exactly*,' said Bulldog, scratching his head. 'I had to do a deal with her. But don't worry about that now, I still have high hopes that this little jaunt is going to pay off big time.'

India shone the torch along a dim concrete corridor that descended towards the heart of the mountain. 'Do you think this is really the way into Ironheart?' she said uncertainly.

'Only one way to find out,' said Bulldog, hoisting his bag on to his shoulder.

They followed the downward slope of the corridor until they emerged into a wider space, shrouded in darkness. Bulldog flicked a heavy switch on the wall and the ancient circuits crackled before the harsh white lights snapped on and a stale breeze began to blow from the air vents.

They stood in a large dining hall, carved from the solid rock. There were long wooden tables and chairs for a hundred people. At one end of the hall, a pair of swing doors led to an empty kitchen with rows of gas cookers and stone sinks. A dusty dormitory was filled with rotting bunk beds and old mattresses with the springs sticking out.

'It looks like there were dozens of people living down here,' said India in a whisper as they picked their way through the broken furniture. 'What do you suppose they all did?'

Bulldog shook his head. 'I dunno,' he said, 'but let's stay close together, this place gives me the creeps.'

They found an office, smelling of decay and showing all the signs of having been abandoned in a hurry. Chairs were overturned, papers were strewn and one of the lights blinked on and off like a bad stutter.

'Look,' said Bulldog, pulling a tattered sheet from the wall. 'It's a map of this whole place.'

'It's in gobbledegook,' said Clench, squinting over his shoulder.

'It's old Russian,' said Bulldog, running a finger over the yellowed paper. 'I've got a smattering of it.'

'Rusty Yakut and a smattering of old Russian,' muttered Clench. 'It's a wonder he's still single.'

Bulldog whistled. 'These tunnels go right underneath the mountain. This level is labelled "*Administration, Staff Quarters and Vaults*". There's another level below this one which says "*Restricted Area, Authorized Personnel Only*".'

Clench's ears pricked up. 'Vaults, eh?' he said. 'That sounds like where we need to go.'

Next door to the office was a guard room with ragged uniforms still hanging from the pegs, and beyond that a pair of double steel doors. The damp air had taken its toll on the ironwork and the bolts were welded shut with a thick coat of rust. Bulldog rummaged through the drawers in the office, found a hammer and, with much bashing and cursing, forced the bolts. The doors yawned open, revealing a tunnel with rough chiselled walls and a high vaulted ceiling.

'After you, *Captain*,' said Clench, slipping behind Bulldog's bulk.

Bulldog stepped into the tunnel and they all jumped as a single overhead light clanked on. They took a few tentative paces into the tunnel. Every few steps the next light would come on and the first would go out so that they walked continually in a pool of light, surrounded by blackness.

The walls of the tunnel were lined with iron bookshelves, so high that they disappeared into the gloom above their heads. The shelves were tightly packed with pulpy, leather-bound books, including technical manuals, medical textbooks and dense novels written in foreign languages.

'They must have every book in the world in here,' murmured India, examining the spine of a scientific text written in Russian. On a low shelf she spotted a row of children's story books and a small volume in a green cover caught her eye. 'I remember this!' she cried, pulling the book from the shelf. 'My dad used to read it to me and Bella when we were little.'

Clench and Bulldog had moved on down the tunnel and didn't hear her. She looked at the book again, then quickly slipped the little volume into her satchel before hurrying to catch up.

In other corridors the shelves were stacked with lifeless computers and racks of shiny plastic disks that reflected rainbow colours in the light. There were dim alcoves with pieces of machinery under tarpaulins and side passages that twisted away into even more remote corners of the mountain. India wondered how she would ever find her father in this maze.

After they had descended for about fifteen minutes, they reached a set of clean white doors. They opened smoothly with a faint hiss and a rush of warm, moist air, and India gave a cry of surprise.

They stood at the top of a flight of stairs above a very large, rectangular chamber. The air was humid and overhead lights warmed her skin like the sun. The chamber floor was divided into sections by low walls, each one filled with thick, chocolatey soil and kept moist with a fine mist from overhead sprinklers.

The room was a living patchwork of vibrantly coloured plants, bushes and trees, growing in neatly manicured lines. She was fascinated by a small tree laden with fuzzy yellow fruits and a twisted vine draped with plump, purple clusters that held the promise of sticky sweetness. Even the fruits she did recognize bore no resemblance to their stunted and shrivelled cousins back home. The tomatoes were a rich, glossy red and the apples were large and crisp. Everywhere the air shimmered with the movement of insect wings.

'It's a garden,' she said, remembering the soggy and barren patch of earth they had at home. 'It's the most beautiful garden I've ever seen.'

'It's not a garden,' said Bulldog squinting up at the ceiling. 'High-intensity ultraviolet lights, automatic irrigation and enough insect life to pollinate the plants. It's a farm! As long as there is power and water, this place could run forever.'

'Fruit and vegetables!' spluttered Clench. His face was aghast. 'Are you kidding me? I've come halfway around the world to visit a bleedin' greengrocer?'

'Take it easy, Archie,' said Bulldog with a grin. 'Vegetables are very healthy, you know.'

'Do I look like I need the vitamins?' he hissed. 'I thought this was the vaults. So where's the treasure?'

India laughed. 'I think this *is* the treasure,' she said. 'Or at least part of it.' She ran lightly down the stairs and walked among the fruit trees, gazing up into the branches.

Bulldog pulled down a bright orange fruit. 'I saw one of these once when I was a kid,' he said breathlessly. 'We had to share it between eight of us but I thought it was the most wonderful thing I'd ever tasted in my life. Here, try this.'

He dug his thumbs into the flesh and pulled it apart, handing India a segment of the dripping fruit. It tasted sharp and sweet at the same time and she laughed as the juice ran down her throat. Soon she and Bulldog were laughing like children as they gorged themselves on sticky fruits and India wished she could have taken some of them home for her sister.

'Don't eat the yellow ones,' said Bulldog, with a pained expression, 'they're as sour as hell.'

A movement in the undergrowth caught India's eye. She pulled apart the leaves and saw a tiny silver machine trundling between the flower beds. It stopped beside a tree and extended one of its wiry steel arms to pluck an apple from a low branch, then it deftly sliced it in two with a thin blade. They watched as it used a narrow tube to suck out the seeds and deposit them in a foil envelope.

'A robot gardener,' said Bulldog in wonder. The little machine jumped at the sound of his voice and promptly turned to scuttle in the other direction. 'Quick, follow it!' he said.

The robot beat a hasty retreat down the rows of crops. When it reached the far wall it pushed its way through a thin plastic curtain. The room beyond was chilled and full of high shelves stacked with plastic boxes. When the robot found the box it was looking for, it deposited the foil pack inside and headed back out to the garden.

'There must be enough seeds in here to plant a garden like this in every country in the world,' said India, gazing up at the shelves.

'More than enough,' said Bulldog. 'According to the map there's at least a dozen other garden chambers like this one.'

'It's the most wonderful place I've ever seen, Bulldog,' said India. She tried to imagine how John Bentley would have felt seeing it for the first time, and the opportunity he would have seen to feed the world. 'My dad's here somewhere, I just know he is. We have to keep looking for him.'

When they got back to the garden Clench was in a state of high agitation and India was amused to see a herd of the tiny silver robots whirring and chattering around his feet. He crashed around in the shrubs trying to shake them off while they tried to repair the damage he left behind. When he aimed a kick at one of them they scattered like frightened chickens.

Without warning, the bright lights were suddenly extinguished to be replaced by a soft red glow.

'Must be night time,' said Bulldog, glancing up.

'Night time!' said India with a start. 'Oh no! Nentu said we only had two days before something terrible was going to happen and that's one day gone already. Come on!'

Bulldog looked as though he would happily have remained in the garden all day but, after much cajoling, she forced him and Clench out of the chamber. Back in the corridor, Bulldog found another switch and the lights surged on in the concrete stairwell. 'Level Two, restricted area,' he said with a grin. 'Sounds like my kind of place.'

They descended dozens of flights of stairs and India felt increasingly aware of the weight of the mountain above them. A door at the bottom opened into a room filled with pale green cabinets where the atmosphere hummed with electrical energy. Every surface was covered with switches and dials and needle-thin pointers that pulsed to an unseen current.

'It's a generator room!' said Bulldog, inspecting one of the panels. 'It's using geothermal energy from deep underground. It could have been running on its own like this for a hundred years.'

A row of windows in the control room overlooked a factory floor where a big turbine hummed powerfully amidst hissing steel pipes and red-wheeled valves. One end of the turbine hall was taken up with a set of huge hangar doors.

'According to the map we've travelled right down through the heart of the mountain,' said Bulldog. 'Those doors open out by the lake.'

The cavern also provided storage for hundreds of dark brown wooden crates stacked in high rows, each one stencilled with a red star. Clench's eyes nearly popped out when he saw them. Before they knew it he had scurried to the nearest one and was lovingly running his hands over it. 'It's treasure,' he said breathlessly, 'I know it is. Find something to open it with, quickly.'

Bulldog pulled out the hammer and used it to smash his way through the wooden panels. Clench looked on with eyes as round as plates as he thrust his hands inside the crate and pulled out stacks of pristine banknotes, bound with gummed paper strips.

'Roubles,' said Bulldog, stuffing a stack of notes in his bag. 'One of the old-world currencies.'

'This is no good,' cried Clench. 'We can't spend this anywhere.'

The crates in the next row contained gilt-framed paintings packed in straw. They showed angels and saints with golden halos painted in dark oils and decorated with splashes of gold leaf.

'Religious icons,' said Bulldog. 'Priceless, actually, or at least they would be if you could find anyone to buy them.'

'Boring!' shouted Clench.

Other crates held portraits of generals on horseback, kings and queens, landscapes and pictures of ancient cities. Pretty soon the floor was littered with wood splinters and wisps of straw. At the sight of each crate filled with fine art, Clench would curse loudly before stomping off to break open another one.

'The stories were right,' said India in a hushed voice. 'These really are the treasures of the old world, aren't they?'

'Looks like it,' said Bulldog. He held up a painting of an angel in an ornate golden frame. 'Do you think this would look good in *The Beautiful Game*?'

'Bulldog!' said India.

'Yeah, I guess you're right,' he said, putting it back with the others. 'It belongs here.'

They were interrupted by the sound of whooping from the next aisle. They found Clench beside a crate from which all manner of jewels was spilling on to the floor. Emeralds, rubies and sapphires lay scattered like Christmas nuts, and splinters of diamond flashed ice-fire in the dim light. There were thousands upon thousands of gold coins and countless pieces of fine jewellery.

'You go and find your own crate,' growled Clench, stuffing handfuls of gemstones into his bag. 'This one's mine!'

His eyes gleamed yellow like a dog's and a small muscle had begun to twitch in the side of his face. India felt faintly disgusted by him. 'We're wasting time here,' she said. 'We're supposed to be looking for my dad.'

'Haven't you got it yet?' said Clench. 'If John Bentley was ever here then he's long dead, frozen to death or eaten by one of those shadow things, I shouldn't wonder.'

'Don't say that!' cried India. 'You don't know what happened, you don't know anything about him!'

She stamped away, wiping her eyes with her sleeve. Bulldog followed. 'Don't pay Archie no mind,' he said kindly. 'He can't see past his own greed.'

'Oh, Bulldog, what if those Valleymen really did get my dad?' she sniffed. 'I've seen what they can do.'

Bulldog placed an awkward arm around her shoulder. 'Come on now,' he said gruffly. 'Let's have none of that. If your dad's here we'll find him.' Then he stiffened suddenly. 'Holy moley!' he said. 'Would you look at that!'

Ahead of them was a row of narrow caves, each filled with a deadly-looking arsenal of equipment. One was lined with racks of rifles and boxes of ammunition while another was stacked with sinister-looking black drums, each marked with a skull and crossbones.

'Chemical weapons,' said Bulldog. 'Nasty things. They drift on the breeze and kill anyone that gets in their way.'

India shivered.

The last cavern was filled with what looked to India like dozens of gleaming white coffins in steel racks. There were angry warning signs in yellow and black on the surrounding walls. Bulldog seemed shocked by what he was seeing. He ran his hand over the glossy surface of one of the coffins. Now that India saw them up close, she thought they looked familiar. Each one had stubby fins and a tail with a painted red star. 'I've seen pictures of these in some of my dad's old books,' she said. 'They're bombs!'

'Not just bombs,' said Bulldog in a hushed tone. 'They're warheads, more than a hundred of them.'

'Warheads?' she murmured. 'That's like what Nentu said about my dad: "He rests among the heads of warriors!" But what are they?'

'Terrible old-world weapons,' he said. 'Just one of these missiles could destroy an entire city in a flash of heat and light. No one knows how to make them any more.'

She reached out to touch one. It gleamed like bone and felt cold to the touch. Like death, she thought. 'Bulldog,' she said slowly. 'Do you think these warheads might be the reason Lucifer Stone wants to find Ironheart so badly? I mean, think about what he could do if he had weapons like these.'

Bulldog let out a low whistle. 'You might be right, India,' he said. 'He could hold the world to ransom if he wanted to. No one could stop him.'

They both fell into silence as they looked at the shiny, coffin-like missiles and thought about what horrors Lucifer Stone might be able to inflict with them.

'Can't *we* stop him?' said India, eventually. 'Couldn't you do something to the warheads before he gets here so that he can't use them?'

Bulldog shook his head doubtfully. 'You don't want to go messing around with weapons of mass destruction, India,' he said. 'You could have somebody's eye out.'

'But we have to do *something*,' she said, her voice cracking. 'This must be the reason my dad tried to keep Ironheart a secret, because he knew how dangerous these things would be in the wrong hands.'

Bulldog blew out his cheeks. 'I dunno, India. This is too big for me. I say we grab whatever we can and get as far away from here as possible.'

'We can't just walk away from this, Bulldog,' she said impatiently. 'Stone's a monster. If he ends up with weapons like these then thousands of people could die. And besides,' she added, 'we still need to find my dad. He could be anywhere in these caverns.'

Bulldog sighed again and stroked his chin thoughtfully. Then he looked up and down the turbine hall. 'You know,' he said eventually, 'there might be something we could do that would spoil Lucifer Stone's plans.' He pointed to the turbine at the centre of the chamber. 'That geothermal plant might do the job. If we shut off the valves to the heat exchanger the whole lot will blow, taking half the mountain with it.'

'What about my dad?' said India.

'We'll search the whole place systematically,' said Bulldog, 'level by level. If he's here we'll find him. Then we'll take our fill of the treasure and blow this place sky high. With luck we'll be a hundred miles away by the time Stone gets here.'

India licked her lips nervously and nodded. 'OK, let's do it. What should we do first?'

Bulldog looked at Clench, who was sitting in a pile of gold coins, tossing them gleefully into the air like a child. 'Well, I don't think we'll get Archie out of here in a hurry,' he said, 'and I wouldn't mind picking up a few trinkets myself. I tell you what, give me an hour to take what I want from here, then we'll spend the rest of the day searching for your dad. After that, we'll blow this place off the map and run for the hills. Do we have a deal?'

India spat on her hand and held it out. 'Free-riggers contract?'

They shook firmly. Then he grinned and his eyes began to shine. 'Come on, Archie,' he yelled to Clench. 'We've got work to do.' He hopped over to where Clench was still stuffing his pockets and whispered in his ear.

Clench's eyes widened. 'Blow it up!' he spluttered. 'What do you mean, blow it up? We've only just arrived. Oi, Bulldog, come back here.'

India stifled a smile as she watched them both disappear. She had her own plans now and her thoughts were set on the rich store of seeds in the rooms above. She would use the next hour to search the other chambers and collect as many seeds as she could. What a difference they could make to the barren shores of North London. But as she made her way along the turbine hall, a deep rumbling noise made her stop in her tracks. There was the sound of metal being dragged over stone and a thin white light split the iron doors from top to bottom as they began to grind apart. She could hear the sound of diesel engines now and she could see the unmistakable shape of a giant rig outside, silhouetted against the night sky, its full beams flooding the chamber with harsh electric light.

Now men with guns were swarming through the gap in the doors and as she put her hands up to shield her eyes, an amplified voice boomed from the black rig.

'Stay where you are!' it said. 'This facility is now the property of the Trans-Siberian Company!'

CHAPTER 23

THE HEADS OF WARRIORS

They were rounded up roughly and made to stand on one side of the turbine hall while the guards quickly located the weapons. Earnest-looking men and women in white coats arrived and began to inspect the missiles, ticking off items on their clipboards as they went. The whole thing had the appearance of a carefully planned military operation.

The hangar doors stood open and a bitter wind blew in off the lake. India gave an involuntary shiver as the troll-like figure of Lucifer Stone strode into the chamber, deep in conversation with Dr Cirenkov, with Sid behind them.

'Excellent, Doctor!' boomed Stone. 'Your hunch about finding these blast doors down by the lake was spot on.'

The guards had begun cutting the missiles from their steel racks, sending showers of sparks raining on to the wet chamber floor while others were setting up pulleys and chains to hoist them free. Cirenkov bared her teeth as one of the missiles swung dangerously on its chains. 'Be careful, you cretins, those warheads are over a hundred years old! If you drop one we could all be vaporized.'

Sid pointed at the treasure scattered across the floor and whispered something in his father's ear.

Stone knitted his eyebrow into a thick V-shape. 'No!' he barked. 'There's no room for anything except the weapons, and they'll make us rich enough.' Stone seemed to noticed his prisoners for the first time and walked over to inspect them. 'Well, bless my dirty, rotten soul,' he said. 'Imagine finding such a bunch of misfits in a place like this.' He stroked his chin with obvious glee. 'Let me see now . . . Captain Aggrovius Bulldog, unlicensed privateer and scourge of the Urals. You're a long way from your usual hunting ground, Captain. And who's this? Archie Fenton! I thought you would have the sense to stay out of my sight, Archie. Never mind, Angel Town always enjoys a good hanging.'

Clench groaned, and sagged at the knees.

'And Miss Bentley, who was so concerned to see fair play for the citizens of Angel Town. I seem to remember giving orders to have you taken care of.' He frowned at Sid. 'It seems if I want someone killed around here I have to do it myself.'

India wasn't listening. She was looking, dumbstruck, at the tall figure that had walked in through the hangar doors. 'Calc?' she said uncertainly. 'Is that you?'

The big android walked stiffly to Stone's side. She recognized his battered body, cracked visor and the steel plate in his chest, but somehow he looked different. He was more rigid and lacking his usual poise and grace. An awful empty feeling started to grow in her stomach.

Stone laughed at her confusion. 'It's no use asking him for help,' he said. 'Your robot works for me now!'

India felt as though she was falling and there was no one to catch her. 'It isn't true,' she said. 'Calculus would never betray his friends.'

Stone laughed a long, nasty laugh. 'I wouldn't be so sure, young lady,' he said. 'We could never have found this place without his help.' He turned and whispered something to Calculus, who nodded and left. 'But don't worry, your robot didn't betray his friends, it was his so-called friend that betrayed *him*.'

Calculus returned through the hangar doors with a familiar figure by his side.

'Verity!' cried India.

He pushed Verity forward roughly. She looked bruised and dishevelled and her expression was grim. 'Hi, kid,' she said with a small smile. 'Fancy seeing you here.'

Stone seemed to be enjoying himself. 'It's wonderful to see old friends reunited,' he said, 'but right now I've got things to do. Calculus, start loading the weapons. Dr Cirenkov!' he shouted up at the control room. 'Why is this taking so long?'

'We're doing our best, Director,' she called down, 'but the chemical drums are badly corroded and most of the systems in here are over a hundred years old. We must move carefully.'

'Yes, but what about my missiles? Do they work?'

'Yes, yes, we've bypassed their security systems, they'll all function perfectly.' She gave a cold smile. 'They don't make weapons of mass destruction like this any more.'

'Good, get them loaded on to the rigs as soon as they are cut free. And do something about all this damned water, will you?' The turbine floor was now ankle deep in freezing water. 'Where's it all coming from anyway?'

Cirenkov shrugged. 'The whole lake seems to be thawing out but I have no idea why. It's playing hell with the systems in here. One of my team has already been electrocuted!'

'Why do you need those missiles, Stone?' said Bulldog. 'You've got more money than you could ever use, isn't that enough for you?'

Stone smiled grimly. 'My dear captain,' he said. 'Money and power are worth nothing unless people are afraid of you. Fear conquers all. Fear sweeps away all opposition. Fear is the destroyer of love and the killer of kindness. With these weapons I will create fear on an unprecedented scale.' Some of the men nearby had stopped to listen to Stone. Sensing he had an audience, he projected his voice even more loudly. 'Firstly, we'll send a message to our Chinese neighbours by blasting one of their cities out of existence.' Sid smiled grimly at this. 'Then, our newly created android armies will take control of their rig yards and they will have no choice but to surrender to me. Nations will bow before the might of the Trans-Siberian Mining Company and they will be proud to call me their emperor!' Stone's eyes gleamed with a strange light and tiny flecks of spittle sprayed from his mouth.

'Blimey. He's a few sandwiches short of a picnic,' muttered Bulldog under his breath.

While Stone raved, India watched Calculus loading a missile on to a steel trolley. 'Calc,' she hissed. 'It's me, India! Are you all right? Can you help us to get away?'

The big android turned slowly to face her. 'Move back, prisoner,' he said coldly. His words cut her to the bone.

'It's no good, kid,' said Verity. 'They've changed his base codes. He's not the person you knew any more.'

'How could you let that happen to him?' said India, tears stinging her eyes. 'You were supposed to be his friend!'

'I had no choice, India,' said Verity sadly. 'I'm sorry I got you into this. You would have been better off staying in London and marrying that slimy little creep.'

'Oi, steady on!' said Clench, peering out from behind Bulldog, where he had been hiding from Stone's gaze. 'That's charming, that is.'

Verity's eyes nearly popped out of her head. 'Holy mother of all riggers!' she said. 'What are you doing here?'

'That's a long story,' said Bulldog and India simultaneously.

Bulldog glanced over at Stone, who was still droning on about world domination, then he dropped his voice to a whisper. 'I have a suggestion.' He pointed to the open hangar doors. 'Those are six-inch, blast-proof doors. If we can jam them shut then Stone won't be taking those missiles anywhere.' He pointed to a steel box on the wall underneath the stairs. 'Mrs Brown, do you think you can shut those doors from that junction box?'

She looked at the box and the wires that ran from it. 'Piece of cake.' She grinned. 'I can re-route the power line and then fuse the electrics so they won't be able to open them again for a week.'

'Oh, great idea, genius,' said Clench. 'Then we'll be locked in here with Mr Call-Me-Emperor, and he's not exactly going to be in the best of moods, is he? I think I'd rather take my chances in an all-out war, thank you.'

Bulldog glanced at the guard and pulled the folded sheet from his pocket. 'I've been looking at the map,' he said in a whisper. 'This whole place is built on top of a network of natural caverns. There's a small door at the end of the hall that leads down to the caves. If we can escape down there while they're worrying about the blast doors, we might get clean away.'

'It sounds foolproof,' said Clench, rolling his eyes. 'I can't think of anything that could possibly go wrong.'

Two guards were standing nearby whom India recognized straight away as Silas and Cripps. While Verity slipped into the shadows to pull away the metal cover from the junction box, India gave them a disarming smile, hoping they wouldn't notice Verity was missing. 'Hello again!' she said brightly. 'This is a fascinating place, isn't it?'

Silas looked at her blankly, his tongue protruding slightly from his mouth while Cripps ignored her and probed the thick white sticking plaster that covered his broken nose.

'Have you seen the paintings in the other room?' she persisted. 'Are you both art lovers?'

Silas gave a confused frown; Cripps looked up and sneered.

An animal roar from the other end of the chamber made India jump. She turned to see Stone striding towards them wearing a furious scowl. 'Where has she gone? Where is the Brown woman?'

'Please, Mr Director,' said Clench in his whiniest voice, pointing to Verity. 'She's over there trying to sabotage the doors. It wasn't my idea, I told them I wanted nothing to do with it.'

'Oh hell!' said India under her breath.

Before anyone could stop her, Verity threw a switch on the junction box. The current sputtered and crackled, and Stone turned aghast as the great iron doors began to grind closed.

The first missile was already halfway out of the door and there was panic among the guards. A few of them tried to push the missile outside while others tried to push it back the way it had come; for a moment it looked like the doors would cut the missile in half. Then the doors shuddered to a halt in a half open position and the junction box exploded in a shower of sparks.

Silas and Cripps stood gormlessly, looking first at the junction box and then at Verity Brown. They might have stood there for some time had another guard not pushed them aside and pointed his pistol at Verity.

Reacting quickly, Bulldog pounced on the man and they wrestled for the gun. Without hesitating, Stone pulled out his own long-barrelled pistol and fired two shots in quick succession. The guard collapsed to the floor and lay still. Stone fired for a third time and Bulldog staggered and sat down abruptly. His breath escaped like steam from a pressure pipe and the colour drained from his face before he keeled over backwards.

'Bulldog!' cried India.

She ran to his side. His face was twisted in pain and his breath came in short gasps. 'I'm hit!' he gasped. 'It's me shoulder!'

Lucifer Stone dragged Verity from the shadows at gunpoint and bellowed at Silas and Cripps, who clung terrified to each other. 'Can't you imbeciles even guard four people? Cirenkov! What did she do?'

Up in the control room, Dr Cirenkov consulted the control desk with a worried frown. 'It looks like she was trying to lock the main the doors, Mr Director, but she was unsuccessful and now the circuits have blown.'

'Damn your eyes,' he yelled, purple with rage. 'Android! Tear the arms and legs off these troublemakers. Here —' he shoved Clench forward — 'start with this one.'

The group gasped as Calculus stepped forward and pulled Clench from their midst. Clench began to make an awful, high-pitched screeching as Calculus lifted him by the arms.

'Calculus, stop it, please stop it!' shouted India. 'This

isn't who you are! When I first knew you, you were gentle and kind. How can you have changed so much?'

'It won't do any good, young lady,' chuckled Stone. 'The Calculus you knew never really existed. He's just a machine, a stone-cold killer!'

Calculus turned his attention back to Clench, who had begun to gibber in fear.

'Don't do it, Calc,' she pleaded. 'You're more than just a machine. You've lived for longer than anyone else here. Long enough for there to be something else inside of you that isn't just a program, something that is just *you*.'

The android looked at her blankly. 'My programming,' he said in a hollow voice, 'is absolute. I am no different from any other machine.'

India sensed she was losing him. 'You are different, Calc,' she said, 'because you have friends. You have people you care about and who love you and that makes you more than just a machine. It makes you a person.' A single tear tracked slowly down her face. 'It means you can *choose* not to do this.'

There was a breathless silence in the hall. Calculus looked at India and cocked his head to one side and, for a moment, she was struck by how sad he looked.

'Stop meddling, you brat!' thundered Stone. 'The android works for me now, do you hear!' He raised his pistol and pointed it at her. But as he took aim, Calculus suddenly let go of Clench and stepped in front of the gun. There was a flicker of fear in Stone's eyes. 'Stand back, android!

Do as I say or I'll have you crushed and fed into the furnaces.'

'I have no wish to injure you, Director,' said Calculus calmly, 'but I cannot let you harm this girl.' As he stared at the Director, there was the faintest suggestion of a red glow behind his visor. Stone backed away and none of the guards made a move to intervene.

'Oh, Calc, my dear, dear Calc, you've come back to us,' said India. She wrapped her arms tightly around him. 'I knew you were still in there, I just knew it.'

The sound of the blast was sudden and loud. Something snicked past India's ear, making her flinch, and Calculus gave a quiet gasp. He moved India gently to one side and put a hand to his chest, looking curiously at the sticky blue ooze that trickled through his fingers. When he pulled his hand away there was a neat, round hole punched in the centre of the steel plate in his chest.

Sid began to shout excitedly and wave his pistol around. 'I got him, Pa!' he cried. 'That damned robot went bad and I plugged him!' He whooped and punched the air.

Like a toppling tree, Calculus sank slowly to his knees and crashed sideways to the floor. A horrid rattling came from his chest.

India screamed. 'Somebody, help him please!' she sobbed.

Verity was at his side at once, speaking quickly into his ear. 'OK, Calc, you know the drill. Activate your injury protocols and switch on your back-up systems. Come on, do it *now*, soldier!'

Sid was still hopping around delightedly when the first blow from Stone sent him sprawling.

'You idiot child,' yelled Stone. 'That android is worth a fortune to us.' He took his own pistol and began to strike Sid repeatedly around the head as the boy rolled on the floor and tried to protect himself with his hands.

'No, Pa!' he cried. 'He was going to kill you! I saved you, Pa! *I saved you!*'

'I'm no pa of yours!' roared Stone. 'I should have drowned you on the same day I drowned your treacherous ma!'

'Quick,' hissed Verity, as the guards turned their attention to the spectacle of Stone's rage. 'Now's our chance. Calc, can you walk?' He nodded weakly. 'Good, let's move, then. Clench, India – let's go.'

As Sid's beating continued they lifted the injured Bulldog to his feet and moved quietly towards the end of the hall.

Bulldog had been right: there was an ancient door there, made of iron-bound wood. Calculus pushed his weight against it and it groaned open. The noise echoed up the cavern, immediately drawing the attention of the guards at the other end of the hall, who started to run towards them as they squeezed through the narrow doorway. Calculus slammed the door shut and drove home the iron bolt as the guards began to pound on the wood.

Once on the other side of the door they found themselves in darkness, clinging to a slippery ledge with the sound of rushing water filling the air. Calculus turned on his visor light, which illuminated a long cavern, studded with sharp rocks. The ledge they were standing on dropped away into a steep gorge and an underground river rushed through the narrow channel, sending foam and spray into the air.

A heavy blow rattled the door and one of the thick timbers split and bent inward.

'Now what?' gasped Bulldog. 'They'll be through that door in no time.'

'There's no other choice,' said Verity. 'We'll have to ride the rapids out of here.' She stepped to the edge of the rocky gorge.

'No,' said Clench anxiously, 'I can't go down there, I just can't.'

'Come on, Clench,' said Verity. 'Now is not the time for an attack of the vapours.'

'No, it's not that.' He wrung his hands awkwardly. 'The thing is . . . I can't swim,' he blurted. They stared at him in silence and then Verity began to laugh.

'Can't swim?' She grinned. 'Hell, don't worry about that. You'll be dashed to death on the rocks before you drown.' She looked at Calculus. 'Calc? Are you still with us?' All eyes turned to the android and he nodded slowly. 'Good,' she said, still watching him closely. 'Then please, take hold of Mr Clench and make sure he keeps his head above water. Everyone else, follow me!'

Without a further word she jumped into the foaming waters and was carried swiftly down the rocky black throat at the end of the cavern. Calculus grabbed hold of Clench and, before he could protest, leaped in after her.

'Come on, let's keep up,' said Bulldog, offering his good arm to India. She took it gratefully and they stood at the edge.

'Ready?' he said.

Before she could reply, the door came crashing inward and the guards spilled on to the ledge. Bulldog jumped into the raging torrent, pulling India after him.

CHAPTER 24

BENEATH THE MOUNTAIN

India braced herself for an icy plunge but, to her surprise, the water was warm. The current immediately pulled her over the lip of the tunnel, tearing her away from Bulldog. She scrabbled to get a purchase on the smooth walls but she was swept relentlessly through the darkness.

Without warning the tunnel floor suddenly dropped away and she found herself free-falling. She fell for three full seconds before she hit the surface of the water with a smack. The impact knocked the wind from her and she tumbled over and over in a confusion of bubbles, uncertain which way was up. A strong hand on her collar yanked her spluttering to the surface. Calculus towed her to the edge of the water, where she found the others huddled on a small shingle beach.

'Is everyone in one piece?' said Verity. Her voice echoed back at them from the darkness.

There were various groans and grunts in reply.

By the light of the android's visor India could see they were in a natural cavern with a high vaulted roof that sparkled with blue-green stalactites and fragments of quartz. A lake filled part of the cavern floor and water cascaded from a hole fifty feet up in the roof. India realized with a gulp that that was where she had fallen from.

'Why is the water so warm?' said Bulldog. 'Not that I'm complaining, mind.'

'Thermal springs,' said Calculus. 'A by-product of the geothermal power plant, luckily for us.'

Before anyone else could speak, Lucifer Stone's voice began to boom from the hole in the roof. 'Damn you all!' His words reverberated around the cave. 'Run if you want to, but you won't get far. I'll see to it that this place becomes your tomb!'

'What does he mean by that exactly?' said India in a hushed voice.

'I don't know,' said Verity, 'but he's been talking about those weapons for days, and nothing's going to stop him taking them now. We'd better focus on trying to get away from this place before he finds us.'

They took stock of their injuries. By the light of her torch, Verity prepared a makeshift sling for Bulldog's arm while India watched Calculus carefully. She noticed that the blue ooze had stopped leaking from his chest and she wondered if that meant he had managed to repair himself. 'Are you all right?' she asked in a small voice.

'My emergency systems have made temporary repairs,' he said. 'I am functioning adequately.'

'I mean, are you *all right*? Are you . . . *you* again?'

There was a long silence before he answered. 'Something incredible has happened to me, India,' he said distantly. 'When Dr Cirenkov changed my base codes I still knew who you were but I cared nothing for any of you. But then, as you talked to me in the turbine hall, I felt something change inside.' He stared across the cavern. 'The incident has somehow corrupted my base codes. I no longer seem to be following my own programming: I seem to have developed a *free will*. This has never happened to an android before.'

India smiled. 'Well, maybe you've lived so long that you've become something new; something wonderful that no one has ever seen before,' she said. 'Who knows what you could do now.'

Verity motioned everyone to be silent. Further along the shingle beach they could hear someone splashing and choking in the shallow waters.

The group picked their way along the beach as Verity trained the torch along the water's edge. The beam picked out a huddled figure by the edge of the lake with knees drawn up under its chin. Black eyes stared back at them from a deathly pale face.

'Sid!' cried India.

'Don't look at me!' he said, holding up his arms. 'This is all your fault, India Bentley!'

'What is?' she said. 'I never did anything to you.'

He dragged the sleeve of his coat across his bleeding nose and India could see he'd been crying. 'I wanted to show my pa I was tough like him but you ruined all that! Since you came along, nothing I've done for him has been right. Then he said I weren't no son of his and he threw me down this damned hole to die with the rest of you.'

'He threw you down the hole? His own son?' India exchanged glances with Verity. 'The man's a monster!'

'Don't you dare say that!' Anger flashed in his eyes. 'He's a great man, my pa!' Then his face crumpled and he began crying again.

'What are we going to do with him?' said India.

'We don't need to do anything with him,' said Verity coldly. 'He's not our problem.'

'I'll second that,' said Clench, peering over Verity's shoulder.

'I don't know,' said India. 'He seems so *alone*.'

'He can die of loneliness for all I care,' said Verity. 'He put a bullet in my friend's chest or had you forgotten that? Come on, let's start trying to find a way out of here.'

Verity and Calculus helped Bulldog to his feet and they prepared to move off.

Sid wiped his eyes and stood up. 'Maybe I can help you.' Everyone turned to look at him. 'I just want to get out of here, same as you,' he said. His eyes flicked back and forth across the faces of the group like a nervous animal.

'And what help do we need from you, son?' asked Bulldog, sticking out his chin.

'Well, it seems to me you're all in pretty bad shape,' he replied. 'And it looks like I'm the only one here with a gun.' He rested a hand on his long-barrelled pistol. 'You don't need to worry. I don't want nothing from you. I just want to get out of here and find my pa, is all.' He spat on the floor. 'Then I'm going to shoot that worthless dog stone dead.'

'Well that's just super,' said Clench under his breath. 'Not only are we buried alive but now we've got a psychopath for company. How much worse can this get?'

'There's no point moaning,' said Verity wearily. 'It looks like we're stuck with him for now. Come on, let's get moving.'

They set off through the cavern with Sid trailing in their wake like a dark comet. In the wavering light of the torch, giant stalagmites cast twisted shadows across the walls.

'Calc,' whispered India as they walked along. 'I've been thinking about what Nentu said to us when we met her. She said there was an Elder Spirit living under this mountain. She said it wouldn't be pleased to see us but that we had to speak to it before two days were up or something terrible would happen.'

'And did you believe her?' said Calculus.

'It sounded real when she said it. Clench was there, he'll tell you. It was as if she could really see and hear things that nobody else could. And, now that we're here, I can really *feel* something too.' She struggled to put a name to what she

226

was feeling. It was like a low oscillation that vibrated within her bones. But there was something else too, something old beyond measure, something *intelligent*.

'I feel it too,' said Calculus. 'The caverns are filled with an infrasonic field, out of range of human hearing. You must be sensitive to it.'

'But something here is *alive*, Calc. I know it is. What if there really is something down here with us?'

By way of an answer, a gust of air passed through the cavern, raising goose bumps on India's skin. Then she heard the familiar hissing voices gathering in the darkness. Valleymen.

'Everyone, get together,' said Verity urgently.

Several indistinct shapes glided back and forth, just beyond the reach of the wavering torch beam.

'*You were warned to s-s-stay away from here, short-lives-s,*' they whispered in ghastly unison.

'Sid,' whispered Verity from the corner of her mouth. 'How many bullets have you got in that gun?'

'Why?' he drawled. 'You want me to shoot you now?'

Like a flash from a nightmare, two of the shadowy forms rushed from the darkness and India caught a glimpse of hard black claws and teeth. A brief image of the white reindeer, terrified and bleating, flashed before her eyes, then Sid's gun blasted once. The creatures shrank back to hover at the edge of the light. As they started to close in for a second time, a burning firebrand dropped to the ground in front of them, followed by another.

'Hey, you fools, get up here quickly,' called a voice behind them. 'Those devils won't hold off much longer.'

They turned to see an open doorway high up in the rock wall behind them. A lean man, silhouetted against a bright light, was reaching out his hand. Clench's instincts for self-preservation kicked in and he was the first to grasp the man's hand and haul himself out of danger. The others followed quickly and Calculus pulled himself up last.

'Good grief, you were lucky,' said the man as he slammed the door shut. 'Those devils can turn a man into a soulless shell in moments.'

They stared at him. He had wild hair and a thick, knotted beard, and his clothes were in shreds. Sid reached for his revolver but Verity pushed his hand down. 'Damn it, Sid, put that away,' she said. 'You start shooting like other people start sneezing.' She turned warily to the man. 'Who are you exactly?'

But India knew who he was. From the moment she had heard his voice, she had known it. She pushed forward and looked up into his strong, blue eyes.

'Dad?' she said tentatively. 'Dad, it's me, India.'

CHAPTER 25

JOHN BENTLEY'S TALE

He looked at her for several long seconds, his blue eyes gradually filling with tears of disbelief. 'India?' he said. 'India, is that really you?' He threw his arms around her, lifting her clean off the floor and squeezing her until she gasped for breath. 'It really *is* you!' He laughed. 'How is this possible? I thought you were in London.'

'I thought you were dead,' she said, her voice catching in her throat.

He held her at arm's length. 'I know, and I'm so sorry, India. There hasn't been a day when I haven't thought about you and Bella.'

'Then why didn't you come home to us?' she snapped.

'I understand how you must feel, India. Staying here was the hardest decision I ever made in my life but I had good reasons, believe me. I think when you hear my story you'll understand why.' He hugged her again and she wrapped her arms around him and buried her face in his chest.

The others watched awkwardly, not knowing quite where to look. But at that moment, for India, there was only John Bentley.

'Is Bella all right?' he said, suddenly concerned. 'Is that why you're here?'

'She's fine, Dad,' said India. 'We've been looking out for each other since you . . . well, for a while now.'

'That's my girl,' he said proudly. 'I should have known if anyone was going to come after me it would have been you. You take after your mother. But damn it, *how* have you got here?'

'Well, that's a long story,' she said, looking at the others. 'A *really* long story.'

Bentley turned to survey the group. There was a flicker of recognition when he saw Clench and his eyes narrowed. Clench shuffled his way to the back of the group.

'I am John Bentley,' he said. 'I apologize if I took you by surprise back there but the Valleymen are evil creatures that can send a man to the afterlife without the company of his soul. I had to wait until you were close enough to one of the service tunnels before I could risk opening a door to let you in.'

'I hate to break up a family reunion,' said Sid sarcastically, 'but we ain't no closer to finding a way out of this hole.'

'I'm afraid he's right, Mr Bentley,' said Verity. 'We could really use your help again.'

She drew him a hasty sketch of how they had arrived at Ironheart, talking him through the stages of their adventure. His eyes opened wide when he heard about their encounter with Lucifer Stone in the missile room.

'Stone's here?' he said in a hushed voice. 'Then it's as bad as I feared. Once he has those weapons, no one will be safe.'

'We tried to stop him,' said India. 'We were going to blow up the geothermal plant before Stone got here. Perhaps we still can still do that?'

'I doubt we can do anything from down here,' said Calculus.

'Calc's right,' said Verity. 'The best we can hope for is to keep out of Stone's way until he leaves.'

'I know these tunnels like the back of my hand,' said John Bentley. 'I can lead you to an exit, but we'll need to lie low for a while. We're safe enough in here but the caverns are thick with Valleymen during the hours of darkness. In the meantime, perhaps I could offer you something to eat?'

He led them to a wide, dry cave that had been partially converted into a living space. There was a camp bed, some personal effects and a small wooden desk spilling over with papers and notebooks. India noticed a cracked and grubby photograph of her and Bella on the desk. Along one wall, a set of shelves groaned beneath a stack of canned goods bearing Russian labels. Bentley lifted down tins of beans, sardines and pears in syrup which he opened while Verity lit a small fire using a stack of Bulldog's banknotes, striking a flame expertly using the edge of her hunting knife against a piece of flint. As the bedraggled group peeled off their wet layers and held out cold hands to the fire, the smell of oil and salted fish began to fill the air. India realized she was salivating.

'You've got enough food in here to feed an army,' said Bulldog as Verity draped a blanket over his shoulders.

'Yes,' said Bentley. 'The rats have been at the dried goods but the tins are mostly fine and I can get fresh fruit and vegetables from the gardens when I need it.'

Bentley asked a stream of questions over the meal. India talked about home in between mouthfuls but she decided not to tell him about Roshanne's scheme to marry her off to Clench just yet.

'What about your friend over there?' said Bentley. 'Isn't he going to eat?' Sid had positioned himself as far away as possible at the other end of the cave and was sulkily cleaning his pistol.

'He's no friend of ours,' said Clench.

On an impulse, India put some beans on a metal plate and took them over to Sid.

'What do you want?' he said suspiciously.

'I thought you might want some food.' She set the plate down carefully and backed away.

'I didn't ask you for nothing.'

'Well don't eat it then!' she snapped. 'See if I give a damn!' She turned to walk away but he called after her.

'Hey – how's your metal man? Is he going to live?' India was surprised to see that Sid looked almost concerned. 'I thought my pa'd be pleased if I shot him. But he's never

pleased about nothing I do, so I'm sorry I done it now.'
India wasn't sure if that was an apology or not. 'You can tell
your friends I ain't about to kill none of them neither. Not
unless they come trying to kill me first. There's only one
man I want to kill when I get out of here and that's my pa.'
He went back to cleaning his pistol. 'And thanks,' he said as
she walked away. 'For the beans, I mean!'

Back at the fire she sat down next to her father and he
patted her hand.

'OK, Dad, tell us what's been going on here – and don't
leave anything out!'

He poked the fire thoughtfully, sending a shower of
paper sparks into the air. 'I first found this place about
three years ago,' he began. 'Angel Town had always been rife
with rumours about a treasure trove in the mountains and
the Company were offering huge rewards for information
about its location. Every rigger had their own theories
about where it might be and I had my own ideas too. I
spent six months trying to talk to the local tribesmen but
they just used to mutter something about mountain spirits
and then refuse to speak to me. Eventually I met a crazy
old woman who lived on her own in the forest – she was as
blind as a stone.'

India's eyes widened. 'You mean Nentu. We met her
too,' she said. 'She gave us a map showing us how to get
here.'

Bentley looked surprised. 'Well she didn't do that for
me,' he said. 'At first she sent me away without telling me

a thing. But that night I had the most vivid dream I ever had in my life. I dreamed I was an eagle, flying over the landscape. I could feel the wind under my wings and sense the small creatures hiding from me in the forest. I saw the whole land; the mountain, the lake, the trees. And then I saw Ironheart, right here on the mountainside as clear as daylight. When I woke up I knew exactly where to find it.' He stared absently into the fire. 'Damnedest thing . . . When I finally got here I found the underground gardens and realized what a treasure trove this place really was.'

'We saw them,' said India excitedly. 'They're beautiful.'

'There are seeds for every major food crop in the world in there. They have the potential to feed millions.' He shook his head in wonder. 'I thought if I could bring the seeds back to London then people wouldn't need to fight over every last scrap of food. It would be a new start for everyone. I wanted to catalogue the seeds properly and bring samples home before Stone or anyone else got here. But it was late in the season and I had to get back to London before the winter set in. I did my best to hide the location of Ironheart. Before I came back to London I burned all my records, then I programmed two small computer chips, one to hold all my notes and the other with the codes to operate the doors.' He glanced at the pendant around India's neck. 'I never thought anyone would use them to follow me here, let alone my own daughter.'

India grinned.

'When I returned in the spring Ironheart had changed.

The mountains were being rocked by earth tremors and even the sky looked strange. When I got inside I had my first encounter with those foul creatures, the Valleymen. Nentu had warned me about them but even so I was absolutely terrified of them. But I was determined to save the seed vaults.' He patted the bulky shoulder bag that lay beside him. 'These are the best samples I could gather: wheat, barley, oats, fruit trees and vegetables, all carefully catalogued and packaged. The contents of this bag will ensure that the Hunger Wars are over for good. But the longer I stayed here, the more I was haunted by the feeling I was not alone. I became convinced that something was watching me, something ancient.'

'I felt that too,' said India with a start.

'Whatever it was didn't much like me being here,' said Bentley. 'The Valleymen were always out looking for me and I began to realize it was controlling them somehow.'

India shivered. 'So why did you stay?' she said. 'Why didn't you just leave once you had the seeds and come home? We needed you, Dad – *I* needed you.'

'I meant to, India,' he said. 'But then I discovered something incredible.' He took a deep breath. 'There is something buried under these mountains, beneath Ironheart itself. Something ancient, an *artefact*, if you like, and its presence here changes everything.'

'What do you believe this artefact to be, Mr Bentley?' said Calculus. 'You make it sound as though it was alive.'

Bentley nodded thoughtfully. 'The artefact protects us,'

he said. 'It has the power to determine whether we live or die. And, yes, I do believe it is alive and possibly even intelligent.'

The words stirred a memory in India. 'Nentu's Elder Spirit?' she whispered.

Bentley nodded. 'Perhaps.'

'I'm sorry,' said Bulldog, 'but you've lost me entirely. What is an Elder Spirit when it's at home with its feet up?'

'Something that mad old crone was gibbering on about in the tent,' supplied Clench. 'No idea what she meant.'

Bentley stood up abruptly. 'There's no way to explain this without sounding like an utter lunatic, so the best thing is if I show you. But brace yourselves for what you're going to see because nothing will ever seem quite the same again.'

CHAPTER 26

THE COPPER CAULDRON

He led them down a flight of concrete stairs to a corroded metal door. The space beyond was the deepest black, making them all hesitate on the threshold. Bentley fumbled for a switch and a series of overhead floodlights clanked on in sequence.

'Holy mother of all riggers!' said Bulldog. 'Would you look at the size of this place?'

They stepped on to a metal gallery that ran around a cathedral of solid rock. The high roof was supported by natural stone columns and India guessed her entire village could have fitted comfortably inside the space. The chamber was dominated by an enormous copper cauldron. The rim stood twenty feet high and two hundred feet wide. At evenly spaced points around the rim, pillars made of the same metal rose towards the roof, curving and tapering gracefully like the petals of a vast copper tulip.

'What is that thing?' said Verity. 'And who built it?'

'It doesn't look like it was built at all,' said Bulldog. 'It looks like it *grew* here.'

There wasn't a hint of a join or a weld anywhere. The metal at the base appeared fused to the rock.

They peered over the lip of the cauldron, which sloped down to a yawning hole at the centre. Bentley picked up a stone and tossed it into the bowl. It rolled down the metal surface and dropped into the hole. They strained their ears for a sound.

'Didn't hear it hit the bottom,' said Clench, using the sort of voice people usually reserve for church.

'That's because it's still falling,' said Bentley, 'and it will be for several hours yet.' He leaned back on the railings. 'When I first came down here and saw this thing I was desperate to know what it was. I searched the offices for clues. That was when I found their records.'

'Whose records?' said India.

Bentley shrugged. 'They were either the government or the military but they were very secretive about their work. All I know for certain is what I read in the files. About two hundred years ago a massive explosion completely devastated this entire region. Eyewitnesses said they saw a huge fireball. It caused a blast which flattened the trees for twenty miles in every direction. They thought it was a meteorite or an asteroid so they sent a scientific expedition out here to search for it. The team spent six months searching and found no trace of a meteorite or a crater anywhere. But what they did discover was this chamber and the artefact, right here under the lake.'

Verity and India exchanged baffled glances.

'Their first thought was that it was some kind of weapon that had been put here by their enemies. But when they examined it more closely they got their first surprise.' He looked at the cauldron. 'What you see here is just the tip of it,' he said slowly. 'It goes down nearly a thousand miles.'

'Nonsense,' said Clench. 'Nothing could go down that far.'

'I hate to agree with Archie about anything,' said Bulldog, 'but that's a quarter of the way to the centre of the Earth. I've been a rigger all my life and nobody's ever made a hole that deep.'

'No one in living memory,' said Bentley. 'Which leads me to their second surprise. When they ran more tests, they found the artefact was over twelve thousand years old!'

'How is that possible – humans were still living in caves then,' said Verity. 'Who is supposed to have built it?'

'They asked themselves the same question,' said Bentley, 'so they looked for anything that would give them a clue. They discovered that this cauldron tapped into the Earth's magnetic energy field and that it had the potential to generate more electricity than all the world's cities put together. After that they started to call it *the machine*. But it was still a complete mystery as to who had built it or what it was for.'

'Then what?' said India eagerly. 'What did they find out?'

'Nothing,' said Bentley. 'Over a hundred scientists came and went, carrying out thousands of tests. But nobody could say for certain what the machine was for or what it did. The only thing that did happen was that nearly everyone who worked here reported an unpleasant sensation of being watched all the time.'

India cast an involuntary look over her shoulder.

'After a while it got so bad that no one wanted to stay here. So they finally locked up this room and forgot all about it. Later on, when the Great Rains started, they used the caverns for storage. The records got patchy after that. The Hunger Wars started and governments began to collapse. At some point during the enduring chaos, Ironheart was abandoned completely. I began to develop a theory. I thought that the machine and the asteroid might be connected somehow. Then it struck me.' He leaned towards them, his eyes gleaming. 'The expedition that first came here never found any trace of the actual asteroid. No craters, no fragments of rock, nothing!'

'Well, meteorites don't just disappear,' said Clench. 'It must have gone somewhere.'

'There was only one explanation that fitted the facts,' he said. 'The reason they couldn't find the asteroid was that it never reached the Earth. Before it could collide with the planet, this machine blasted it out of the sky – hence the explosion.'

Everyone began to talk at once.

'You can't shoot down an asteroid,' said Verity. 'They're too fast.'

'I know it sounds impossible,' said Bentley, 'but the facts

240

back up my theory. This machine detected an asteroid while it was still in deep space and destroyed it before it could hit the Earth. Somehow the shamans in the region knew it was coming and led their people to safety. Incredible as it sounds, this is a machine designed to protect the Earth, and after twelve thousand years it's *still working*!'

An eerie feeling stole over India as she listened to her father's story. She thought of the empty tents by the frozen lake, the absence of animals in the forest, and the earth tremors and shooting stars that had become more and more frequent on their journey. 'It's starting again, isn't it?' she whispered. 'That's what Nentu was trying to tell us. The machine, the thing she called the Elder Spirit, has detected another asteroid.'

'I'm afraid you're right,' said Bentley. 'Something is shifting underground, causing the earthquakes. Not to mention –' he dropped his voice – 'the cauldron storms.'

'What's a cauldron storm?' said Clench, looking nervously at the machine.

'It's a term I came up with. Some sort of electrical energy storm that moves across the surface of the metal. The first time I saw one I made the mistake of trying to touch it and I got this for my trouble.'

He rolled up his sleeve and showed them an angry red scar that ran from his wrist to his elbow. India winced. 'It's always the same: first the earth tremors and then the cauldron storm. It scares the hell out of me every time. The first time was after I'd been here for eight months, then it happened again four months later and then eight weeks after that.'

'Half the elapsed time between each event,' said Calculus.

'It's a countdown,' said India in a hushed voice.

'Exactly,' said Bentley. 'I think it's measuring the time until the asteroid arrives. What's more, the storms are only a few hours apart now. I think the asteroid must be quite close.'

There was a stunned silence as they absorbed the implications of his words.

'Well, what's going to happen then?' said Bulldog. 'Is the machine going to shoot it down?'

'I don't know for sure,' said Bentley, 'but it is capable of producing an enormous amount of energy. If it did fire, it would probably release enough radiation to vaporize everything in Ironheart.' He shook his head sadly. 'The gardens, the seed vaults, everything would be lost.'

'But not the warheads,' said India. 'Stone will have taken them. They'll be the only thing that gets saved.'

'There's nothing we can do about that now,' said Verity. 'How long do we have before the asteroid arrives?'

'Nentu said a "bringer-of-death" called Nibiru was going to come. She must have been talking about the asteroid. If she was right, then we have less than a day left.'

Bentley's eyes widened in surprise. 'Good grief! I had no idea it would be here so soon.' He looked around anxiously. 'I must collect my seeds and then we have to leave immediately, before the machine fires.' A faint tremor ran through the cavern and a light fall of dust and stones descended from the roof. 'Come on,' he said, 'I'll show you how to get out.'

He led them around the outside of the chamber to a ventilation grille, which he pulled away to reveal a broad tunnel bored into the rock. There was a steady trickle of water running from it.

'These tunnels drain the meltwater from the lake in the summer,' he said. 'It's how I get in and out when I go hunting. They come out on the far side of the lake and I have a snow wagon parked up in the old boat shed.'

Verity crouched down and shone the torch into the narrow opening. 'It's a bit tight in there,' she said, 'but if we leave now we should have plenty of time to get to the lake and then make some distance before the machine goes off. Let's collect everything together and get moving.'

'Wait,' said Calculus. 'I am picking up some strange readings from the machine. I think one of Mr Bentley's cauldron storms may be starting.'

They turned to look but nothing seemed to have changed.

'We're wasting time here,' said Clench, 'I say we—'

He stopped short.

A sound like distant thunder rumbled around the chamber and the gallery began to sway. India gripped one of the handrails for support as the floodlights crackled and dimmed.

'It's starting again!' shouted Bentley. 'Take cover and whatever you do, don't go anywhere near it!'

CHAPTER 27

AWAKE IN THE DREAM WORLD

The air shimmered with a blue haze as a hot breeze sprang up from the cauldron. Waves of electrical energy shivered across the surface of the metal and every few moments a bolt of white lightning arced across to the steel gantry.

'How long does it do this for, Mr Bentley?' said Calculus, raising his voice over the din.

'About half an hour usually,' he shouted back. 'We'll be all right as long as we stay out of the way.'

'Them lightning bolts look like some kind of defence mechanism,' said Sid, regarding the cauldron warily.

'I don't think so,' said Calculus. 'I can detect a signal within the electrical field. It's a repeating pattern that resembles some computer authentication protocols.'

'What does that mean in English?' shouted India.

'What I mean,' he said, 'is that it may be waiting for someone to give it instructions.'

'It's been here for thousands of years,' said Bulldog. 'No one ever had to tell it what to do before.'

'Perhaps they did,' said India. 'Nentu said the job of the soul voyagers was to speak to the mountain spirit. She said they'd been doing it for a hundred generations. Maybe the shamans have to actively ask the machine for help.'

'That's what I mean to find out,' said Calculus. 'If I can replicate the same signal it might recognize me as a friend. I might be able to initiate some sort of log-on procedure.'

'It might also decide to vaporize you on the spot,' said Verity. 'Forget it, Calc! It's too risky.'

'I understand the risks,' he said, 'but this machine was built by someone with technology far more advanced than our own and it may be at least partly intelligent. I am going to try and speak to it.'

He walked towards the crackling cauldron. When he got within ten feet of it, he held out his palm. A white arc of electricity shot abruptly from the metal surface and connected with his hand. He stiffened and arched backwards.

'It's attacking him,' cried India.

'I don't think so,' said Verity. 'I think it's working, I think he's actually talking to it!'

The electricity ran lightly over the android's metal skin, forming a latticework of connections. It really did look as though some sort of communication was taking place. Suddenly the lattice grew brighter and more intense. With a sound like a thunderclap, Calculus was sent flying backwards across the floor.

Verity was by his side in an instant. 'Calc, speak to me, let me know you're still in there.'

When he spoke, his voice had none of its usual resonance. 'I think,' he gasped, 'it didn't like the way I spoke to it.'

She hooked her arms under his shoulders and tried to pull him clear. 'India, help me to move him.'

But India wasn't listening. She was staring at the point where the arc had emerged from the cauldron. The bright spot had now elongated into a tall rectangle of brilliant light. Like a doorway, she thought to herself. Mesmerized by the blue-white glare, she walked slowly towards it. The sound of the storm receded and she heard only a faint hum and a voice that spoke clearly in her head.

'*Only a true soul voyager can enter the dream world,*' it said.

She didn't see her father rush forward to grab her and she didn't notice as he was forced back by the bolts of raw energy. Oblivious to the shouts of her companions, she extended her hand towards the white-hot metal. In the moment of contact she felt a pulse of energy in her palm, then a sudden rush of coldness surged up her arm as the light overwhelmed and engulfed her.

A sea of sparks danced around her like a shoal of fish before scattering in all directions. Then she was alone, floating on a dark sea, not black but deep red, the colour of blood. It felt good against her skin and all she wanted to do was let herself sink into its warm saltiness.

'*Wake up, soul voyager.*' Nentu's voice was suddenly loud in her head. '*Wake up and find your wits, your kujaii is already dead.*' An image flashed across her mind. The white deer, eyes glazed, blood running from its mouth.

She opened her eyes. The place in which she stood was so dark that she could barely see, but she could tell she was no longer in the cavern; it felt closed in and uncomfortably hot. She sensed there was another presence in here too; the same ancient, brooding intelligence she had first felt when they entered the caverns.

As her eyes adjusted, she thought she thought she could make out three shapes, like dark spheres, floating against the blood-red background.

'You are not Nentu.' Three voices spoke in perfect unison and a flurry of tiny lights danced over the surface of each sphere.

India wondered what response was required and she struggled to make her mouth work. 'No,' she said thickly. 'No, I'm not Nentu.'

The sphere on the left floated a fraction closer to her. 'Then you are another soul voyager?' it said. It sounded female and clinical, as though it was partly artificial. Violet and blue lights flickered when it spoke.

'Well, no, not exactly,' she said. The heat was starting to make her feel faint. 'Who are *you* exactly? Where is this place?'

The sphere drew back.

'She is confused,' said the sphere. 'She is still partly in the dream world.'

'She must be a soul voyager,' said the middle sphere. 'Even if she does not know it yet.' It flashed lights of gold and silver and its voice combined both male and female tones.

'I said who *are* you?' said India more insistently.

'We are the mind of the machine,' said the first sphere. 'The mind is made of three parts. I am the voice of Compassion and these are the voices of Wisdom and Logic. Only when all three parts of the mind are in agreement will the machine make a decision.'

'Why is Nentu not here?' said the last sphere. 'Nentu was trusted but you have not earned any trust.' It sounded cold and irritable. India guessed this was Logic.

'Nentu couldn't come,' said India, 'she wasn't strong enough any more.'

'Then how do we know you can be trusted?' said the voice of Logic. 'What assurances do you bring?'

'*The bag, child,*' said Nentu's voice in her ear. '*Show them the bag.*'

She pulled the half-remembered fur bag from her pocket and emptied the collection of pebbles and small bones on the floor in front of her. 'I have these,' she said.

The three voices went quiet and the spheres drew nearer. Then the voice of Wisdom spoke. 'She holds a nexus,' it said.

'Is it important?' said India faintly.

'The nexus is the key to the portal,' said the voice of Compassion. 'We have granted them only to a few soul voyagers. Without it, the portal would have killed you.'

She was feeling horribly hot and longed for some fresh air. 'If you're a machine, then who built you?' she said, trying a different tack.

'We were created by the long-lives at the start of the last great cycle, many millennia ago,' said Wisdom. 'They built the machine to protect their world. Now they are gone and only we remain. Nentu calls us . . . the Elder Spirit.'

'And what about the Valleymen?' said India. 'Did the long-lives create them too? I've seen them kill a man.'

'The Valleymen protect the machine from the inquisitive,' said Compassion. 'They reflect only what men bring with them into the forests.'

'There's an asteroid,' said India, remembering why she was there. 'It's heading towards the Earth.'

'We know this,' said Logic. 'We have detected the coming of the rogue planet named Nibiru.'

'You have to shoot it down,' said India. 'I mean, *could* you shoot it down? If it's not too much trouble. Please?' She wondered how you were supposed to ask a machine to save the world.

'Why should we do this?' said the voice of Logic. 'This machine was built to protect the makers. Short-lives like you are not our concern.'

'But . . .' India struggled for words. 'The people who

made you, the long-lives, wouldn't they want you to help us, even if they weren't here any more?'

The three voices fell silent. India felt there was a conversation going on between them.

Compassion spoke next. 'You speak the truth,' it said. 'But still we cannot help you.'

'But why not?' said India. 'Isn't that what you're supposed to do?'

'There are tools of war in this place,' said Compassion. 'We can sense the greed and fear that surrounds them.'

'Do you mean the warheads?'

'The man of blood will take what he wants and then he will destroy Ironheart,' said Logic. 'He has set one of the warrior heads to explode. This machine will be destroyed before the asteroid comes within range.'

India's head swam. 'Lucifer Stone's going to set off a warhead? Here, in Ironheart? But then what will happen?'

'The course of nature will run true,' said Logic. 'Nibiru will enter the Earth's gravitational well in approximately three hours. The impact will destroy all higher-level life forms on the planet.'

'What? But there must be something that can be done?' said India. She was finding it hard to breathe now.

'This is no longer our concern,' said Logic. 'The short-lives sow the seeds of their own destruction and care nothing for the consequences. Now we must shut down the machine to preserve the mind.'

India struggled to focus. 'But you can't just leave us to die,' she cried.

The room spun and the spheres began to fade to blackness.

The three voices spoke as one. 'Our time in the dream world is at an end and your world will soon be gone. Goodbye.'

India felt herself slipping away.

'*India!*' hissed Nentu's voice. '*This is your last chance!*'

'Wait,' said India, though she was not sure if anyone was still listening. 'What if we could stop Lucifer Stone and prevent the explosion? If we could do that, you could still shoot down the asteroid, couldn't you?'

'Do you know how to do this?' said the voice of Logic.

'*Speak only what is in your heart, India.*' Nentu's voice was suddenly loud. '*Say nothing less.*'

India sighed. 'No,' she said. 'No, I don't know. But I'll find a way. Whatever it takes I will find a way to stop that bomb. I give you my word.'

'Whose word do you give?' said the voice of Wisdom.

'My word!'

'And who are you?' said the three voices together.

India felt groggy, as if she might faint.

'*Now, India,*' said Nentu. '*Now is your last chance. Say what is in your heart.*'

'Who are *you*?' demanded the voices.

'I am a soul voyager!' she shouted with the last of her strength. 'I am a soul voyager and I give you my word. Now will you help us?'

There was no response, just silence and blackness and the sense that the whole scene was slipping away from her.

'Answer me!' she shouted. 'You have to answer me, it's not fair!'

'Steady now, steady.'

'I'll find a way. Whatever it takes, I'll find a way.'

'Give her some space. Here, drink this.'

A bottle was pressed to her lips and her eyelids flickered under a harsh light. She coughed as cold water was poured into her throat.

'Go easy now,' said a voice that sounded like Bulldog's. 'That thing gave you a helluva jolt.'

India pulled herself up to rest on her elbows and the pain in her head seemed to split her skull in two.

'I think she's going to be OK,' said Verity. 'India, can you hear me? You've been out cold for the last ten minutes. You gave us a real scare there, but don't worry, everything's going to be all right.'

India shook her head, sending more waves of pain through her skull. 'No, it isn't,' she said with as much force as she could muster. 'Everything's not all right. It's a long way from being all right. We're all going to die!'

CHAPTER 28

THE END OF DAYS

It took a long while to make her tongue work so that she could be understood. Then they wouldn't let her speak until she had taken a drink.

'Just sit still for a moment, India,' said her father, wide-eyed with anxiety. 'Give yourself a bit of time.' So she drank the water and took a deep breath, feeling that the frustration might kill her.

'There *is* an asteroid coming,' she managed to say eventually, 'and it's going to hit the Earth.'

Verity and her father exchanged looks.

'We already know that,' said Bentley. 'I told you, remember, just before you got knocked out.'

'But the machine can't defend us!' she said, pulling herself up. The pain in her head redoubled. 'They can't fire the machine because Stone's going to explode one of those bombs and destroy everything.'

'Calm down, India,' said Verity. 'You were hit by a

lightning bolt and you've been unconscious, you must have dreamed it.'

The fragments of her memory started to fall into place. 'Where's Calc? He'll believe me – he spoke to them too!'

A look passed between her father and Verity.

India turned to see Calculus sitting against the wall of the chamber about twenty feet away. His head was drooped on his chest and his sinewy body was limp and lifeless. Worst of all, a black, clotted liquid had begun to bubble from the hole in his chest plate.

'Calc!'

She scrambled over to where he lay, ignoring the pain that flooded her body. A faint rasping came from deep inside his chest like the sound of metal gears grinding without enough oil.

'He's been like this since he was struck by the lightning,' said Verity.

India put her mouth close to his ear. 'Calc, can you hear me? It's India. I need you to wake up and tell the others what you heard.'

'Let him rest, India,' said Verity, placing a hand on her shoulder.

'No!' she cried. 'It's too important. Calc! You have to wake up!'

'That's enough, India!' said Verity firmly.

'Did somebody call me?' Calculus's voice was weaker than before. He sat up slowly and placed his head in his hands. 'There is an asteroid coming,' he said eventually.

'India is right. But the machine can't shoot it down because Lucifer Stone is going to destroy Ironheart first.'

'Then you *did* hear them too,' said India. 'The voices, I mean?'

He shook his head wearily. 'No. They spoke to you because you are human. When they realized I was a machine, they tried to download information directly to me. The entire history of the ancient people who built the machine was fed into my brain in a microsecond.' He looked down at his scorched body. 'I'm afraid it took it out of me a little.' He made a sound like a cough and the grinding noise increased.

'Well, the hell with it,' said Clench. 'Asteroid or no asteroid, if Stone's going to blow the place up, then let's just get out of here. Who cares where the asteroid lands as long as we're not underneath it.'

'The asteroid is over five miles wide and made almost completely of iron,' said Calculus. 'It's bigger than the one that made the dinosaurs extinct. When it hits the Earth it will cause widespread earthquakes and tsunami. After that it will throw up enough dust to blot out the sun for a hundred years and create a new ice age. Nothing will grow and nothing will survive except for a few bacteria . . . and, well . . . me,' he added.

'"*First comes the iron and then comes the snow,*"' said India under her breath, '"*and then comes the winter when nothing will grow.*" It's what Cromerty was trying to tell me and it's what Nentu meant when she talked about the end of days.

If Stone lets off that bomb, he'll not only destroy Ironheart but the rest of the world too!'

'Then it makes no difference what we do,' said Verity. 'Either way, we're going to die.'

'I told them,' said India, 'that we'd stop the explosion if we could. Couldn't we try?'

Verity shook her head wearily. 'It's not that easy, India,' she said. 'Shutting down a sophisticated warhead isn't just a matter of throwing a switch. They have security systems and codes that have to be entered.'

'But didn't Dr Cirenkov say they had already bypassed the security systems?' said India.

Bulldog snapped his fingers. 'You're right, she did say that!'

'That doesn't help us,' said Clench. 'We've still got no way of getting back to the turbine hall. There's a maze of tunnels between here and there and they're full of Valleymen, remember?'

'Mr Bentley,' said Verity, 'is there any way back to that control room without going through the tunnels?'

Bentley shook his head. 'You could get out through the drainage tunnels and then double back through the forest but that would take hours, and you'd still risk running into the Valleymen.'

'Come on, Bentley, you've lived here for a year and a half,' said Bulldog. 'There must be another way. Think, man!'

Bentley shrugged and held up his hands. 'The only other route between floors is the conduits that carry the pipes and cables. The rats used to use them but they're way too small for a person. Believe me, I've tried.'

'Show me!' said Verity.

He took them to a tiny rectangular opening high in the chamber wall with cables running out of it. It was gushing with icy water.

'I might get in there at a push,' said Verity, biting her lip. She slipped off her jacket and Clench and Bentley gave her a boost. By turning her head sideways she could just about squeeze it into the slot but there was no room for her shoulders. She tried leading with one arm and then the other as freezing water cascaded over her. After ten minutes she clambered back down, soaked and filthy and with nothing to show for her efforts but some fierce scratches on her hands and arms. 'It's hopeless. I couldn't get in there if I starved myself for a month. I'm running short of ideas.'

'What about Calculus?' said Bentley. 'If he went up the main tunnel, couldn't he run back through the forest to the control room?'

Verity shook her head. 'He's in no fit state,' she said, lowering her voice. 'He's too badly damaged.'

'I could get in there,' said India quietly.

'Maybe we could climb up the waterfall to the cavern roof and get out that way?' said Bulldog.

'I said I could go,' said India. 'I could climb up that conduit, I'm the only one small enough to get in there – look!'

257

She peeled off her jacket and heavy jumper. After nearly three weeks of missed meals she was as thin as a pencil.

'It's too dangerous,' said Bentley. 'You could get stuck, and even if you get through, Stone's men might still be up there.'

'Now's not the time to get all fatherly on me, Dad. Look, if they've set a bomb to explode, they'll be trying to get away from here, the same as us,' said India. 'Besides, if we do nothing we're all going to die anyway, so what's the difference?'

'It might work,' said Bulldog.

'It won't work, said Verity. 'Bombs like that have fail-safe devices attached to them so it takes more than one person to turn them on or off. Usually two people have to press a button or turn keys at the same time. You can't do it on your own.'

'I reckon I can fit in there if she can,' said a voice from the shadows. Sid had already removed his coat. If anything, he was even thinner and scrawnier than India.

Clench snorted. 'There's no way we'd trust you with this.'

'I got the same stake in this as you,' he said, 'and it don't make much difference anyhow. Either we die trying or we die without trying and I reckon it's better to die trying.'

'Well put, my friend,' said Bentley, patting Sid on the shoulder. He looked anxiously at India. 'If there was any other choice, India, I wouldn't let you go, but I think you are right. This may be our only option.'

It was settled swiftly. John Bentley would lead the rest of the group up the drainage tunnel while India and Sid made their way to the control room. Once they had shut down the bomb they would all rendezvous on the far side of the lake. Nobody spoke about what would happen if they didn't succeed.

They made their preparations quickly. Verity packed their few belongings and Bentley returned to his quarters to collect his precious seed samples. Meanwhile India stripped down to her long underwear and a pair of thick socks and Sid removed his heavy boots and shirt but kept his pistol tucked into his trousers. India was shocked to see his body was covered in red weals and scars – the result of dozens of beatings.

Verity pulled India to one side. 'You watch that boy,' she said. 'I don't trust him any further than I can spit. He might easily decide to double-cross all of us just for the hell of it.'

'I don't think so,' said India. 'He seems pretty determined to get even with his father, and who can blame him?'

'And that's another thing,' said Verity. 'Don't get in the way of that fight. If he goes after Stone you need to be as far away as possible. As soon as that bomb's disarmed you get away from him and keep running.'

India went to see Calculus, who was still slumped against the wall. 'Will you be able to manage the climb?' she said.

'I need to talk to you, India.'

'I know what you're going to say,' she said quickly, 'and

259

Verity's already warned me about Sid. Don't worry, I can look after myself.'

'It's not that.'

A chill ran through her body.

'The machine has shut itself down to protect the mind from the explosion,' he said. 'Before it can start up again, I will need to speak to it and tell it the bomb has been disarmed.'

India wasn't sure why this conversation was making her so uneasy. 'Well, that's OK. You can do that, can't you?'

'To communicate with the machine I will need to make direct physical contact,' he said. 'It means I will have to stay here.'

'But what about your communicator? Couldn't you use that?'

'My communicator does not work on the same frequency as the machine,' he said. 'I have thought carefully about this, India, and I have discussed it with Mrs Brown. There is no other option, I have to stay behind.'

A hot tear ran down her cheek. 'But why you? Why should you be the one that has to stay? It's not fair, you could still live for hundreds of years.'

'No, I couldn't,' he said quietly, 'because I am already dying. My repairs were only temporary. From the moment I was shot, I knew I only had hours to live.'

She put her hand to her mouth.

'Don't be sad,' he said. 'Now I have a chance to do something really important. It means I will be remembered for being more than just a war machine.' He reached out and took her hand. 'I can't think of anything more . . . human.'

She wanted to scream at him and tell him he was wrong but the words wouldn't come. 'I hate the thought of you being on your own down here,' she said in a small voice. 'You know, after we've gone.' A thought occurred to her. She scrabbled in her bag and pulled out the slim, green volume she had found earlier in the day. 'My dad would read this to us when we were little,' she said. 'He used to tell me I'd have an adventure of my own one day.' She handed it to him. 'There's a character in it that reminds me of you.'

He took the book and looked at it carefully.

'*The Wonderful Wizard of Oz*,' he said, reading the title. He opened the book and turned the pages, pausing at a picture of a metal man holding hands with a young girl. 'It's a story about an android,' he said with surprise. 'Thank you, India, I shall treasure it.'

India forced herself through the final preparations for the task ahead. Verity hugged her and Bulldog ruffled her hair. Then her father squeezed her tightly and clapped Sid on the back.

'Good luck, young man,' he said. 'I'm trusting you to take care of my daughter. When we all get out of here we should talk about your future.'

Sid looked at him as though he was speaking a different language.

Then India put her arms around Calculus for the last

time. His metal skin felt warm and sticky from the clotted, black ooze which mingled with her tears.

'When you have shut down the bomb,' he was saying, 'use the wrist communicator to let me know straight away.'

She blinked at him. 'I have to go now,' she said.

'Will you be all right?'

'Sure,' she said, wiping her eyes. 'But I think my anticipatory sub-routines might register your absence from my immediate environment.'

'I'll miss you too, India,' he said.

She hugged him tightly again as he rested a hand gently on her hair. No one spoke and the silence was broken only by the sound of Bulldog blowing his nose into a large red hanky.

She took one last look at Calculus, now holding hands with Verity, and then turned away quickly. She accepted a boost up from Sid to get to the tiny space in the wall, then squeezed her head into the hole and began to drag her body forward over the pipes, crawling, inch by inch, away from the chamber.

CHAPTER 29

THE CONDUITS

The climb was incredibly hard going. The narrow space was so tight that India could not lift her head or turn it around and the roof scratched her back as she dragged herself along. Only the pencil-thin beam from Verity's pocket torch showed the tunnel ahead. Sid grunted and cursed behind her.

'You OK back there?' she called, after they had gone some distance.

'Don't worry none about me,' he replied from the darkness. 'Just watch out for yourself. I don't want to find no corpse blocking my way.'

'Charming,' she replied.

They crawled on in silence through the freezing water. India struggled to keep out the thought that a sudden surge might drown them both in the narrow space. After fifty yards or so they came to a junction box where the tunnel met several others. A single shaft rose vertically from the junction and more freezing water cascaded down it. India crawled from the narrow pipe and stood beneath the deluge.

'Looks like this shaft goes all the way to the next level,' said Sid. 'Let's start climbing, that lake must be melting good and fast and I don't reckon much on getting drowned like a rat in a pipe.'

No sooner had he spoken than there was a rumble from somewhere deep within the tunnels. White water began to gush from the pipe around Sid's feet.

'Get up there quick!' he shouted above the roar.

India scrambled up the pipes, trying to stay ahead of the foaming waters, with Sid close behind. The shaft seemed to be never-ending, her lungs burned and her arms trembled as she tried to pull herself up.

Just when she thought she could climb no further, the torch picked out a reflective surface above them. She pulled herself quickly up the last few feet but her elation turned to despair. A heavy steel grille was fastened across the top of the shaft and secured with a padlock. She rattled desperately at the metal. Sid bobbed up beside her but even with both of them pulling, the grille wouldn't move an inch. The water rose around their shoulders; in a moment, it would be over their heads.

'What are we going to do?' she said, her voice cracking with fear.

Sid kept clinging to the grille with one hand and pulled out his pistol with the other. 'Better hope the cartridges aren't wet,' he said, pressing the barrel of the gun against the padlock. The gun clicked and nothing happened. 'Damn thing's soaked through,' he said. He pulled the trigger again.

A deafening blast filled the tiny space and the padlock snicked away with a singing noise. Sid pushed open the grille and they dragged themselves on to a concrete floor where they lay spluttering as the water bubbled out of the shaft around them.

'That was quick thinking,' said India between coughs.

'Slow thinking gets you dead,' he grunted.

'What I meant,' she said, sitting up, 'was thank you for saving my life.'

He glanced at her and gave the briefest of nods. 'Weren't nothing.'

The shaft had brought them to a narrow service corridor, filled with pipes and multicoloured cables. The corridor was too low to stand up in but it felt spacious compared to the conduit.

'Which way to the control room, d'you reckon?' he said.

She shrugged. 'My guess would be the one with the most cables. Let's try that way.'

'Are you sure about that?' he said, squinting into the darkness.

'No. I'm just making an educated guess. For all I know it leads to the Commanding Officer's personal toilet!'

Sid looked at her for a moment, then unexpectedly his frown evaporated and he broke into a huge grin. 'Damn!' he laughed. 'Wouldn't that be a bummer?'

'You should do that more often,' she said, laughing too. 'You wouldn't be half as scary if you did.'

They followed the tunnel until they found a glimmer of light from a ventilation grille near the floor. It was rotten with rust and India kicked it out easily. She squeezed through the vent and lowered herself gently to the floor. Sid followed her and collapsed into an undignified pile, cursing and spitting.

They had landed in a small storeroom. The door was locked but a single kick from Sid sent it bursting from its hinges. Once outside, they made their way along an anonymous-looking corridor and through a final set of doors to find themselves standing again in the great turbine hall. They stared at the vast space for a moment, then India whooped for joy.

'We did it, Sid! We made it!' she cried.

They hugged each other ecstatically, then realized what they were doing and jumped apart with embarrassed smiles.

The hall was silent, except for the humming of the turbine and the giant steel doors that stood open to the bitter night. The missile racks were empty and the warheads were gone, save for one that sat like a sarcophagus in the middle of the floor. A cable attached to its nose ran across the floor. They followed it up the steps to the control room where it disappeared into one of the metal cabinets.

'Can't we jus' pull it out?' said Sid, scratching his head.

'Verity said it didn't work like that. We need to find the

fail-safe to switch it off. There should be two buttons or switches, some distance apart.'

'Like them?'

He pointed to two small panels at opposite ends of the control desk, painted with red and yellow warning stripes. There was an empty silver keyhole in the centre of each one.

'Yes!' said India. She looked around the room. 'The keys have to be in here somewhere.'

They scoured the control room with increasing urgency. India was just about ready to sit down and cry when Sid upended a waste basket in frustration and two silver keys on short lengths of chain clattered across the floor. He tossed one to India and they stood ready at each end of the control desk.

'They need to be turned at the exact same time,' said India. 'Ready? Go!'

The keys would not turn.

Sid let out a cry of anguish and drew his gun. 'A pox on this, I'm going out there to put a bullet through that damned bomb.'

'Calm down, Sid,' she said. 'We've just got the wrong keys. Here, take this one.'

The keys crossed in the air and they tried them again. This time they both turned with a click. They looked at each other expectantly. A buzzer sounded, making them both jump, and a green light glowed on the control desk. Sid broke into a grin. 'Hot damn, we did it!' He punched the air. 'We shut that damn thing off!'

India was busy unfastening Calculus's bracelet. 'I need to speak to Calc,' she said. 'I have to tell him it's safe.' She pressed the little button on the side of the bracelet but all she got was static hiss. 'I guess all this electrical stuff is interfering with it. Let's try outside.'

They clambered back down the steps to the turbine hall and skirted around the dead missile as though it might bite them. The body of the guard shot by Stone was still lying on the floor.

Sid pulled the blood-soaked jacket from the body and offered it to India. 'You want this?' he said. 'It could be pretty cold out there.'

She shuddered and shook her head. Sid shrugged and put it on himself. Then they walked out through the hangar doors to stand on the hillside overlooking the lake. The night air stung like sharpened steel and a billion stars glittered and whirled above their heads. But when she looked up, the night sky struck terror into India's heart. High above them was the brightest star she had ever seen, larger than the moon and shining with an intense white light, shot through with streaks of red and blue.

'It's Nibiru,' she said breathlessly. 'The asteroid is here already.' They watched the gleaming apparition hanging silently above them like a sword, neither of them speaking. With shaking fingers she tried the bracelet again but it returned only more hissing. 'I need to get further away from the turbine hall,' she said.

But Sid was not listening to her. He was staring out over

the lake and the look of cold hatred had returned to his hard, bony features.

A short way down the hill were the unmistakable shapes of two rigs, black and gleaming in the starlight, rolling carefully down the slope. Now India could hear the sound of their engines carrying faintly on the breeze.

'It's the *Ice Queen* . . . and the *Prince of Darkness*,' he said between clenched teeth. 'My pa's rig.' His whole body quivered with anger as he watched the rigs roll away.

India touched his arm gently. 'Forget about him, Sid,' she said. 'He can't hurt you any more. Why don't you just let him go?'

He shook her arm away. 'I'm not letting that dog get away,' he said spitting on the ground. 'He murdered my ma, the sweetest woman that ever lived, and he told me it was pirates that done it.' He pulled out his pistol. 'Well, now I'm going to get him if it's the last thing I ever do.'

'We've got more important things to do, Sid. The asteroid is nearly here and I need to get Calc to tell the machine.'

'No!' He turned on her. 'If that ancient machine goes off now it'll blast everything on this mountain, including him!' He pointed to the receding rigs. 'Then I won't never get a chance to get even. You're not taking that away from me, India Bentley. Do you hear? Never!'

As quick as a snake his hand darted out and he snatched the bracelet from her grasp. Then he was off and running down the slope towards the rig, leaving her gasping in horror.

'Sid!' she called after him. 'Come back, we need that bracelet!'

In desperation she looked up at the asteroid, and then at the receding figure of Sid. Before she had time to think about what she was doing, she began to run down the slope after him.

CHAPTER 30

OUTSIDE

Verity leaned against the tunnel wall and closed her eyes. They had been crawling on their hands and knees for over an hour now and the effort had taken its toll on all of them. John Bentley crouched beside her and offered her some water, which she drank gratefully.

'How are you doing?' he said.

'I'm about done for after the last few days. Stone's men aren't exactly the best of hosts but it's the Captain I'm worried about.'

Bulldog sat a short way off with his eyes closed. His breath came in rattling gasps.

'He's too heavy to carry,' said Bentley. 'We could really use your android about now.' Verity turned away. 'I'm sorry,' he said, noting the pain on her face. 'That was insensitive of me.'

'It's OK,' she said. 'Calculus knew what he was doing. I think staying behind with the machine was what he wanted

271

more than anything else. I'll miss him though. We were together for a long time.'

Bentley nodded. 'Siberia is a hard place and I've lost a lot of good friends out here.' He looked at Clench, who was counting a stack of coins. 'And some of them I've lost because of that miserable creature over there. When we get back I'm going to see to it that he gets brought to justice.' He rubbed his palms over his face. 'If we ever get back.'

'Don't worry,' said Verity. 'If anyone can shut down that bomb it's India. She's as tough as old boots!' She laughed. 'I guess she takes after her old man.'

'That's what I'm most worried about.' Bentley smiled. He turned and sniffed the air. 'Can you smell that? It smells like . . . pine needles.'

'It must be the end of the tunnel,' said Verity. 'Come on, we'll be out of here in no time.'

On the other side of the lake, India ran down the hill towards the two rigs, cursing at Sid as she went. A low cliff ran along one side of the track and Sid sprinted along the top of it, looking down on the rigs for an opportunity to leap.

A door opened on the upper deck and a crewman looked out. Without a moment's hesitation, Sid leaped from the rocks and crashed down on top of the man, pinning him to the deck. Seconds later, India arrived at the edge, but pulled up sharply. It was a fifteen-foot drop on to the icy deck and the rig was rolling past steadily. In another few moments it would be out of reach.

Taking a deep breath she leaped into the darkness and crashed into the deck, crying out as a white-hot pain spiked through her twisted knee. She climbed to her feet and limped down the walkway to where Sid sat astride the helpless crewman, holding the gun to his head.

'How many?' said Sid through gritted teeth. 'How many are in there?'

'At least fifteen down below and another twelve on the *Ice Queen*,' sneered the grizzled old veteran. 'Plenty enough to kill you, boy. Though when your pa finds out you're still alive I reckon he'll want to take care of you personally, just like he did that ma of yours.'

Sid's eyes bulged and before India could stop him, he brought his pistol down on the man's skull with a dull crack. He climbed from the man's unconscious body and made for the open door.

'Sid, wait,' said India, struggling to catch up with him. 'You have to give me the bracelet.' He ignored her and disappeared inside the rig. Once again, she had no choice but to follow him.

Verity Brown and John Bentley helped a haggard-looking Captain Bulldog from the tunnel. They found themselves on the far side of the lake, at the edge of a forest.

Verity laughed out loud for sheer joy. 'It's so good to be out of that damned hole,' she said. 'Remind me never to go in any abandoned treasure caves ever again.'

Bentley was making Bulldog comfortable against a rock.

'Don't celebrate just yet,' he said. 'We've got company.'

Several dark, ghostly figures were moving through the trees, trailing wisps of greyness.

Bentley picked up a fallen branch. 'Get moving,' he said. 'I'll hold them off as best I can.'

'I don't think we need to,' said Verity. 'Look.'

The Valleymen were moving erratically through the trees. Their dark bodies seemed paler and more transparent than before, and they shrank back from the humans like timid animals. In a few moments the last of them had melted back into the trees.

'What was *that* all about?' said Verity.

'Perhaps that's the answer,' said Bentley, pointing at the brilliant sight of Nibiru in the skies above them.

'The asteroid,' said Verity under her breath. 'Is that why the Valleymen are retreating?'

'Who knows?' said Bentley. 'But I think we should get moving in case they decide to come back again.'

'Good idea,' she said. 'Mr Clench, will you give us a hand to—'

She stopped abruptly. Thaddeus Clench was standing ten feet away, holding a small, silver pistol. 'Just how dumb did you think old Thaddeus was, eh?' he sneered. 'You didn't think I was just going to let you to turn me in, did you? I've got very good hearing, you know, and I never go anywhere without this trinket in my boot.'

'You won't get far,' said Bentley. 'Sooner or later they'll find you.'

Clench laughed again. 'You were good enough to tell me where you kept your snow vehicle.' He chuckled. 'So I might get further than you think. Now then, Mr Bentley, I'll have those seeds of yours before I go, please.'

Bentley clutched the bag closer. 'For God's sake, man!' he said. 'These seeds are for the benefit of humanity. You've already got your gold, what could you possibly want these for?'

'Profit, Mr Bentley,' he said, holding out his hand for the bag. 'Food is scarce and I know people who will pay top money to have control of the world's food supplies. So hand them over or Mrs Brown gets it.'

John Bentley paused, then held up his hands. 'Wait, Thaddeus, don't do this. Hasn't there been enough destruction and violence? These seeds could mean an end to years of misery. And think about it. Whoever brings them back will be a hero.'

Clench looked at him suspiciously. 'What you saying?'

'I'm saying if you help me to bring them back to London I'll see you get the credit for it. You can live out your days as "*The Man Who Saved the World from Starvation*". Isn't that better, Thaddeus? Wouldn't you rather be loved than be rich?'

Clench looked confused. He licked his lips and long seconds ticked by. 'People would love me?'

'Yes,' said Bentley. 'They'd be eternally grateful to you for what you'd done. These seeds are more important than any amount of gold.'

Clench snapped back to attention. 'Of course, the gold! That's what this is really about,' he hissed, his eyes narrowing. 'You want my gold! You nearly had me believing you there with all your talk of "being loved". But I'm not buying any of it, see! Money is the only certainty in life, Bentley, if you don't have that then you've got nothing. So I'm going to take those seeds and I'm going to sell them to the highest bidder. I'll die a rich man while you starve in your mud hole.'

He darted forward and snatched the bag from Bentley's shoulder and then, with a triumphant cackle, fled through the trees at a sprint. Bentley started after him but Verity grabbed his arm. 'Let him go. I need your help with the Captain.'

'But I have to go after him,' he said desperately. 'Those seeds could save millions of lives.'

'And who's going to save us?' she snapped. 'Maybe you haven't been keeping up with current events but this whole area is about to become toast. Our priorities are to find India and then get out of here.'

'And how are we going to get away if Clench takes the snow vehicle?' said Bentley. 'Do you really want to walk through five hundred miles of wilderness?'

'Shut up, both of you and listen to me!' Bulldog had hauled himself painfully up on one elbow. 'The Beautiful Game is on its way here, but Tashar won't wait around for long. We need to build a fire so they can spot us.'

'A pirate rig?' said Verity. 'You don't really expect them to keep their word, do you?'

'There's honour among riggers, Mrs Brown,' said Bulldog solemnly. 'Our word is our bond. And besides,' he added, 'I told them if they came I'd make 'em rich.'

CHAPTER 31

THE *PRINCE OF DARKNESS*

The engine room of the *Prince of Darkness* was larger than the one on *The Beautiful Game*. The floor was clean, the pistons gleamed under a slick layer of oil and the polished brass gauges flickered obediently in the half-light.

Sid stood by the door checking his pistol. He looked up as India came in.

'Give me that bracelet,' she said impatiently.

'Not until I've taken care of my pa,' he said, baring his teeth.

'What are you planning to do?'

He looked at her blankly as though he had not thought this far ahead. 'He'll be up on the main deck,' he said. 'I'll run in there and put a bullet between his eyes before they can stop me. I reckon I can take two or three of them with me besides.'

'And then what? They'll just shoot you down where you stand.' She looked around the engine room until she found what she was looking for. 'There's a better way to stop him, Sid. Look!' She went to the instrument panel on the opposite wall where a row of brass dials showed readings for engine temperature and oil pressure. Underneath were four large valves. 'Pieter once told me these valves would shut off the coolant system. He said any rig would blow sky high if you turned them off. I don't want anyone to get killed if I can help it but then again, millions of people could die if your father takes those missiles back to Angel Town.'

Sid looked thoughtful and then nodded. 'OK, as long as it takes out my pa, then do it!' he said.

The valves were made of heavy brass and terminated in a red wheel the size of India's hand. Sid watched the door while she shut off the first one. The needle on the gauge began to drop.

'Get on with it!' he hissed. 'Shut 'em all down.'

She closed the second and the third valves but the last one was stiff and caked with grease. He tutted impatiently and crossed the room to help her.

'Get a lever,' he said, pointing to a rack of engineer's spanners on the wall behind her.

She reached for a spanner and turned back just in time to see the door swing open and the bulky figure of Lucifer Stone step into the room. He took in the scene and let out a howl of rage.

Sid's reactions were fast. He reached for his gun but a massive hand dealt him a crushing blow and he collapsed into a corner like a wet shirt. India tried to heft the spanner at Stone's head but he swatted it away and a blow across her cheek made her teeth rattle. Before she could regain her senses, Stone had grabbed her by the throat with both hands. She struggled to get away, but his meaty fingers were clamped tightly around her neck. A sound like rushing water grew in her ears and her vision began to go black around the edges. Suddenly the relentless pressure around her neck stopped and India fell choking to the floor.

Stone had dropped to his knees, clutching the back of his head, and Sid was standing behind him, holding the engineer's spanner. Stone looked up in surprise but, as he opened his mouth to speak, Sid brought the spanner crashing down for a second time on his father's temple and his head hit the deck with a metallic clang.

They stood over the slumped figure, watching a thick, crimson puddle form on the deck-plates.

'I think you killed him, Sid,' said India in a hushed voice.

Sid said nothing; he just clutched the spanner tightly and stared down at the body with wide eyes. They were jolted back to life by a sharp explosion as one of the pressure gauges burst, releasing a rush of steam and sending shards of glass across the room.

'Sid!' she croaked, shaking him out of his daze. 'This engine could blow up at any moment. Come on, we have to get off.'

Sid tore his gaze away from the body and crossed to the cabin door, jamming the spanner in the locking wheel. They left the engine room together and stood outside on the main deck, where India gasped at the bitterness of the wind. The *Prince of Darkness* had reached the lake and was picking up speed as it rumbled across the ice in tandem with the *Ice Queen*. Sid led India to a small gantry that stuck out beyond the thundering caterpillar tracks and allowed for a clear jump to the ice fifteen feet below. He turned to her with a strange look in his eyes and thrust the bracelet into her hands.

'When you get down there, you start running,' he shouted over the engines. 'You find your friends and you get the hell away from this place.'

'Sid, what are you talking about?' she said. 'We can both get off this rig.'

He shook his head. 'There ain't no place for me now my pa's dead. There's nothing I know how to do except his killing and now he's dead I'm no use to no one. I'll just stay here until it's over.'

'That's crazy! You don't need to die. Captain Bulldog, Verity, my dad, they could all help you.'

He shook his head. 'Your Mrs Brown was right,' he said. 'You don't want nothing to do with me. I'm just a stone-cold killer and I'm never going to change.'

'Everyone can change, Sid,' she said. 'Look at Calculus. It doesn't matter what anyone expects of you, you can always change yourself. But you've got to want to make it happen.'

He looked at her strangely, as though unable to find the right words, and for a moment she saw the lost boy again.

'Do you think I really could?' he said. 'Do you think I could change things?'

She opened her mouth to answer but the words froze on her lips. The grotesque figure of Lucifer Stone loomed from the engine room behind them. His face was a mask of blood, his ear was torn away and his hair stuck out in clotted streaks. He looked like a creature escaped from hell.

Stone grasped Sid by his collar and jerked him off his feet. Sid wriggled out of the jacket and scrambled across the deck towards India. 'India, get away from here!' he shouted. 'Get away and run as fast as you can.'

Before she could react he shoved her in the chest with both hands and she sailed backwards off the gantry. She landed with a blow that knocked all the air from her body, and struck the back of her head on the ice.

The two rigs continued on their way, rolling relentlessly across the ice. High up on the deck of the *Prince of Darkness* she could see two figures locked in a mortal struggle in the moonlight: the huge frame of Stone and the slight figure of Sid, flailing and clawing at his father as though all the rage in the world were pouring out of him.

She called out to Sid, but her words were carried away on the wind. The battling figures stumbled through the open hatchway and disappeared from view. She scrambled to her feet and began to hobble after the rig but she had not gone more than ten paces when the *Prince of Darkness* exploded in a ball of flame.

A blast of heat and air knocked her off her feet once again. Then came the noise. A great, roaring, metallic explosion that sent tongues of flame high into the air and hurled pieces of burning wreckage across the ice. One of the giant caterpillar tracks broke and unravelled, bringing the big rig to a shuddering halt.

There was a moment of complete stillness before the ice splintered into huge triangular shards and the *Prince of Darkness* pitched violently into the lake in a cloud of steam and foaming water. The *Ice Queen* revved her engines and tried desperately to reverse away but there was no escape from the shattered surface and it too plunged into the icy depths after its sister, carrying its deadly cargo to the bottom of the lake.

India's ears rang in the silence and she stared at the great hole in the ice for a long time before her body began to shiver uncontrollably. Her long underwear was frozen to her skin and she felt more intensely cold than she had ever felt in her life.

There was something she was meant to do now, she felt sure of it, but she could not quite remember what it was. It was getting difficult to make her legs obey and she weaved a ragged line across the ice towards the shore. She threw back her head to gulp the night air and it made her feel better. She didn't feel so cold now; in fact she felt pleasantly warm and sleepy. It would be just perfect, she thought, if she could lay down here and watch that beautiful star overhead while she waited for sleep.

'*Remember your duty, soul voyager!*'

She opened her eyes again. Nibiru hung in the sky above her like a giant locomotive bearing down on the world, filling the night with its deadly brilliance. Then she saw the bracelet in her hand and remembered her friend who was waiting for a message from her. She held the communicator and pressed the button with fingers that were numb and lifeless. There was a brief crackle of static and then a familiar rich tone sounded over the speaker.

'India?'

'Hello, Calc,' she said in a whisper. 'It's good news. We stopped the bomb, you can tell the machine that it's safe.'

There was a brief pause before he replied. 'I knew you could do it.'

He sounded vague and distant.

'Calc, I don't want you to die,' she said.

There was a long pause at the other end.

'I am not afraid of dying, India,' he said. 'Because now I have a heart. Thanks to you.'

She gave a faint smile. 'Just like the Tin Man,' she said.

The pause grew longer.

'I'll never forget you, Calc,' she said.

'Then once again, I have become immortal.'

'Goodbye, Calc.'

'Goodbye, India.'

The line went dead. The tiredness was overwhelming and she closed her eyes, feeling the silence wash over her.

She didn't notice the movement in the trees or the spindly figure that dashed across the ice towards her.

Clench smiled thinly to himself as he approached the girl lying on the ice and grasped her by the arm.

'Got you, you little witch!' he said.

CHAPTER 32

THE PILLAR OF FLAME

Clench dragged India across the ice towards a paint-blistered boathouse on the beach. She tried to put up a struggle but the intense cold had penetrated her bones and her limbs would not work properly.

'Thought you'd get the better of old Thaddeus,' he muttered, half to himself. 'You'd all have given me up the moment we got back to Angel Town, wouldn't you? Well I've got news for you, missy. You and me are taking that snow vehicle across the border to China where I intend to live very well indeed.' He patted his shoulder bags, which made a dull chinking noise.

'Wh-why are you doing th-this?' she stammered. 'Why don't you just take the gold and go?'

'Why?' He stopped dragging her for a moment. 'Payback of course, for all the time I spent running and hiding and having to be pleasant to that revolting old trollop Roshanne. Not to mention being humiliated by a spoilt brat like you.'

As he spoke there was another earth tremor, a strong one that shook the mountains and dislodged large rocks from the cliff face.

India noticed that there was water flowing freely beneath the surface of the ice. 'Thaddeus! The ice is too thin here, it isn't safe.'

'Your tricks won't work on me. Nothing's going to get in the way of my plans now.' He pulled her closer and felt a strand of her hair between his fingers. 'Oh yes,' he murmured. 'You'll fetch a good price in the flesh markets of New Peking. Before long you'll look back on my offer of marriage and wish you'd taken it when you had the chance.'

She tried to pound him with her fists but he just laughed at her. Before he realized what was happening she had slipped her hand into his pocket and pulled out one of the gold ingots. Summoning every ounce of strength she had left, she hefted the bar in a wide arc at the side of his head. If it had connected it would surely have knocked him out cold, but it didn't.

Clench stepped nimbly out of the way and laughed pitilessly. 'Is that it?' he sneered. 'Is that the best you've got? This is going to be easier than I thought.'

She leaned on her knees for support. 'I'm not afraid of you,' she gasped. 'You're just a bully.'

He looked taken aback. 'What did you call me?'

'You're only brave when you can make other people scared of you, people who are smaller and weaker than

287

you are. But whenever you're not in control you're just a snivelling little creep!'

His eyes narrowed. 'I'm in control now though, aren't I?' he said. He pulled the silver pistol from his pocket. 'So you'd better do what I say, India Bentley, and *give me back my gold*.'

She looked at the gun and knew there was nothing else left to do. She held out the ingot and he grinned, showing his yellow teeth. But as he reached for it, she let it slip from her fingers. It fell in slow motion, tumbling end over end before passing straight through the frozen surface of the lake like a cricket ball through a pane of glass. The thin ice immediately caved inward and they both plunged into the black water. Panic consumed her as the raw, biting waters closed over her head and the freezing pain took hold of her. She burst back to the surface, flailing and gasping for breath.

'I can't swim,' squealed Clench. He thrashed around the frozen pool, churning the waters to foam and grasping at the brittle edges of the ice.

'Thaddeus!' she shouted. 'Stop panicking and drop those bags. The gold is dragging you down.'

'Never. It's mine. I'm never letting it go, never!'

He lunged forward and wrapped his arms tightly around her in an attempt to stay afloat. She tried to scream but the water rushed into her mouth as she was dragged under. Her lungs heaved desperately for air and when she opened her eyes she could see the bright light of the ice hole receding above them.

Just as quickly, the panic left her, to be replaced by a sense of deep calm. She no longer cared that they were sinking or that Clench was still clutching her tightly. Even dying didn't seem so bad.

'*Be awake, India.*' Nentu's voice was close by and harsh.

India closed her eyes and tried to ignore it. 'I have to go now,' she said in her mind.

'*You do not have the luxury of dying. You are a soul voyager.*'

'I can't be a soul voyager any more,' she said listlessly.

'*You still have work to do, soul voyager, and now is not your time to die. Before this story is over it will take you to the ends of the earth. Then you will really know what it is to face death.*'

The severity of Nentu's voice disturbed her sense of peace and she tried to push it away. But at the very moment she thought she was about to die, there came a tug at the back of her shirt and she found herself being hauled back to the surface. She slipped free of Clench's grasp, bringing one of his bags with her as she was pulled from the sinister waters. She burst back into the light as though being reborn.

Pain reawakened her desperation to survive. She clawed at the brittle edges of the hole and through sheer force of will, pulled herself on to the ice, dragging the bag after her. She looked around to see who had pulled her out but there was no one there. She was alone.

A sudden bump beneath her made her look down and she recoiled from the terror-struck face of Thaddeus Clench, trapped beneath the ice, his face contorted into a soundless scream. She watched in horror as he slid slowly along the underside of the ice until his body was finally dragged down into the blue depths.

'Rich for the rest of your life,' she murmured.

By now her body was drained of any last dregs of energy. She collapsed on to the frozen lake and stared up at the glittering jewel of Nibiru, shot through with the colours of a diamond. It no longer seemed threatening: it was beautiful. She closed her eyes.

Time passed; she wasn't sure how long. But then, once again, her peacefulness was disturbed. Someone was shaking her and calling her name.

'India, can you hear me? Please speak to me.'

She looked up into intense blue eyes that mirrored her own.

'Dad?' She could see he was weeping.

'I was afraid I'd lost you.' He clutched her tightly and shouted to someone unseen. 'She's here, come quickly.'

And then there was another noise, a fierce rumbling that vibrated the ground, accompanied by an acrid smell. Her eyelids flickered and she caught a glimpse of something large and familiar. A battered white hulk, crashing its way through the trees towards them, tracks biting deeply into the snow.

She remembered the rest in bursts of images. There was more shouting, people crowded around her, then she was lifted up and wrapped in something warm.

'India, don't go to sleep!'

Something vaporous was held under her nose and her

eyes popped open. She winced under the bright cabin lights and the harsh noises that crashed in on her. 'Dad?' she murmured again.

'Right here, sweetheart,' said Bentley. 'You're safe now.'

Verity's face moved into view. 'Well done, kid,' she said. 'I knew you'd make it. Did you . . .' Her voice dropped. 'Did you speak to Calculus?'

She nodded weakly. 'Where are we?' she said.

'You're on *The Beautiful Game*,' said Verity. 'I don't know how Bulldog managed it but they got here just in time.'

Bulldog appeared with his arm in a sling. The colour had returned to his face as though he was drawing energy from his beloved rig, and he wore an ear-to-ear grin. 'Never underestimate the Captain, ladies. I've always got a plan, me.'

India sat up painfully. Now she was back in the warmth, her hands and feet felt like they were on fire and her knee was sending bolts of pain up her leg.

Tashar stuck her head out of the cockpit and gave India a cursory nod. 'We're not out of the woods yet, Captain,' she said. 'Rat says the seismic readings have gone off the scale. Something huge is happening right underneath our feet. And the lake – it seems to be draining away.'

From the window they could see the water level in the lake had dropped and the icy surface was now thin and translucent. Wisps of steam curled into the air.

'It's starting!' said Bulldog. 'Better get moving, we don't want to be anywhere near that machine when it goes off.'

'Machine? What machine?' said Tashar. 'What have you got us into now?'

'I'll explain later,' he said with a grin. 'Right now we need to make some distance, Tash. My guess is this whole area will be completely devastated in about, ooh I dunno, ten minutes?'

Tashar's eyes widened. 'My God, Bulldog,' she said. 'You are a total madman. We should never have come back here for your crazy ass!' She fled to the cockpit.

'Er, that's *Captain* Bulldog to you,' he called after her.

The giant engines fired up and Tashar twirled the rig expertly on its tracks. She pressed on the drive levers and they leaped forward up the forested slopes. *The Beautiful Game* carved a straight line up the mountainside, cutting a deep swathe through young pine trunks, and the deck-plates rattled and groaned as though they would shake apart. But as they ploughed up the mountain they became aware of another, more powerful vibration that could be felt over the roar of the engines. It was like a surge of energy deep in the earth that peaked and died away like a giant pulse that was getting faster and faster.

'Step on it, Tashar,' shouted Bulldog. 'Give it everything she's got.'

'What do you think I'm doing?' she yelled back. 'Taking in the damned scenery?'

India shrugged off her blanket and limped to the window. Outside the sky had turned black and thin, with silvery clouds forming concentric circles over the lake. A great booming filled the air and a crack ran down the hillside like a tear in a sheet of paper. The water had completely drained from the lake now, leaving a circular pit that glowed with a ghostly blue light.

'Make for the ridge,' shouted Bulldog as they neared the top of the slope. 'Get the mountain between us and that damned lake.'

The glow brightened and a vast pillar of blue energy began to rise from the pit carrying a white sphere on its summit that pulsed and arced like the cauldron in the cavern. A monstrous howl filled the air, drowning out the engines and making them press their hands over their ears. As *The Beautiful Game* crested the ridge, India looked back to catch a last glimpse of the brilliant sphere, spinning rapidly on top of a flaming blue column a hundred feet high. She thought the noise of it alone might split the world in two.

'It's going to blow!' shouted Bulldog. 'Brace yourselves!'

At that very moment, in a chamber deep beneath the ground, the android stood alone before the machine, bathed in its intense white light as he reached out his hand to touch it. And, in the instant before the energy field vaporized him in a flash of radiation, he was joined with the ancient machine and all the knowledge of other worlds filled his mind.

'My God!' was all he said.

And then he was gone.

CHAPTER 33

THE PRAYING TREES

For a moment, the cabin of *The Beautiful Game* was filled with a brilliant white light that bleached all the colour from the room. An instant later a colossal explosion lifted the rig high into the air and flung it back down with a crash that shattered windows, burst deck-plates and broke open steam pipes. The crew tumbled around inside the broken rig like dolls in a box, and India pressed her hands over her ears as the almighty noise seemed to roll on and on.

Gradually the roar diminished. An uneasy silence fell over the rig, save for the hiss of escaping steam. India brushed away the debris as the others picked themselves out of the mess of glass and splintered furniture.

'Bit of a nasty bump back there,' said Bulldog, clambering from the cockpit. 'Everyone still in one piece?'

Miraculously, no one was injured save for a few minor cuts and bruises, but Tashar climbed from the cockpit with a face like thunder. 'Damn it, Bulldog!' she yelled. 'What have you done to my rig?'

'Not yours yet, Tash,' he said, 'we had a deal, remember?'

'Which you haven't kept.'

'In good time,' he said casually. 'Well, that thing certainly went off with a pop. Shall we have a look around outside?'

The nose of the rig was buried in a mound of snow and rock and the forward doors were jammed shut. They followed Bulldog through the tangle of wires and pipes to the rear hatch, where he had to apply all of his weight to the door to shift the debris behind it. One at a time, they squeezed through the narrow gap and stood on the top deck in awed silence.

The clouds had cleared and the scene was lit by the sharp silver light of the moon. In the valley below, the lake had been completely gouged out as though by a giant hand. The steep sides of the crater dropped away into a vast black pit and the meltwaters ran over the sides in gushing waterfalls, sending clouds of steam into the night air. Most astonishing of all, every tree in the valley, and for as far as the eye could see, had been knocked flat, each one perfectly aligned with the direction of the blast so that they looked to India like praying multitudes, honouring the spot where the great machine had been beneath the ice.

'Look,' said Verity. 'The asteroid, it's gone.'

Nibiru had disappeared and in its place a million tiny

shooting stars streaked across the sky from horizon to horizon.

'Very pretty,' said Tashar drily. 'But what exactly do we have to show for all of this, Captain? You promised that if we met you here you would make us rich or the rig would be ours. A rigger's promise! Now all I can see is a wrecked rig and no money.'

'Have a bit more faith, Tashar,' he said, grinning.

He pulled something heavy from inside his coat and two enormous gold ingots dropped with a resounding clang on to the deck, where they gleamed dully in the moonlight. They crowded around the treasure and Rat let out a low whistle.

'Holy mother of all riggers,' said Tashar. 'There's enough gold there to buy three new rigs.'

'This one will fix up just fine,' said Bulldog. 'And afterwards we'll split what's left between all of us – including you too, ladies,' he said to India and Verity.

'Wait a minute,' said Verity. 'That gold must weigh forty pounds. Was that in your pockets all the time we were carrying you around down there?'

Bulldog looked sheepish. 'Yeah, well, I never quite found the right moment to tell you.' He broke into another grin. 'Come on, we've got a bit of clearing up to do.'

Sometime later, India sat wrapped in a blanket on the top deck of *The Beautiful Game*, watching Bulldog build a fire in an upturned oil drum. Tashar and Rat were inside, fixing the heating with some well-meaning advice from India's father, and Verity was investigating the galley.

'What will happen now?' she asked him. 'Do you think the crew will stay?'

Bulldog looked serious as he stared into the flames. 'Difficult to say,' he said eventually, 'but Tashar's not nearly as hard-nosed as she makes out and Rat's pretty much family. So my guess is we'll all be back next season after the money's gone, looking for something to turn up.' Then he grinned. 'And you know me, something always turns up.'

After he had gone to check on the repairs, Verity returned from the galley and gave India a mug of hot milk with some of Bulldog's chocolate grated on top. India sipped it gratefully.

'How did you manage to live with these people?' said Verity, holding out her hands to the fire. 'Bulldog's barking orders like a madman, Tashar keeps looking at me as though I'd crawled out from under a rock, and Rat is showing your dad his collection of pressure gauges.'

India grinned. 'Oh dear, do I need to go and rescue him?'

'No, you're all right,' said Verity. 'Actually I think he's quite interested.'

India giggled and clapped her hand over her mouth. Then they both convulsed with laughter until the tears rolled down their cheeks.

'It's a total mess down there,' said Verity when she had recovered. 'Bulldog's pretty confident he'll have it in some sort of working order by morning, although, to tell you the truth, I think Rat's the one doing all the hard work.'

They gazed at the fire for a while.

'What do you think you'll do when you get home?' said Verity.

India shrugged. 'I'm looking forward to spending some time with my dad and Bella.' She grinned. 'I think we'll both have some great stories to tell her. But, after that I don't really know. Maybe I'll buy that scav-boat and see if I can dredge up any interesting old-tech.' She looked down at the lake crater. 'Although anything I find is going to seem a bit tame after all this.'

Verity nodded knowingly and they fell quiet again. 'You really did it, India,' she said after a while. 'You saved all of us.'

India smiled. 'Not just me,' she said. 'You, me, Bulldog . . . even Sid. It was down to all of us in the end.' She stroked the dull steel bracelet on her wrist. 'And Calc of course.'

They looked up as a solitary shooting star streaked its way across the sky and fell to Earth.

CHAPTER 34

ON LONDON SHORES

It was the first day of May when the ancient motorcycle and sidecar pulled up to the top of the hill overlooking Highgate Village. The three passengers stretched their limbs and looked down on the smoky stone cottages where the junk piles gleamed in the late afternoon sun and long shadows crept across the grass. A small crowd gathered at the bottom of the hill and began to point up at them.

'I never thought of this place as beautiful,' said John Bentley. 'Functional maybe, but never beautiful. But there were times, under that wretched mountain, when I longed to see Highgate again.'

India smiled and put an arm around his shoulder, and Bentley was struck by how much taller she had become. Several weeks of Mrs Chang's home cooking had put some muscle back on her bones, her limp was mostly gone, and she looked strong, lean and brown-skinned. And there was something different about her eyes.

'Mrs Brown,' he said, 'thank you for everything you've done.'

'The thanks go to India,' said Verity. 'There wouldn't be much of anything left if it hadn't been for her.'

'If you don't mind, India,' he said, 'I think I'd better go on to the house first. Roshanne and I are going to have a serious discussion.' He grinned. 'Mostly about where she's going to live from now on.'

They all laughed.

'Any ideas what you're going to do now, John?' said Verity. 'Will you go back to the oil fields?'

He shook his head. 'No, I'm finally done with that,' he said, patting his shoulder sack. 'After India rescued these seeds, I knew I had the chance to do some good here. I'm going to become a farmer. I'll use the spare land around here for fields, and we'll grow the crops with the highest yields. In no time we'll be able to feed everyone on these shores, northsider and southsider alike.'

'I'm not sure what Mehmet will have to say about that,' said India.

'Don't worry about him,' said Bentley. 'He's thrown his weight around for too long and the position of constable is overdue for re-election. I might even decide to stand myself.'

Verity and John Bentley shook hands, then he walked down the hill, raising his hand in salute as he went. As he reached the village a small, golden-haired figure broke away from the crowd and ran towards him with a squeal that could be heard all the way to the top of the hill.

John Bentley lifted Bella on to his shoulders and the crowd gathered around them. India smiled – she couldn't wait to see Bella again – but for now that time belonged to her father. Then India's eyes were drawn to a wild-haired creature sitting alone on the earthworks. As usual, no one was paying much attention to Cromerty, but the old woman was staring at India with an intensity she had felt once before, in a tent in a far-off land. India raised her hand in a half-wave and the old woman nodded in reply.

'I hear Bulldog offered you a job,' said Verity, breaking into her thoughts.

'Yes,' she said. 'Assistant engineer on *The Beautiful Game II*, as Pieter's replacement. I think the Captain wants to make sure he doesn't hire another spy by accident.'

Verity looked impressed. 'That's a good position. Are you going to take it?'

'I don't think so,' said India. 'I've had enough of Siberia for a while. I'd like to be somewhere a bit warmer. And besides, I can't see myself getting on with Tashar in that tiny rig, can you?'

They both laughed and then an awkward silence fell between them. Verity began checking the motorbike, kicking the tyres and tightening the straps on her few items of luggage.

'What about you?' said India. 'What will you do?'

Verity shrugged. 'Well, we may have saved the world but the pay was pretty lousy. Bulldog's gold barely covered my expenses and now Trans-Siberian has collapsed I'm out of a job too. I'm going to look up some people who owe me money and then I'm going to do what I do best: go tech-hunting.' She looked up from the bike and her eyes twinkled. 'I've heard about a tech-mine just outside New Peking where they've discovered technology no one's ever seen before, hundreds of years ahead of what we have now. But, apparently, it's all controlled by a local tech-lord who . . .' She stopped and then laughed. 'But I guess that's a different story, huh?' She paused as though she still had something to say. 'I've been thinking,' she said. 'I might look for a new assistant. You don't know anyone who would fit the bill, do you?'

India grinned. 'I just might,' she said. 'I'll give it some thought and let you know.'

'You do that, kid,' said Verity. 'I'll be back this way in a couple of months and we can talk about it then.' She stepped forward suddenly and gave India a fierce hug. 'Take care of yourself, soul voyager,' she said. Then she turned away quickly and fired up her motorbike.

'Do you think,' said India, raising her voice over the roar, 'that I could really be a tech-hunter?'

The bike backfired and pulled away sharply.

'Sure you can, kid,' shouted Verity over her shoulder. 'You can be any damn thing you want to be.'

ACKNOWLEDGEMENTS

The process of writing a novel is a bit geeky to say the least. It involves long hours closeted in a room like a mad monk while you try to make words behave themselves on the page. It means you don't go out much, your friends have conversations about you that begin, 'Whatever happened to . . .' and you miss loads of good TV. That's OK, I was expecting that.

What I didn't expect was that the process of turning a novel into a published book was anything but a solitary activity. *Ironheart* only got here because a lot of people were prepared to give me their help, advice and support when I needed it and they had faith in the outcome even if I doubted it myself at times.

I would particularly like to thank my agent, Julia Churchill, for investing so much time and effort in my work without any certainty of a return (just kidding). Also, thank you to the truly lovely people at Macmillan, particularly Emma Young and Rachel Kellehar for their incisive editing, and for Rachel's boundless creativity and truly splendid ideas.

At home, any lack of inspiration is always quickly dispelled by my kids, Ryan and Katie, who are funnier than me and more disobedient than a roomful of rig pirates. But, most importantly, my biggest thanks go to my wife, Carol, who has unflinchingly managed the inconvenience of living with a hermit whilst only ever making one demand of me – that I follow my dreams.

And look, I did!

REFERENCES

I have drawn on many books and articles on Siberia and its people to try and get my facts straight and I am indebted to the many authors of web pages and articles whose work has informed and inspired Ironheart. I would particularly like to acknowledge and extend my thanks to the following:

Reindeer People: Living with animals and spirits in Siberia, by Piers Vitebsky, published by Harper Perennial, 2005

Fingerprints of the Gods: The quest continues, by Graham Hancock, first published by William Heinemann Ltd, 1995

Soul Hunters: Hunting, animism and personhood among the Siberian Yukaghirs, by Rane Willerslev, published by University of California Press, 2007

Shamanism in Siberia: Aboriginal Siberia, a study in social anthropology, by M. A. Czaplicka, first published in 1914, reissued 2007 by Forgotten Books

Yakutia: Valley of Death: Hidden Mysteries of Siberia (Parts 1, 2 & 3), by Valery Mikhailovich Uvarov. Web articles: http://www.astrologycom.com/yakutia1.html, http://www.valeryuvarov.net/

Fluid Dynamics: Wikipedia article: http://en.wikipedia.org/wiki/Fluid_dynamics

The Wonderful Wizard of Oz, by L. Frank Baum, first published by the George M. Hill Company, 1900

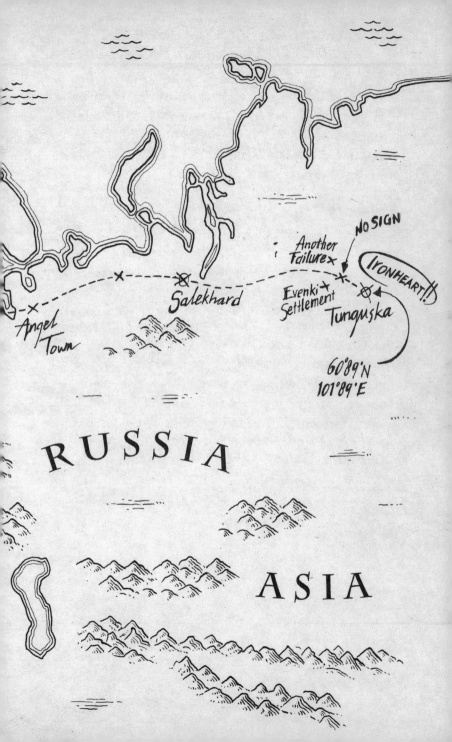

and the local geology is mainly crystalline
basement rock with sedimentary layering.
I have journeyed from Angel Town under the
pretence of carrying out a long-range mineral
survey but I am suspicious of Fenton.
He is eager to please and attempts to
ingratiate himself at every opportunity.
Does he suspect my true purpose?

October 14th

A pirate rig has delivered me as far as Lake
Baikal and I will make the remainder of the
journey on foot. It is essential my destination
is kept secret from the eyes and ears
of the Trans-Siberian Mining Company.
Moving North near the Podkamennaya River
I have noticed several small earth
tremors since I have been here. There
are several Evenki hunters in the area
although most are reluctant to talk.
Their Shaman, a woman, has warned me
away from the high forests for fear of
the spirits called the 'Valley men'.

I have no time for her superstitions but
I confess I find the forests to be
eerily quiet.

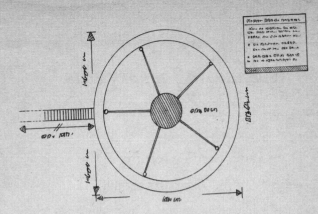

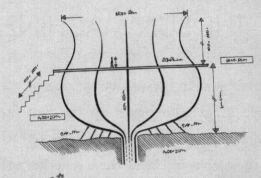

October 29th

60° 89' N, 101° 89' E. I am at The place indicated by Nentu. The earth tremors have returned accompanied by strange lights in The mountains and, by now, I am certain This is no natural phenomenon. I long to return home and I am desperate to see my girls once more but I cannot turn back so close to my goal. Truly this is a cursed place, it is little wonder they call it Ulinu Cherkechekh.

October 31st

There's something wrong with The sky...

Coming in January 2015

India Bentley returns in the
epic *Ironheart* sequel

THE SUN MACHINE

'Aren't you interested in the legend of the three kings who broke up the Sun Stone?' India said excitedly. 'Wouldn't you like to find all the pieces and bring them together again?'

The boy's eyes opened wide and he looked aghast at the suggestion. 'That must never be allowed to happen,' he said darkly.

'But why ever not?' asked India.

'Mankind is not yet ready for its secrets.' He shuddered. 'If the pieces are brought together too soon . . . they will bring about the end of the world.'